MISS DELACOURT
SPEAKS HER MIND

MISS DELACOURT
SPEAKS HER MIND

●

Heidi Ashworth

AVALON BOOKS
NEW YORK

Published by Thomas Bouregy & Co., Inc.
160 Madison Avenue, New York, NY 10016

Library of Congress Cataloging-in-Publication Data

Ashworth, Heidi.
    Miss Delacourt speaks her mind / Heidi Ashworth.
        p.   cm.
    ISBN 978-0-8034-9926-3 (acid-free paper)
    I. Title.

PS3601.S58M57 2008
813'.6—dc22   2008023178

PRINTED IN THE UNITED STATES OF AMERICA
ON ACID-FREE PAPER
BY HADDON CRAFTSMEN, BLOOMSBURG, PENNSYLVANIA

To Mom, Louise, and especially Shirley.
Without the encouragement of each,
this book would never have been written.

To my husband who proves each day
that real life is better than fiction!

Chapter One

Impatient, Sir Anthony Crenshaw, baronet, took a turn about the elegant gold study of his grandmother's London townhouse. How long had it been? Two, maybe three years since he was last summoned? He remembered it had something to do with her grandniece, the pious one who had some namby-pamby ideas about true love and the like. What was her name? Janey? Jenny. Ginny!

Whatever Grandmama wanted this time, he wished she would bestir herself to attend to it. He hoped she wasn't going to read him another lecture on the ills of his frivolous existence or indulge in her when-was-he-going-to-settle-down-and-set-up-his-nursery monologue. It was far too early in the morning for such things, and, after all, it wasn't as if he were a duke. His uncle, the seventh Duke of Marcross, held that position, and Sir Anthony wished him joy in it.

He took up a chair before the fire, stretched his legs into a tolerable position and consulted his watch. Ten A.M. Stifling a yawn, he cursed the early morning habits of the elderly.

At length, the study door opened and a small woman bustled into the room. Her tiny stature belied the great strength evident in her fierce eyes. Crossing the room with astonishing speed, she plucked the timepiece from Sir Anthony's hand.

"Anthony, you have no need of this when in my home. I shall inform you when pressing matters necessitate your departure."

Sir Anthony rose to his feet. "You are in good looks this morning." He gave the Dowager Duchess of Marcross a deep bow and kissed her hand. The one holding the watch.

He curled his fingers around it and tugged.

"Not a chance," the dowager snapped and turned away.

Sir Anthony inclined his head. "Very well. I have little enough to occupy myself of late. May I sit?"

At his grandmother's nod, Sir Anthony settled himself in the chair, lifted his legs to the ottoman, and stretched his hands behind his head. "I am completely at your disposal, madam."

"Good. Then we can get to matters of importance." her grace proceeded to lose herself behind a large satinwood desk, shuffling papers to and fro with apparent disregard for her grandson.

Sir Anthony longed for his timepiece. Why was he here, anyway? He could be enjoying a gallop through the park, a round at Jackson's, or better yet, his bed. He brought his eyes to rest on his grandmother, whom in private he called "the virago."

What changes had three years wrought in her? He allowed his eyes to rove over her person. None. No changes at all. One would suppose a woman of eight and sixty might have shown some signs of age, but there it was. The same flame-red hair. The same proud tilt of the chin. And could it possibly be the same puce satin she donned the last time she required his presence?

The dowager rose majestically from her desk and moved to Sir Anthony's chair with her characteristic swift stride. "These are they." She thrust a thick packet of papers beneath her grandson's nose.

Sir Anthony gazed at the documents, then raised his quizzing glass to her face. "Pray, have the goodness to tell me, are these . . . rose pedigrees?"

"Excellent! I have long suspected there was something going on in that head of yours. Your father wouldn't hear of it, but I told him otherwise."

"Yes. Well, in spite of my late father's lack of faith in my abilities, I did manage to catch a word or two. 'Rose' and 'pedigree' were the most enlightening ones that came to eye," he said dryly. "What I am not astute enough to discover is what they have to do with me. I crave your indulgence." Sir Anthony inclined his head and looked up at his grandmama.

"Don't be obtuse! You know exactly what they have to do with you. Think a moment. My pedigree roses are my pride and joy. Many of them are as old as the manor. Why, Henry the Eighth admired some of them!"

"Was that before or after he admired your great-grandmother?"

"That will be enough of your nonsense, Anthony. I need you to go to Dunsmere to check on them."

"Check on whom?" He tapped his riding crop against his boot.

"My roses, of course."

Sir Anthony stopped his whip in midair. "Roses? You are asking me to undertake a journey of considerable length to admire roses? Grandmama." He arched an eyebrow. "Tell me you are funning."

"No, I am not," she said with a snap, then returned the papers to her desk. Folding her hands against her stomach, she frowned at him in that way which usually spelled displeasure.

"I see," Sir Anthony said through thin lips. The truth was, he saw nothing at all. The frown, however, was something with which he was most familiar. In spite of it, he was quite fond of his grandmama and hated to displease her. He sighed. "May I ask when I will be required to depart for the nether reaches of the kingdom?"

The dowager walked around the desk and seated herself in her chair. "It is only as far as Bedford. You can be there tonight. That is, if Ginerva is ready."

"Ginerva?" Sir Anthony felt a spark of alarm. "By that you can't mean Ginny, that grandniece of yours? I daresay her governess would not allow it."

The duchess glared at him, an imperious gleam in her eye. "Ginerva is now one and twenty. You only think of her as seventeen. That is how old she was when first she came to live with me."

Could that slip of a girl truly be a woman grown? He remembered her to possess large, dark eyes, a tangle of brown hair, and some annoying opinions. Well-voiced ones. Sir Anthony felt his composure slipping. "What has Ginny to do with your roses, anyway?" he demanded. "If she comes along, I shall have to return home for my cattle and rig."

"You shall take my barouche. I won't have Ginerva bounced about in that curricle of yours for the better part of the day. Not that she would mind," the dowager said with a fond smile. "She is quite the nature lover. It is she who cares for my roses. She prefers the company of the garden over that of the multitude of rakes and rattles one finds in the city. Being a forthright young woman, she doesn't quite know how to deal with society's way of never saying what they mean." Grandmama pressed her lips together. "For this reason, she always spends the season at Dunsmere, but this year I insisted she come with me." Her voice became low and worried. "She is looking rather pale of late."

Sir Anthony rose from his seat and made ready to depart. "She was always pale, Grandmama. She never did anything but sit inside all day and dream of true love. As if such a thing exists." If it did, it had certainly eluded him. No matter; marriage was not for him. "If you wish me to go on a madcap journey to take a look in on your roses, I will do so, but *must* you saddle me with the chit?"

The duchess did not respond, for just then the study door opened. A young lady, tall and willowy, walked into the room, her eyes wide with reproach.

Good Gad, it was Ginny. When had she turned into this lovely girl in the fashionable green gown? He stared at her, at her perfect oval of a face. The graceful curves of her figure. The enormous gray-green eyes and the full lips set above a dimpled chin. They were all he recognized of the girl he had met years before, the childishly round face now turned to elegant planes and angles. Even her once-indifferent brown hair hung in rich chestnut coils against her neck and shoulders. Astonishing! And most delightful.

"Come, Ginerva." The dowager duchess waved an authoritative hand, then motioned at Sir Anthony. "This addlepated exquisite is my grandson, Sir Anthony Crenshaw, as you may recall. He will see you to Dunsmere if you still wish to go."

"I should not wish to trouble the gentleman," Ginny replied in a clear, well-modulated voice. Her words were polite, but the look she gave him was one of cool condescension.

He was surprised to find he felt a bit sorry for her. In spite of her insouciance, there was a spark of real distress in her eyes. Sir Anthony bowed. "Rest assured, Miss Delacourt, it would be no trouble." When she made no reply, he lifted his gaze to meet her cool stare.

"Come now, Ginerva. You needn't be so nice in your ways. You wish to go home—I have provided you with a perfectly acceptable escort. We all get what we desire most."

Sir Anthony bent a look through his quizzing glass at his grandmama. "And which desire of mine will be realized through this experience, my dear? Aside from a day spent in the company of the charming Miss Delacourt, that is," he added with an apologetic smile for Ginny. He was startled by the positive glare his grandmama gave him.

"You don't know a good thing when it's nibbling on your nose, young man. Now, be off with the both of you and don't let me see your face again until you are prepared to give me a full report on my roses!" With that, the dowager bent her head to her papers.

Sir Anthony bit his tongue and regarded his fingernails. No doubt this was another one of Grandmama's misbegotten schemes to see him in leg shackles. Ginny had turned into quite a taking little thing, but it would take more than a pretty face and figure to bring an end to his bachelor days. He had eluded the parson's mousetrap so far, a plan of action he had absolutely no intention of abandoning anytime in the near future.

Deeming it best to quit the room before his annoyance became evident, Sir Anthony favored each lady with a bow. "Your servant, Miss Delacourt," he said and, retrieving his watch from the desk, headed for the door. "Oh, and Miss Delacourt, I shall return within the half hour. I hope the arrangement allows you sufficient time to prepare for our departure." He paused, then added, "I look forward to it."

Ginny lifted her chin. "Very prettily said, sir, but nowhere near the truth. Never fear, I shall be ready and waiting long before you arrive. I travel light, you see."

Sir Anthony was struck speechless. True, the young lady had filled out her gown to admiration since last they met, but she was sadly lacking in address. He sketched her a slight bow and, flourishing his whip, strode out.

Precisely one half hour later, Ginny watched the English landscape fly past through the carriage window, the nodding head of Nan, her young abigail, on her shoulder. She glanced at Sir Anthony, looking very much asleep on the bench opposite. London's elite were all the same. They were arrogant. They were amoral. They feigned sleep on long journeys. She wrinkled her nose in disgust.

She should have stayed with Grandaunt Regina rather then subject herself to Sir Anthony's company. But no, her grandaunt, the dowager duchess, would insist that she attend the endless balls, routs, and soirees replete with the glib of tongue and faint of heart.

Dejected, Ginny laid her head against Nan's. She would not have been able to get through the last few weeks of a rather humiliating London season without Nan, not to mention the last three years. She was more companion than servant, despite being four years younger than Ginny, and they had been together since the vicarage days when Ginny's father had been alive.

Best not to think about home now, she thought. Ginny sighed and checked Nan's cheek. Goodness, she felt warm, even feverish! Most likely she was overheated from being cooped up in the carriage for the better part of the day. Ginny loosened the ties of Nan's cloak to let in some air.

"You should be restored to your roses by nightfall, Miss Delacourt," a deep voice drawled.

Startled, Ginny glanced into the languid gaze of a pair of penetrating blue eyes. She could determine no other sign of Sir Anthony's wakefulness. His hat still teetered at a jaunty angle along his brow. Against his silver-striped waistcoat his hands were still. Even the steady rise and fall of his chest indicated that he slept.

Flustered, Ginny busied herself with Nan's cloak fastenings. "I should be glad to get Nan home and into her own bed. I fear she is not feeling well." She settled Nan against the cushions, then made a point of staring out the window to indicate she was not interested in conversation.

"If I didn't know better, I would think you were the abigail, Miss Delacourt."

"And why is that, sir? Is it my gown or my lack of gentility that most betrays me?" Her voice held a particle of censure.

Sir Anthony arched a brow. "Why, neither," he answered, in some surprise. "However, I find your costume charming." He smiled, a lazy, one-sided affair, then reclaimed his hat and placed it firmly over his eyes.

"I see. As you reserve judgment on my gentility, may I inform you that even amongst the fashionable, there are some who deign to treat their servants as human beings? My mother was one such, and she was the beloved niece of your grandmother, the Dowager Duchess of Marcross."

"Yes, I believe your mama was a Wembley," he commented into the curly brim of his hat. "*Hers* is a very fine name."

"If what you mean by that remark, sir, is that my name leaves something to be desired, why do you not simply say so?"

The impudent man lifted his hat, regarded her for a moment, and replied, "Clearly, there is not the need." He let the brim of his hat fall once more over his eyes.

Ginny fumed. He had insulted her family name and had insulted her as well. And he had been so polite throughout. The man was a charlatan. Why, even his air of languid repose was an affectation.

"No response, Miss Delacourt?" Sir Anthony drawled.

Ginny was aghast. Why, the man didn't even have the decency to remove his hat when conversing. Hefting her reticule in her hand, she considered lobbing it at his arrogant head, but owned that even her belief in unrestrained communication could not uphold such a hoydenish act. Ashamed of herself, she moved to place the reticule by her side, when the carriage lurched and the bag was sent flying across the velvet interior, smack into the center of Sir Anthony's high-crowned hat. There was a crunching noise followed by a loud thunk as the reticule bounced off his hat into the carriage squabs, coming to rest against his shoulder.

Sir Anthony did not move.

Ginny gasped. He was unconscious. No—dead! There was no other explanation. A man simply did not sit still through such an assault, not when the weapon was a reticule containing scissors, a flask of rose water, and a bottle of Denmark lotion.

Her former indignation forgotten, Ginny leaned closer to Sir Anthony and searched for signs of life. The silver threads of his waistcoat still wavered. She trembled with relief. With great care, she put an unsteady hand to his hat and lifted it from his brow.

Sir Anthony regarded her out of one eye. "Would you be so kind as to leave it be?" He reached behind him and restored the reticule to her. "You wouldn't want to be without that."

Ginny jumped and let the hat drop with a thud. Odious man! He was polite to a fault. If having sophisticated manners meant letting her Nan die of fever, she would have none of it.

"By the way, Miss Delacourt," Sir Anthony mumbled, "hadn't you better attend to your girl?"

"Whyever do you ask, Sir Anthony?" Ginny replied, feeling haughty.

"Why, she looks as if she is about to launch her breakfast," he drawled with a smile.

While Ginny fussed over Nan, Sir Anthony studied Ginny through the hole she had made in his hat. She must have had a loaded cannon in that dratted bag. Nevertheless, he had to admire her spirit. She had bottom, spunk. She was an original. He groaned inwardly. No use wrapping it up in clean linen, she was a hoyden. In point of fact, she was the perfect choice to guard Grandmama's roses. No doubt she was a whirlwind of destruction. He had a vision of obliterated blight, eradicated black spot, and coshed beetles.

She had been under Grandmama's thumb far too long. Someone ought to marry the girl and save her from turning into a shrew and then an out-and-out virago like his grandmother. That is, somebody other than himself.

His scrutiny of the girl became more intense. Was she aware of Grandmama's intentions? Surely Ginny was not so dim-witted to believe the dowager's prattle about roses. Perhaps she was not only aware of Grandmama's plans to throw them together, but party to them as well. The thought made him squirm.

Ginny must have noticed how he shifted about, for she regarded him with surprise. "Oh, Sir Anthony," she said with relief. "You were so silent, I feared you might have been injured after all."

Guilt nudged him out of his negligent sprawl. "Not at all. Truth be told, I was lost in contemplation of roses."

"Truly? Do you admire roses?" She seemed pleased.

"Not especially."

"Oh."

The lack of pleasure in the chit's voice had made a hole in his detachment. Exasperated, he turned his gaze out the window with a groan.

"You *are* hurt!" Ginny settled Nan against the squabs and took up a seat next to him. "Here, turn about and let me see."

Sir Anthony presented her with his profile. "Miss Delacourt, pray be at ease. I have sustained no injury. Now, would you be so kind as to attend to your abigail?"

There was a tiny pause, then a rustling of skirts as Ginny did as he asked.

"Sir Anthony?"

"Yes, Miss Delacourt?"

"Nan feels a bit feverish. Would it be out of our way to stop at an inn so she may rest?"

Sir Anthony consulted his watch. Past luncheon. "It is getting rather late, but heaven knows it doesn't matter what time we pull into Dunsmere. I believe the Swan and Flute is just ahead. We will stop for tea and perhaps consult a physician for the unfortunate Nan."

"That is kind of you," Ginny said, her voice grave and thoughtful.

Kind? What would make her say such a thing? He was merely doing what was necessary. Any gentleman would have done the same. "Not in the least. Your servant, as always, Miss Delacourt."

She cocked her head. "Do you always say just the right thing?"

"I beg your pardon?"

"There. You did it again! I provoke you; you are polite. I compliment you; you are polite. I suppose if I were to drink myself silly at the Swan and Flute and dance on the table with my skirts over my head, you would still have that prim, polite smile plastered to your face."

Sir Anthony broadened his smile. "I shall be sure to bespeak a private parlor in the case you feel such an urge."

She threw up her hands in exasperation. "Does nothing ruffle you?"

Sir Anthony considered. "My personal grievances are not meant for the ears of such as you." However, he could think them. Religious fanatics. Rose fanatics. Fanatics who flung reticules at the heads of unsuspecting gentlemen.

"I suppose it would not be polite to mention them to, perhaps, a vicar's daughter?"

"That is correct. Even were you not, I would not deem it in good taste."

"To whom could you mention them without risking a scratch on that fashionable veneer of good breeding?" She gave him a glittering smile.

Sir Anthony's, in return, was freezing. It was the same smile that had his tailor, bootmaker, and hatter on the run. "Have you something against good manners, Miss Delacourt?"

"No. Against hypocritical, self-serving lords who always remember to say 'please' and 'thank you' when passing the butter boat, but who let the poor go cold, hungry, and ill clad, yes."

Sir Anthony was taken aback. Surely she was painting him with the same brush as some of the more self-indulgent nobility littering London. He had every right to feel angry, but one could not scold the gently bred as one would a groom or a tailor. Besides, it was difficult to determine how she would respond to a tongue-lashing. The tailor usually fled out the back door and did not benefit from it.

With great effort he curbed his speech. He had learned long ago good breeding made up for many lacks. He would desert his personal code for nothing: not to earn another's approval, not to save his own life, and certainly not for this slip of a girl who looked at him with such determination.

With a rap of his cane to the roof of the carriage, Sir Anthony found the only safe response. "I shall inform the driver of your wish to stop at the next inn."

"Have you no reply to my rude words, sir?"

Sir Anthony smiled with amusement. "Could it be you are purposely provoking me?" No answer. The woman could try the most placid man's patience! Which he was not. Perhaps he should change tack. "Miss Delacourt. It is the duty of a gentleman to remain one, even in the face of his greatest challenge."

Ginny left off her ministering to the sleeping Nan. "And what would you say presents you with the greatest challenge to your code of manners?" she asked with great interest.

"A shrew, Miss Delacourt. I find I cannot abide a shrew."

Ginny's eyes grew very wide. "Are you calling me a shrew, Sir Anthony?" She looked as if she would be glad to learn that was precisely his intention.

"I would never do so, madam, for I am never rude." At least, not out loud.

She dropped her gaze to her lap. "No. I don't suppose you are. There is something to be said for speaking one's mind, however."

Sir Anthony could make very little of that response and was glad when the carriage ground to a halt.

"This can't be the Swan and Flute!" Ginny exclaimed upon alighting. "I daresay Beelzebub himself wouldn't set foot in the place."

"Then we shan't invite him in, shall we?"

Ginny looked at him, her eyes rounded with surprise. "Why, that remark skated perilously close to sounding surly, sir." She smiled, a delicious pink curving of the lips.

"A regrettable oversight," he said, biting back an answering smile. "Pray, forgive me."

Leaving the abigail in the care of the driver until a room could be procured, Sir Anthony offered Ginny his arm and they headed into what he suddenly recalled to be the most disreputable establishment in all the county.

It was a good thing the girl had a sense of humor. She was going to need it.

Chapter Two

Ginny was wrong. The Swan and Flute was everything Beelzebub could wish. It was dirty, derelict, and dingy with the accumulated dregs of society: regulars who never left, who hadn't moved in about twenty years, from the looks of them.

Every corner of the room seemed to sport a leering, toothless smile fixed to the pasty faces of ne'er-do-wells, knaves, thieves, and murderers. Ill at ease, Ginny picked her way among overturned chairs and puddles awash with something foul. She fixed her gaze to the center of Sir Anthony's well-dressed back. It was too disconcerting to look into the overbright eyes of the locals.

One of them waved his tankard at her. "Hey, missy, you can do better than that bit o' blood." He winked and passed out, spilling his ale in a great puddle on the floor. A filthy dog appeared from nowhere and lapped it up. With an ecstatic wave of his tail, he disappeared into the muck from which he had come.

Ginny shuddered. How could she take tea in such an establishment? Why, the odor of the place was enough to make one gag.

Sir Anthony must have sensed something of her thoughts, for he stopped and subjected her to close scrutiny. "Is something wrong? You look a trifle pale."

"Do I? Sir Anthony, does this place not seem to be all that it should?"

Sir Anthony looked about him with some surprise. "It looks precisely the way such establishments do. Oh, perhaps this one is a bit worse than some, though it is a sight better than others I've seen."

"You've seen worse? Than this?" Ginny could not believe it was so. She sensed he was once again glossing over the truth.

Perhaps that was why he took her hand. "If you are frightened, we could leave. We should be to Bedford in another few hours or so."

"Oh, no," she protested. "I am persuaded it would be best to secure the opinion of a physician for Nan first." She felt braver with his strong fingers curling about her own.

"Yes, of course, the suffering Nan. The proprietor can tell us the whereabouts of the closest physician." Sir Anthony tightened his grip on Ginny's fingers, drew her to the bar of the taproom, and rang the bell.

An enormous woman, her filth-encrusted apron woefully insufficient for her girth, answered the summons. "Well, what d'we 'ave 'ere?" she demanded, rolling her wandering eye at Ginny in scornful amusement. "Come 'ave a lookee 'ere, 'usband, at the fine-lookin' swells."

Ginny edged closer to Sir Anthony. She was aware of how she gripped his hand and was suddenly mortified. She hoped the physician would come with all speed. The sooner she left this godforsaken place for the safety of the carriage, the better.

Sir Anthony gave her hand a little squeeze and smiled, his eyes nearly sparkling. "It looks as if we are to be waited on by Tubbins himself."

"Most reassuring," Ginny mumbled. At least Tubbins couldn't be any worse than his wife. Not unless he bathed in dirt, was the size of a horse, and *both* eyes wandered.

Tubbins proved to be as short as his wife was tall. He appeared to be possessed of two ordinary eyes, though this was difficult to determine beneath his thick brows and forbidding expression. He said nothing, only stared at them with those frightening orbs.

Ginny considered screaming, but who would be her rescuer? Everyone at the Swan and Flute, including Sir Anthony, seemed to think this place was perfectly acceptable. And, of course, there was Nan. Something needed to be done about her and time was wasting.

"Excuse me, sir, but is there a physician to be had in this town?"

Tubbins gave no response.

"The man is quite deaf," Sir Anthony said, then shouted, "Tubbins, we are in need of a physician. Is there one hereabouts?"

"There be one in Bedford, I 'spect. Will you be 'avin' a drink, Sir Anthony?"

"Bedford!" Ginny exclaimed. "That is our destination! We might as well continue on home to Dunsmere rather than wait here for him to come to us."

"In either case, we should take some refreshment. The brandy here is among the best I've tasted."

Ginny pulled her hand free. "I don't drink, sir." How could he discuss alcohol when her Nan was so ill?

Mrs. Tubbins ambled forward, wiping a glass with the corner of her apron. "You know whats they says," she whispered, one eye staring straight ahead and the other aimed at the hearth yonder. "Look to the wall, me darlin'." Well, she certainly had that covered.

"Well then, what shall it be, Miss Delacourt? Do we press on, or are you hungry?"

Ginny realized she was famished. "We are like to miss supper at the rate we're going. Perhaps we should take some tea and make Nan comfortable in bed for a spell." If there was such thing as a comfortable bed in this establishment. She tried not to think about the food.

"Very well. Tubbins!" Sir Anthony bellowed. "We will be needing a private parlor for our tea and a bed for the lady's abigail. Oh, and see to my horses." He flipped a guinea into a crock on the counter and turned to Ginny. "Will you be all right while I fetch Nan?"

"Yes, I think so. I shall wait for you in the parlor."

Mrs. Tubbins appeared with a tea tray and led Ginny into a small chamber off the taproom. She put the tray on the table with a clank. "I'll be back with some food."

Only after Ginny had closed the door on Mrs. Tubbins did she feel some relief. Sir Anthony would return in a moment, and she would feel even better after she had eaten something. She noticed Mrs. Tubbins hadn't bothered to ask what she wanted for her supper. Ginny was so hungry, it didn't matter. Plain bread and water sounded like ambrosia at this point.

She had drunk a mere cup of tea before Mrs. Tubbins made her laborious way into the room with a tray loaded with platters of food, each with its own fragrant curl of steam rising into the air. She spread the food out on the table with clean hands, Ginny was gratified to notice, and left the room. Now, if only Sir Anthony would come, she could see herself clear to making short work of the lot. The food was so inviting and her stomach so noisy.

Just when she thought she could wait no longer, the door finally opened. Only it wasn't Sir Anthony. It was two men, one short and ugly, the other tall, thin, and uglier.

"This parlor is spoken for," Ginny hastened to tell them.

"Not right for a pretty lady like you to be here all alone, now is it, Seb?" the first man said.

Seb shook his head. "Nope. Sure aren't, Dobbs."

"I'm not alone. Sir Anthony Crenshaw is merely out attending to his horses. He will be along any moment." She treated the two of them to what she hoped was a scathing glance. "He will be very angry if he finds you here." What was she saying? He was far more likely to invite them in to take tea. It would be the polite thing to do.

"Sir Anthony Crenshaw." The short one mused, licking his lips. "Would that be the mort what drives that pretty black carriage?"

"Why, yes, as do any number of gentlemen. It is my aunt's carriage, actually, and . . . oh! I don't see how this is of any of your concern. It would be best if you were to leave."

"I hadn't known you were expecting guests, my dear." Her heart leaped at the sound of the familiar voice.

"Sir Anthony!" Ginny jumped up and ran to his side. Grandaunt Regina would deem it an action unbecoming of her grandniece, but Ginny thought it prudent under the circumstances. As Sir Anthony placed himself between her and their unwanted guests, she thought perhaps he agreed.

"Be assured, Miss Delacourt, our friends here were just leaving, were you not?" Sir Anthony gazed steadily at the so-called Seb and Dobbs, a picture of easy calm.

"Come along, now, Seb," Dobbs declared, "we'd not be wanting to disturb the gentleman's tea, now would we?"

Seb nodded, a wicked grin splitting his mouth. "Sorry we be intrudin' on your afternoon pleasures, wot here in this private parlor and all."

Ginny's cheeks grew warm. How dared they imply— She returned to her chair, humiliated.

When the two left, punctuating their bawdy laughter with slaps to each other's backs, she almost wished they had stayed. She didn't relish the thought of sharing tea and conversation with Sir Anthony after their remarks. Alone. In a private parlor. Without Nan to lend them countenance, it looked for all the world like an elopement, or worse.

Sir Anthony closed the door with calm deliberation and turned to Ginny. She was startled by the cold light in his eyes. "Your tea will be growing tepid," he said, taking a seat.

"It wasn't better than tepid when it arrived." Like Sir Anthony at his best. Most likely it was now stone cold. "You are not angry with me?"

"Why? Because of those two? Not unless you invited them in."

He sounded sure she would do no such thing, but the look in his steely gaze implied she might.

"Whyever in the world would I desire the company of those two?" Ginny exclaimed.

"Did I say that you had?" Sir Anthony asked in surprise. "I do beg pardon."

"No, but you looked it."

"Come to think on it," he replied with exaggerated nonchalance. "I seem to recall Grandmama telling me how she came down to dinner one fine day to find she had unexpected guests. A traveling tinker and a trio of carolers, I believe."

"That was a very long time ago." Ginny felt a rush of humiliation at his quizzical smile. "I don't suppose she told you it was Christmas and excessively cold that night? Besides, Mr. Simms and the Varleys were much more respectable than those two."

"No doubt you learned your lesson after the tongue-lashing Grandmama must have given you." Sir Anthony picked up his knife and buttered a piece of bread.

"Grandaunt is always kind to me, even when correcting my behavior," Ginny explained.

Sir Anthony, a bite of bread in his mouth, swallowed. Hard. "You mean to say, she didn't comb your hair with a footstool for it?"

"Of course not! Grandaunt Regina is a lady."

"She must have become one sometime recently, then. It can't have been that long since she last gave me a thrashing for some offense or another," he mused. "More to the point, I am the one who should be doing the scolding. If you didn't invite our friends in out of charity, perhaps you did it out of spite."

"Spite? Me? What reason could I have for that?"

"I recall having said something about not inviting Beelzebub to dine with us. You thought it surly of me."

"Did I? How ungenerous of me," Ginny said, smiling. "Well, it seems that you have done just the opposite. Invited *me* to eat with Beelzebub. This place would most likely suit him very well, indeed," she murmured as she glanced around the room.

Sir Anthony had to admit she had the right of it. This room was not too bad, but the taproom and the clientele—well, he should never have brought her here. He had thought it a great lark to ruffle her self-righteous sensibilities, but he hadn't remembered the Swan and Flute to be quite so ramshackle a place until it was too late.

"Shall we consign Seb and Dobbs to the devil, then, and be off?" Sir Anthony asked when they had finished eating.

"Yes!" Ginny placed her napkin on the table. "I will just check on Nan and see if she feels up to leaving."

"Very good. And I will request our transport stand ready." Sir Anthony rose from his place at the table and bowed.

The warmth of her smile stunned him in return. "Thank you for supper," she said. "Whenever I think of the Swan and Flute, I shall remember how delicious the food is here."

"That is most generous of you." Indeed, it was excessive. The food was barely edible. And that was the best anyone could say about the Swan and Flute. Perhaps she was learning it wasn't always best to tell the exact truth. Then again, she could be agonizingly charitable. He hoped she resisted the impulse long enough to get to Bedford. He could just imagine her wishing to take up every stray dog or sniffly-nosed child from here to Dunsmere.

"I believe it is you who are being generous," she replied, extending her hand. "I haven't thanked you for being of such service to myself and poor Nan."

Sir Anthony pressed her hand, noting how tiny and delicate it felt in his own before releasing it. He watched her leave the room and, with a brave tilt to her chin, make her way through all manner of rabble to the stairs. He hoped she thought to lock the door to Nan's chamber until he sent word that the carriage was waiting, and repressed an urge to run after her. After all, he was her escort for the day, not her beau, and he mustn't forget his resolve to distance himself from his grandmother's plan to see him wed.

Out in the yard twenty minutes later, the carriage had still not arrived. When an ostler hurried by, Sir Anthony caught him by the scruff of the neck. "Where is my carriage?"

No response. Sir Anthony peered into the pinched face topped with a thatch of straw-colored hair. Why, the boy was trembling and would not meet his eye. Surely his simple request could not have inspired such fear in the fellow. What was about?

He let the ostler go and returned to the taproom. "Tubbins! Where is my carriage?"

"It be gone, Sir Anthony." Mrs. Tubbins stood at the counter, drying glasses with her grimy apron.

"I think you must be mistaken. I had it ordered out and it has not yet arrived. I believe that boy you have is minus a hinge in the attic."

"T'ain't there. Had it of the boy hisself. A pair o' bridle culls hopped on't and took off down the road."

"Since when are highwaymen in the business of carriage snatching?" Sir Anthony demanded.

"Since one landed on't their front door." Mrs. Tubbins shrugged. "A body's got to earn a livin' somehows."

Reminding himself it did no good to shout, he asked, "How long have they been gone?"

"Couldn't say for sure. Maybe ten minutes or so."

Sir Anthony flew out the door in three great strides and ran into the yard. How could he have missed them? He hastened around to the stables to investigate. Sure enough, there was evidence of fresh wheel marks going toward the main road in the opposite direction from the yard. Apparently, no one had the gall to face him, for the place was deserted. A quick look into the horse stalls revealed no hired hand or cowering thief, only a team of ancient work nags. And even they looked nervous.

Sir Anthony considered his options. They could stay the night at the inn—and risk having the likes of Seb and Dobbs as bedmates. Or, he could have the nags pulled from their stall and pressed into service. Hacking their way into Bedford seemed preferable to spending another moment at the Swan and Flute. They would have to leave Nan behind, but he could give the coachman charge of her.

He retraced his steps to the inn to inform Ginny of his decision when he was approached by Tubbins.

"Heard you was having a mite o' trouble, sir."

Sir Anthony doubted he had heard any such thing. "Do you have an alternative solution for me?"

"Gots ol' Bess and Bobby out in the stall. They's job horses, but they oughta get ye as far as Bedford." With a nod Tubbins indicated a decrepit, tumbledown shack behind the stables. "That's wheres I keeps the church-going carriage. You're welcome to hitch 'er up if you can spare someone to see it back, safe and sound."

"That is a very agreeable solution, Tubbins. Now, if you will see to matters here, I will inform Miss Delacourt that we are finally ready to depart." Sir Anthony returned to the inn and collected his things from the parlor, Ginny and Nan from upstairs, and his coachman from the taproom, where he was drinking his pay. It really wasn't like the gruff coachman. If he had stayed with the carriage, perhaps they would not be forced to resume their journey in Tubbins' conveyance. At least

Tubbins had indicated it was his best, used only for church.

Sir Anthony waited in the yard for the carriage while the coachman assisted Ginny with Nan. Before long, Bess and Bobby, the nervous nags he had spied in the stable, appeared around the corner of the building. Hitched to them was a small, open carriage of indeterminate years.

Sir Anthony considered the little landaulet with a censorious eye. It looked too frail to carry the combined girth of the Tubbinses down the road, let alone to church. He realized he should have known at once the barkeep was lying through his jagged teeth. Tubbins and church went together like fire and water.

He turned to his coachman. "It looks as if you will have to sleep it off here. I shall be fortunate to find room for our luggage, and that's only if Miss Delacourt consents to sitting up on the perch with me. Would you have any objection to that, Miss Delacourt?"

"No, I am accustomed to handling the reins, even. I think the seat is large enough that we can stretch Nan out quite comfortably."

Sir Anthony, with the coachman's help, laid Nan, feverish and lethargic, on the backseat. Ginny rushed to make her more comfortable, folding a cloak beneath Nan's head and placing a hatbox beneath her feet.

When she had finished, Sir Anthony handed Ginny to her place on the high-perched bench. "I hope you shall not mind. It will be later than we thought when we arrive."

Ginny turned her face to the sun, the wind riffling through her hair. "It won't be dark for another few hours.

Thank goodness it is May." She tied tighter the ribbons of her chip-straw bonnet against the breeze. "Then again, we wouldn't be off to smell the roses if it weren't spring, would we?"

Sir Anthony sat next to her and took up the reins. "No, I don't suppose we would." If someone had asked the same question just that morning, he wouldn't have thought such a thing possible at any time of the year. Now, seated next to Ginny, with the sun on her lips and the brim of her bonnet throwing a cool shadow over her lively eyes, it seemed most natural. Even desirable.

They were halfway to their final destination when Sir Anthony was forced to bring the landaulet to a creaking halt. In the middle of the road stood two masked highwaymen, one short, one tall, with pistols at the ready. Behind them was a carriage remarkably like Grandmama's.

"Put up your 'ands and toss out your valuables," the tall one demanded.

"Make that toss out your valuables and then put up your 'ands," corrected the short one. "And ifs I see the flash o' metal, I'll shoot."

Sir Anthony noticed that Ginny did immediately as she was told.

"Have I permission to withdraw my watch?" he said. "It is metal and could be mistaken for a pistol." He wasn't willing to take any chances with the idiot Seb, as it surely must be.

"All right. And all your money too. But no guns, you hear?"

"A trusting soul, is he not, Miss Delacourt?" Sir Anthony drawled.

"Yes, indeed. Now, please hurry and do as he asks. My arms are getting tired."

"That is a fine thing to say when you have nothing of any value on your person. I suppose you think it is my duty to give what I have to these poor unfortunates."

"Pray, Sir Anthony, what will they do to us if you do not?" Ginny replied in a strained voice.

Realizing she must truly be frightened, Sir Anthony threw his money purse, ring, quizzing glass, and fob onto the road along with his watch. He wished he hadn't been so punctilious about retrieving it from Grandmama. "You may rest easy, Miss Delacourt. It is only those two idiots from the inn."

"Dobbs and Seb?" Ginny gasped, dropping her arms. "How is it that they have Grandaunt Regina's carriage? And why are they holding us up?"

"I understand it is the way such men earn their living," Sir Anthony replied, biting back a sharper retort. "They must have stolen our carriage from the inn."

"Why, how ungrateful of them! And after I gave them each some money!"

"You did what?" Sir Anthony felt an unaccustomed tide of emotion threatening to sweep away all his carefully crafted nonchalance.

"Well, they wouldn't have been in our parlor if they weren't hungry. If they had money, they wouldn't have to steal. When I went upstairs, they were waiting outside Nan's door, and so very sorry for disturbing me earlier that I gave them each a coin."

Sir Anthony stared at the two scrambling in the dust over his things. "You have money, Miss Delacourt?" he drawled.

"Yes, a little, but it's mine." She drew one of her hands to her lap and clutched a fold of her skirt.

"You will take that money you have secreted in your gown and give it to Dobbs and Seb."

"Ya," Dobbs said, who appeared to have heard their conversation. "Give it over, priddy lady. We knows yous gots it."

A flash of anguish skittered across Ginny's delicate features. "Perhaps it *is* partially my fault. But don't lay this all in my dish. You are the one who is turned out fine as a new penny." She took the money out of a pocket concealed in the folds of her gown and threw it into the road.

Sir Anthony saw that Dobbs was quick about scooping it up and hustling Seb into Grandmama's carriage. With a savage flick of the reins that made Sir Anthony wince for the sake of the horses, the two catapulted down the road. A cloud of dust rose up behind them.

Sir Anthony lashed the reins against poor Bess and Bobby, who flew into action.

"What are you doing?" Ginny cried, her hair wind-whipped and her bonnet askew.

"I am going after them. I have a trick or two of my own, I'll have you know. If only these two could just go—"

A sickening *crunch* robbed Sir Anthony of words. The landaulet tilted forward with a harsh thud, and he felt the reins ripped from his hands. With a final lurch, the carriage tipped forward, spilling its contents into the road.

Chapter Three

There was a moment of intense silence followed by the sound of settling dust. Ginny struggled to a sitting position and checked her arms and legs. They moved as they should, but her hip ached a little. There would be a bruise there before the day was over.

"Are you all right, Miss Delacourt?" Sir Anthony, his face spattered with mud, was kneeling in the road attempting to brush dirt from his silver-threaded waistcoat. A long streak of mud smeared his trousers, and he would never be able to wear that expensive jacket again. He looked up and dust cascaded into his eyes.

Ginny held back a giggle. "Yes, I think I am."

"You look a little worse for your fall," he said, giving her the once-over.

"*I* do!" She glanced down at her skirt. Drat! It was her favorite outfit, emerald green with a sage overdress, and now it was ruined. She scrubbed at the mud with her handkerchief. "Well! Weren't they bold as brass? Imagine, being held up in broad daylight." She had heard of such happenings in the dark of night, but never to anyone she knew. And certainly not to her.

"No doubt it is most common in these parts." Sir Anthony stood, his face twisted with pain.

Ginny repressed an impulse to run to him. "Are you hurt?"

"It is only my ankle. I gave it quite a turn." Sir Anthony took a tentative step. "It's not too bad. I don't think we can say the same for the landaulet, however." He limped over to the tumbled carriage and examined it. "Just as I thought. The axle has been cut almost clear through, and the traces have been tampered with." He unhitched the frightened horses from the badly tilting carriage.

Ginny felt the blood drain from her face. "You mean we were meant to crash? Seb and Dobbs waited for us?"

Sir Anthony nodded, his expression grim.

"Well," Ginny said, brightening, "at least we have the horses." She gave Bobby a cheerful slap on the rump, who snorted, reared, and came down within inches of Bess. Frightened, she took off down the road. Bobby followed, kicking up a colossal cloud of dust.

"Don't go!" Ginny cried. She turned to Sir Anthony. He was bound to be angry with her. She hesitated to meet his eyes. "I hadn't meant to send them off."

He pressed his lips together. "You led me to understand, Miss Delacourt, that you have had some experience with horses."

"Oh, I have, indeed, I have. These were very skittish, I think. I only meant to give her a pat of encouragement." It wasn't her fault the horse misunderstood. "There is a difference between that and a slap of dismissal," she added, braving it out.

"Her? It's a wonder no one thought to educate Bobby," Sir Anthony said, with a humiliating lack of emphasis on the word *Bobby*.

Ginny felt her cheeks turn to flame. "What does it matter if I can't tell which is male and which is female? I can handle the reins, and I can make them go and make them stop. That is, most of the time."

"I trust you are a better hand at gardening than at horsemanship, Miss Delacourt? Otherwise, our trip out here is sadly unnecessary."

Outraged, Ginny forgot to avoid his gaze. She was surprised to see how his eyes danced with amusement. "I refuse to answer that question," she replied. He might throw her answer back in her face at some later date. In the politest way possible, of course.

"There, there, Miss Delacourt, I shan't quiz you anymore. Quite a sacrifice, I must say, as your cheeks turn the loveliest shade of rose when I do."

Ginny felt her cheeks betray her with another rush of color. She gasped and clapped her hands to her face to hide her shame.

Just then, a moan came from the back of the landaulet.

"Oh, poor Nan!" Ginny cried. She picked up her skirts and moved briskly to the little carriage. How could she have forgotten the abigail for even a moment? And what was she to do for her now? They should have left her at the inn while they brought a doctor back.

A vision of the taproom at the Swan and Flute rose into her mind. Ginny shuddered. Perhaps Nan was better off lying in a broken-down carriage in the middle of a dusty road with no place to go and no way to get there, accompanied by two people who had no money and less wits between them. She felt her stern resolve to stay cheerful desert her. "Sir Anthony, what are we to do?"

"I suppose I shall have to go for help and try to find someone who can take us up." He gazed down the long length of the road, the setting sun shining in his eyes.

"You can't mean to walk to Bedford! Not before sunset. Not on that ankle." Ginny could hear the panic in her voice. It wasn't only his ankle she was worried about. Seb and Dobbs were long gone, but there could be more of their ilk just down the road.

Sir Anthony looked a shade worried as well. "You stay here with Nan and tidy things up a bit. I'm going to walk down to the next crossroads and try to find a passing carriage." He retrieved his hat from where it was wedged beneath the seat and placed it on his head.

Ginny wanted to tell him how beyond hope the hat had become, all crumpled and misshapen. And that hole! On the other hand, the mud on his face and that limp were so fascinating, she rather doubted anyone would notice.

"Well, I'll be off then," he said, walking over to where she stood. "Don't speak to strangers and try to stay out of the way of any more thieves." A smile tugged at the corner of his mouth. "We haven't anything left to give them, after all."

"We would have if you hadn't made me give them the money I had hidden in my gown."

Sir Anthony moved closer. "Ah, now, Miss Delacourt, you know that to be faulty reasoning. Those two knew exactly where to look, did they not? You might thank me for saving you the indignity of having them go after it themselves."

Ginny willed the rising tide of color from her cheeks. Must she always blush like a schoolgirl? "I wasn't afraid of them," she said coolly, despite the warmth caused by his nearness. In truth, she had feared Sir Anthony might have been the one to remove the money from her gown. As abhorrent as it would be to have Seb and Dobbs paw through her skirts, the thought of Sir Anthony doing so terrified her. Madly, her cheeks continued to burn.

"I don't think I'm wrong to suppose your charity only goes so far?" Sir Anthony was asking. He cocked one odious eyebrow at her.

"It is money that only goes so far, Sir Anthony," Ginny replied. Only, she didn't think it was money to which he was referring. "Ah, it is charity that never faileth, I believe," she said.

One corner of his mouth lifted just a fraction. "Let us hope we find someone possessed of a goodly amount of that before it gets much later."

Ginny felt a spasm of guilt. The whole of this wretched affair was her own fault. "Do you think someone will be along soon?"

"Be brave." Sir Anthony put a finger under her chin and tilted it up. "We shall come about all right. Some-

one must pass by soon. Someone respectable, that is."
He dropped his hand to his side. "Remember what I
said, watch out for yourself and stay out of trouble." He
shook a finger at her and limped down the road.

Ginny watched him march away from her and tried
to believe what he had said. She hoped he wasn't simply trying to be polite.

Sir Anthony's thoughts at that moment were anything but polite. In fact, they were positively rude. What
else could one expect of a perfectly good specimen of
masculinity, usually most attractive and always expen-
sively dressed, now reduced to walking down the King's
Highway? In tatters. Begging for a ride.

If he were lucky enough to get picked up, it would
most likely be for the purpose of transporting him to
Newgate, he looked so disreputable. That's all the thanks
he'd get after the trouble he had gone to for that chit.
Most likely she would be gone when he finally dragged
his broken body back to where he had left her. She had
the least common sense he had ever encountered in a
young woman.

He supposed the fault for that could be placed in her
father's dish, raising her to be so naive and trusting.
And Grandmama! She hadn't helped any in the years
Ginny had lived with her. If only she hadn't cut short
Ginny's very first season! Any number of fellows might
have offered for her by now, and she would be some
other poor sot's problem. Devil take her eyes!

They were extraordinarily fine eyes, he had to admit.
Gray, with just a touch of green to them. Like a stone
statue overrun by a creeping moss. But not dead-looking,

never that. These eyes were alive; they sparkled with wit, flashed in great gleams of anger, danced and capered in the sunlight.

What was wrong with him? He was turning into a cursed poet, making odes to eyes and the like. Sir Anthony turned his thoughts to the road and the sound of his uneven pacing along the dank earth. The sun was setting and it was growing dark. He began to worry about Ginny, alone, in the shadows, with only Nan for protection. The thought was appalling. His ankle pained him and, in the dark, it would take him longer then he had already been gone to get back. He must return soon.

And then what? They could carry Nan back to the Swan and Flute. He could just imagine their arrival, wild-eyed, filthy, their clothes in tatters, sagging with fatigue. Between them would be the fevered Nan, looking half dead. That ought to clear the place in a hurry. If they were lucky. Otherwise, it would be a long night with no sleep, watching guard.

That is, if Ginny was still there. Anything could have happened to her by now. He should not have left her. Having reached the crossroads, he was about to turn back, but hark? What was that? The jingle of a harness, perhaps? Sir Anthony strained to determine which direction the sound had come from. If his ears did not deceive him, a one-horse conveyance should approach the crossroads in a matter of moments.

Ah! There it was, a pony-drawn cart driven by a round-faced man. In his profound relief, the pony looked the veriest high-stepper; the cart, sturdy and spacious;

and its driver, an honest fellow dressed in the first stare of fashion.

"Hail, sir." Sir Anthony waved his linen handkerchief, no longer white, over his head.

The driver pulled on the reins, bringing the cart to a halt inches short of Sir Anthony's injured ankle. Unfortunately, the back wheel rolled across the toe of his other foot. It hurt like the devil, but no matter. He had transportation. Once he was on that cart and down the road, someone could amputate both feet and he would be glad of it.

"Needin' a lift?" the young man inquired. His glance flicked from Sir Anthony's dusty hair to the mud on his trousers, the hole in his hat, and then lingered on the pocket of his waistcoat where his watch should have been. "Can you pay?"

Sir Anthony felt sadly lacking under his scrutiny. "Why, no. I don't have any money. That is, not on me. That's why I'm wishful to be taken up." Something about the way the lad was eyeing him made him hesitate to mention Ginny and Nan. "I had a carriage wreck a ways down the road. Where are you headed?"

The boy, as Sir Anthony could now see, gathered the reins in one hand and pulled a cheroot from his pocket with the other. "The Swan and Flute."

With a sinking feeling Sir Anthony had to own that he was not surprised. "My things are down the road in that very direction if it would not be too much trouble to take me up."

"I will, in exchange for somethin' valuable." The boy's eyes fell again to Sir Anthony's waistcoat. "Somethin' you might be havin' about your person, if you knows wot I mean."

"Sorry, my dear fellow, but some of your friends have already relieved me of everything I had on me." All of a sudden this fellow didn't look quite so honest, his cart not so large, and his pony not so sharp.

"You don't say? Well, in that case, I'd be willin' to trade you a ride for that fine-lookin' waistcoat you gots on. Bang up to the mark, that one is."

"What!" Sir Anthony ran a hand over the silver threads of his favorite waistcoat. It was the only article of clothing on his person that had not suffered irreparable damage. Even one of his boots was scarred from the encounter with the cartwheel.

"I have an eye for fine clothin'," the boy confided. "From wot I can see, that's about all you have worth taking off ya."

"Very well," Sir Anthony said with a cold smile. He jerked off his overcoat, easily done without the aid of his valet due to the rents in the shoulder seams, and tossed it into the cart.

"Don't be so hasty with the waistcoat," the boy demanded. "Don't wants no tears in it."

Sir Anthony glared at him, then removed the waistcoat and handed it to the boy, who whistled a low *coo,* slipped off his own tattered coat, and donned the waistcoat with the greatest reverence. As the boy replaced his own attire and tilted his hat at a jauntier angle, Sir Anthony realized the lad's entire wardrobe seemed to be made up, piece by piece, from various others.

With a growl, he jumped onto the cart and took the reins from the boy, who whistled a happy tune. Sir Anthony flicked the reins and the cart went into motion. Thankfully, the boy soon ceased his infernal whistling and fell to rubbing his very dirty hands over the dove-gray stripes.

The cart groaned with every turn of the wheel, the pony nickered and neighed if induced to go faster than two miles per hour, and the grubby boy eyed Sir Anthony's fine lawn shirt. Sir Anthony contented himself with thoughts of his success. Ginny would be relieved when he returned with transportation. It was a little slow-moving, but there was room for Nan to stretch out on the seat, with some to spare for their things. Once he dropped the boy at his destination, there would be room for Ginny up on the box.

He supposed the boy would ask for his shirt in return for payment of the horse and cart. He hoped Tubbins would vouch for him, assure the boy that he would return with money when he could. Not that the vehicle was worth more than a few shillings.

After what seemed an interminably long time spent imagining Ginny's relief at his return, Sir Anthony turned a bend in the road. It was all that stood between him and Ginny's rescue. He was surprised at his own relief when he saw her standing by the landaulet, peering inside. It seemed to have grown in the dark. Surely it was never so elegant, even when it was new. He was about to shout out in greeting when he saw the crest on the door, vividly gold against the shining black, and he knew the dusk had played a trick on him.

The moment of triumph he had imagined turned into a nightmare when two man-sized shadows detached themselves from the carriage. They moved toward the landaulet, which Sir Anthony could now clearly see a little farther down the road. They removed something from the backseat, which must have been Nan, and placed her inside the waiting coach, then helped Ginny step up to disappear into the inky blackness.

"Ginny, no!" he shouted, but the carriage was already in motion. His voice could not be heard over the rattle of the wheels.

Inside the carriage, Ginny thanked providence the Barringtons happened by. If left much longer in her predicament, she felt sure she would have had to succumb to a fit of the vapors. Hysteria was not Ginny's weakness, but she had had enough of wringing her hands.

"It is wonderful to see you my dear, wonderful!" Squire Barrington reached over and patted her hand. "How are your roses this season?"

Ginny suppressed a sigh. How could she have forgotten the man's obsession with Dunsmere's roses? He rode over nearly once a week to discuss pruning tactics and talk sweet to Grandaunt Regina. No matter how often the squire hinted, Grandaunt refused to allow him a single cutting. Nevertheless, the squire persevered and made it known far and wide that his fondest wish was to have her famous roses growing in his own garden.

"To tell the truth, she is a bit anxious about them. I've left them too long to the gardener's sole care." Ginny did not add that the gardener was more than qualified to tend the roses. Grandaunt felt better when one of them supervised his actions, and Ginny treasured her tranquil afternoons amongst the blooms.

Squire Barrington clucked his surprise. "You were in London? I didn't know, didn't know. I hadn't realized. Well then . . ."

It was amusing to see his face fall when the luckless squire realized his misfortune. Three whole weeks when he could have pilfered his own cuttings with no one the wiser! Not only was he conveying the source of this wondrous opportunity but also the instrument of its demise. Ginny could almost taste his disappointment.

"Whatever are you doing here then, and whyever were you standing, simply standing about in the road?" the squire demanded.

"I was waiting for Sir Anthony." Ginny peered out the window, hoping to spot him.

"Crenshaw? Sir Anthony Crenshaw?" piped in Mrs. Barrington. "Why, isn't he your aunt's grandson? One would think we would bump into him more often, living only fifteen miles from Dunsmere as we do, but we haven't laid an eye on him in ever so long. Is he very much changed?"

Ginny smiled at Mrs. Barrington. "If by that you mean, is he less top-lofty and stylishly dressed, no, he is not." Ginny turned again to the window. "Oh, there he is now. *Do* stop."

"Of course. We wouldn't think of anything else," the squire spluttered. "After all, he's the grandson of a duke." He signaled the driver to stop and open the door for the new arrival.

Mrs. Barrington stepped over Nan and crowded to the window. "Lucinda will be so pleased. She has had to miss her very own come-out—lingering spots, you know—but to have Sir Anthony land on her very own doorstep! Well! She will have stolen a march on—" Her gush of words came to an abrupt halt.

Puzzled, Ginny followed Mrs. Barrington's gaze out the door. In the road was a pony cart, the reins held by a chubby lad smoking a cigar. His ill-fitting clothing lent him an air of gentility in spite of the bawdy tune he was singing at the top of his lungs. It was the man stepping gingerly down from the box who claimed everyone's profound attention. The hole in his hat was indiscernible in the dark, but the moonlight picked out every other defect in Sir Anthony's ensemble in glaring detail.

Ginny was surprised to see the decline in Sir Anthony's apparel. She felt sure the look of utter amazement on Mrs. Barrington's face was for his lack of a coat of any kind, the stains on his trousers, and the scar in his Hessians. If she had known him better, she would be amazed as well by the fury in his face when he caught sight of Ginny in the carriage.

"Sir Anthony?" Squire Barrington's voice was tremulous and unsure. "Do I have the pleasure of addressing the grandson of Her Grace, the Dowager Duchess of Marcross?"

Sir Anthony froze. A cool smile replaced the jaw tight with anger, and a wash of color flooded his features. "I don't believe I have had the pleasure of meeting you before, sir." The polish of his reply was in jarring contrast to his appearance.

Ginny knew he must be humiliated. A part of her wanted to laugh at his plight, but her disappointment at the quick recovery of his façade overpowered the giggle in her throat. That white-lipped look of fury had brought the beginnings of a wild hope to her heart, but it had gone too quickly. If there was a true man under all that protocol, Sir Anthony would never let him out.

The squire threw a look of dismay into the carriage before rising to address Sir Anthony. "I am Squire Barrington. We have property halfway between here and Dunsmere, where we have met on more than one occasion."

"Ah, yes, of course, I beg your pardon. It has been a long time." Sir Anthony moved as if to lift his quizzing glass, but his grasping fingers found only air. He flicked an accusing glare at Ginny through the window. "I have reason to believe you have found my charge along the road. Would it be too much trouble to speak with her?"

"No, not at all, not at all. Just . . . just a moment." Squire Barrington brushed his wife away from the window and sat down, closing the door behind him. "Sir Anthony wishes to speak with you, Miss Delacourt."

"Of course. It will just take a moment." Ginny reached for the door but was stopped by the squire's hand on her arm.

"Miss Delacourt, this is a delicate question, a delicate question, indeed. You wouldn't be running off with him, would you?"

Ginny hoped she looked as shocked as she felt. "No! We . . ." She felt herself blush. "We had every reason to believe we would be home before nightfall. It has been the most dreadful afternoon. You can't possibly know how grateful I am that you happened by."

"Oh dear, oh dear, and what if we hadn't? We are in the middle of nowhere." Squire Barrington seemed much struck by the role he had played in Ginny's rescue. He gave her a broad smile. "Well then, glad to be of service, aren't we, my dear?"

Mrs. Barrington's reply came small and indecipherable through the handkerchief she held to her nose.

"There, you see, you see, my wife agrees. Poor dear, she has suffered a bit of a shock, I fear. Yes, oh yes," the squire said with a sad shake of his head. "The Sir Anthony we were acquainted with very little resembles the Sir Anthony of today."

Ginny laughed. "The Sir Anthony you see very little resembles the Sir Anthony of this morning, even."

"Oh my, yes, well, a very dreadful afternoon, indeed. In that case, we should invite him up, wouldn't you say so, my dear?"

Mrs. Barrington pressed herself into the squabs with alarm. Her eyes above the handkerchief grew very wide.

The squire's smile faded. "Perhaps, Miss Delacourt, it would better if he sat with the driver. Very little room in here, what with your girl and all."

"I will just get out now and ask him," Ginny managed to say. It was all she could do to keep from laughing, especially when she stepped down and faced Sir Anthony. He smiled at her as if he were dressed in knee breeches and tights, a glass of Almack's orgeat in his hand.

"Miss Delacourt," he purred. "It is a pleasure to see you again."

"Is it?" Ginny asked with a knowing smile. "It seems to me that you would much rather consign me to the devil."

"Whatever gives you that impression?" Sir Anthony gazed at her through wide eyes, every inch himself in spite of his sad reverses in attire.

"Pray, don't be angry. I would never have simply left. We stopped for you, after all."

"Angry? What purpose would it serve to be angry?" He forced his lips into a tight smile.

Ginny cocked her head to one side and narrowed her gaze. "I think I have caught glimpses of a true person in there somewhere. If you are lucky, one day someone shall come along and set him free."

"That person would do better to leave well enough alone, Miss Delacourt." His voice was soft and dangerous.

"As you wish," she said crisply. She reached for the handle to let herself back into the carriage.

"Allow me." Sir Anthony opened the carriage door and extended his arm.

When Ginny put her hand into Sir Anthony's strong one she was very much aware of the warmth of his skin and the ease with which he assisted her up the steps. His fingers lingered on hers for a fraction longer than necessary, and Ginny gave him a questioning look.

"What is it, Miss Delacourt?"

"I . . . nothing. Thank you." Ginny took her seat, careful to avoid the naked curiosity in the Barringtons' eyes.

Sir Anthony limped over to the boy on the cart, who had whiled away their exchange blowing smoke rings on his noxious cigar. For an anxious moment, Ginny thought Sir Anthony meant to leave with the boy and was relieved when he drew his ruined coat from the back of the cart. This morning she would have rathered anyone else be her traveling companion. Now, a tightness gathered in her chest at the thought of his so easily leaving her to her own devices.

With a longing look in Sir Anthony's direction, the boy started down the road. Ginny thought he looked a trifle sour but was too startled by the fact that he wore Sir Anthony's waistcoat to wonder why. As he watched the boy drive away, Sir Anthony looked to be feeling a trifle sour as well. With a jerk of his head, he leaped up the steps of the carriage, no small feat, considering his sore ankle.

When he placed a mangled boot inside the door, Ginny met his eyes. "Oh. I failed to mention it," she said. "It will be necessary for you to ride with the driver."

Sir Anthony betrayed no hint of emotion, almost as if being suffered to ride with the coachman were an everyday occurrence. "Delighted," he said. With a bow to the occupants of the carriage, he swung himself gracefully up to the box.

Ginny settled herself into her seat, vaguely dissatisfied. Why did she have to challenge him? Now he would be more on his guard then ever, and she would never get the chance to find out if there was more to him than he allowed to show. If only she could think of a way to get him to betray his emotions! At least they were finally on their way. She was hungry and dirty and so very tired!

She glanced at Nan, huddled in a miserable heap against the far side of the carriage. Drawing the abigail against her shoulder, she whispered, "Nan, dear, do you feel any better at all?"

"No, miss. I feel worse. Are we there yet?"

"No, dear, but soon. I will prevail upon our hosts to keep us for the night. I can get you to bed much sooner that way."

Nan did not reply, but she relaxed and her head drooped farther down Ginny's shoulder.

"Squire and Mrs. Barrington, would it be too terribly inconvenient to put us up for the night? My abigail has caught a chill somewhere and is suffering with a fever. I hate to have her out any longer than is absolutely necessary."

"Oh, yes, well, I, ah . . ." Squire Barrington glanced to his wife, who still clutched the handkerchief tightly to her nose. "I don't see why not. I daresay Sir Anthony will wash up fairly well, don't you think? We just had a new bathing tub built into one of our closets, complete, oh, very complete with running water." He drew his flabby stomach into his thin chest. "I shall order it filled upon our arrival."

"Thank you." Ginny smiled her gratitude. "I am certain you will find us both more the thing once we wash away the dust of the road."

Ginny noticed Mrs. Barrington still seemed doubtful. She removed the handkerchief from her nose long enough to say, "My, he has changed!" Then, with a little choke, she added, "My poor Lucinda!" and threw herself on her husband's neck.

Squire Barrington consoled his wife with an awkward pat on the cheek. "There, there, my dear, it will be all right." He gave Ginny an uncomfortable, calculating look, his wet lips twisted in uncertainty. "Miss Delacourt," he ventured to ask, "about your roses . . ."

Ginny thought frantically of what to say in response, but was robbed of breath when the carriage lurched and began moving at a furious pace. Sir Anthony had taken charge.

Chapter Four

Mrs. Barrington emitted a wild shriek and tossed her handkerchief into the air.

"See here, what's going on?" Squire Barrington attempted to rise from his seat, but the carriage was traveling too fast. Grasping his cane, he beat upon the ceiling. The coachman must have received the message, for the carriage immediately slowed and came to a halt.

Soon, his grizzled head appeared in the window. "What's toward?"

"Why, I must say, *why* are we going so fast?"

"The gen'lman and I were havin' a bit of a debate. He says he could make the horses go at least fourteen miles per hour. Not on this terrain, says I. The next thing I know, he's grabbed the reins and drivin' your cattle hell-bent-for-leather."

"Well, make him stop!" Mrs. Barrington had rallied.

"Yes, mum." The coachman clapped his hat to his head and disappeared from the window. The carriage lurched and swayed with his ascent to the box, but it was some time before they were once again in motion.

Ginny tried to imagine how the interview between the driver and Sir Anthony had proceeded. She found it difficult to picture him meekly handing the reins over without a murmur. Then again, perhaps he had spent all his pent-up anger on the backs of the horses.

A crack was beginning to show in Sir Anthony's smooth veneer, and Ginny fell to thinking of ways she could make it grow wider before his return to London on the morrow. He was Grandaunt Regina's favorite relative—barring herself—but why? Who was the real Sir Anthony Crenshaw and how would she ever learn? She did not lack for ideas; however, one after another was discarded as being too dangerous. She sensed Sir Anthony was a loaded cannon, and she didn't want to make herself a target. If only she could think of an idea that would keep her out of harm's way, one with a long fuse.

By the time the party arrived at Rose Arbor, home of the Barringtons, Ginny was weary of thinking. After seeing Nan to bed and ensuring all her needs would be attended to, Ginny retired to her own room. There would be time enough for food and a bath in the morning.

The next morning, Ginny was awakened by the smell of toast and eggs and something else she couldn't quite place. Whatever it was, she meant to have some imme-diately. The growling of her stomach almost drowned out the din of water cans being carried down the hall to her room.

A maid entered, her face flushed from the fire that heated the water for Ginny's bath. The girl was younger than Nan and looked tired and spent. Ginny sprang from her bed and pulled one of the cans from where it hung suspended on a stick across the girl's shoulders.

The maid's eyes grew wide with horror. "No, miss. You mustn't do that! T'would be my job if anyone was ta see ya."

"Fiddlesticks! I am accustomed to drawing my own bath. Besides, there is no one here to see what we do." Ginny dumped the water into a hipbath and shivered with anticipation at the prospect of washing away the layers of dust she had collected since leaving London. The other cans followed, and the maid helped Ginny step out of her night rail and into the still-warm water. "The mistress says I'm to attend ya seein' how your girl is still ailin'."

Ginny settled into the bath, feeling guilty. "Poor Nan. She isn't really an abigail. She's more of a friend, really. When my father died and I went to live with my grandaunt, I couldn't leave her behind. My grandaunt thinks I have had an abigail all along, but actually I am quite accustomed to doing things for myself."

"Oh." The maid looked down at the floor, and her shoulders slumped in a frail little heap across her back.

Poor dear. She must have viewed her new duties with pleasure. If it meant she would no longer be responsible for providing bath water, Ginny could understand her disappointment. "What is your name?"

"Maren, miss."

"Very well, Maren. My name is Ginny Delacourt. I will be happy for your help while I am here, but only if you promise not to stand on matters of propriety." Ginny was amused by the delight and terror that passed across Maren's face. "Naturally, we shall be most careful not a word of this reaches Mrs. Barrington's ears."

"Oh, yes, miss!" Maren gasped with delight. "Shall I fetch you something to wear?"

"You will find a clean shift and stockings in the portmanteau. I believe I even thought to bring an extra gown." Ginny was grateful Seb and Dobbs had no interest in stealing clothing.

When she was dressed in a white-sprigged muslin tied with a saffron sash and her everyday shoes, she felt much refreshed and ready to formulate a plan of action against Sir Anthony. That is, once she had eaten. Her empty stomach was now her primary concern. Maren insisted on brushing out Ginny's hair and redressing the brown curls, but the moment she was done, Ginny wasted no time in finding the breakfast room.

The enticing aroma of bacon and eggs led Ginny through a maze of unknown corridors and rooms until, mouth watering, she was standing on the threshold of the gold-and-green breakfast room. The floor-to-ceiling drapes were pulled from the windows, flooding the room with light that glanced off the highly polished surfaces of the furniture. On the sideboard lay a sinful array of breakfast foods, steam curling from every dish.

At the far end stood Sir Anthony, a spoon poised in his hand and a question in his eyes.

"Miss Delacourt! You are not dressed for travel."

"Of course I'm not dressed for travel. Ummm, what is that heavenly smell?"

"Kidney steak in mushroom and wine sauce. What does your breakfast have to do with our departure? Certainly you could eat in your traveling suit."

"Certainly I could. Are you quite finished with that? There are some lovely coddled eggs on the other end of the board there."

Sir Anthony dumped another boatful of sauce onto his steak. "Had some."

Ginny was somewhat startled by the shortness of Sir Anthony's reply. He hadn't even addressed her by name.

Sir Anthony continued. "If you think I wish to waste my time kicking my heels while you change from that ill-suited frock into yesterday's costume, you are quite mistaken. I intend to leave for Dunsmere before the hour is up. If we hurry, we can be back in London before nightfall."

"You mean you wish to hasten off, just like that? Why, we haven't even summoned the physician yet."

"That's another bone I've been meaning to pick with you. Why you insist on a physician to attend to a mere fever is beyond me." Sir Anthony took a seat at the table and smiled. "Now, shall we enjoy our food?"

Ginny dropped into a chair across from him and gazed into her plate. Aromatic steam curling from her steak and eggs sent her stomach into tumultuous rumblings. A corner of her mind screamed at her to eat, but the voice seemed small and far away. "Sir Anthony, I do believe you are being rude."

"Isn't that what you wished? For me to say what I think?"

"Is that what you think? That Nan does not warrant a physician? That she be treated like a mere servant?"

"Well, isn't she?"

"No, she is not!"

"Oh. I have been led to believe that she is. I have referred to her as such on numerous occasions and you have never corrected me. Tut tut, Miss Delacourt"—Sir Anthony waved his fork at her—"we must always be sure to tell the truth."

"The truth is, Sir Anthony, I shall not be returning to London. So, you may take your airs and manners off and return forthwith. I'm confident Squire Barrington can see me the rest of the way home."

"Wonderful! I shan't have to worry about dodging flying reticules, wandering all over the countryside for a doctor, or trudging down the road on a sore ankle."

Ginny winced. How true his words were. "I had quite forgotten about your ankle. How is it this morning?"

"Sore. And my bath last night was cold. But, after donning a clean suit of clothes this morning, I feel like a new man." Sir Anthony pushed his plate away and leaned back in his chair. "It is refreshing to say what is on one's mind, Miss Delacourt. I am a changed being, and it is all because of you."

"If you must know, this wasn't exactly what I had in mind."

"What exactly did you have in mind, pray tell?"

Ginny fiddled with her eggs. "I don't know precisely, but rest assured, you have thoroughly discouraged me from finding out. You are an odious, odious man. I have always thought as much."

Sir Anthony looked a bit struck, almost as if her words had stung. "I daresay you've been wanting to say that for a long time. It does feel good to express one's feelings, does it not, Miss Delacourt?"

"Yes, indeed it does." But it was a lie, an unaccountable lie.

"Well, then, that leaves little to say but farewell."

In spite of the foolish constriction of her throat, Ginny managed to speak. "Good-bye, Sir Anthony. Thank you for all you have done. I will write to Aunt Regina today and have her make restitution for the damages. The hat and your waistcoat, to name a few."

"That won't be necessary." Sir Anthony threw his napkin on the table and rose. "Well then, no doubt Grandmama shall send me back for you, so I'll be seeing you again soon."

"Oh, no," Ginny said. "Aunt Regina and I are quite agreed. I shall remain at Dunsmere indefinitely. It seems I and high society are not a good mix."

"I see." Sir Anthony lingered at the table, his expression unreadable. Standing in front of her as he was, it was difficult for Ginny not to notice the way his dark hair curled crisply away from his brow. Brows that hovered over intensely blue eyes, accentuated by the dark blue of his elegant coat. From the coat, it was but a small feat to take in the snug fit of his buff pantaloons, encasing well-muscled thighs and tucked securely into the tops of shining black Hessians. "Well, then I suppose this is good-bye." His boot tassels twirled from view as he spun away and headed for the door.

"Why, you muth be Thur Anthony," lisped a girlish voice from the hallway. "You look much better than Mama thaid."

Ginny attempted to get a glimpse at what kind of creature this could be, but the girl was hidden from view by Sir Anthony's broad back.

"That is most kind of you," Sir Anthony replied. "May I ask whom I have the pleasure of addressing?"

"But of courth! Thilly moi! I am Luthinda Barrington."

Lucinda Barrington. It couldn't be! True, she was barely out of the schoolroom so Ginny was little acquainted with her, but she hadn't a lisp the last time they had spoken. She did, however, contrive to turn heads everywhere she went, even then.

Lucinda took Sir Anthony's arm and drew him back into the room. "I was juth about to partake of my breakfast," she lisped on, "and la! What a thurprise! Oh, Mith Delacourt, Mama thaid you were visiting. Tho good to thee you again."

"Yes, what a surprise, indeed," Ginny said. "Sir Anthony and I were just discussing the benefits of speaking truth, were we not, Sir Anthony?" Surely he would have many home truths for this girl.

"Yes, we were, Miss Delacourt. A delightful conversation. Would you like some kidney steak, Miss Barrington? It is very good."

"Ooooh, yeth, I love kidney steak."

Ginny watched in rapt fascination as the creature actually clapped her hands and giggled like a baby. There were girls in London who behaved in just such a nauseating fashion, but such airs were unknown in the provinces. Until now.

Sir Anthony served up a dish of the steak and placed it in front of Lucinda.

"Thank you oh tho much, Thur Anthony," Lucinda squealed. With another clap of her hands, she picked up her fork and ate. Sir Anthony sat nearby and smiled his encouragement.

Ginny wondered if Sir Anthony could possibly be taken with the pitiful girl and what it was about her he could admire. True, she had hair like spun gold and a mouth like a bow, but couldn't he see past the china blue of her eyes to that hideous beauty mark? It was set above a dimple in her cheek—one of a pair—and Ginny was sure it was false.

She took her plate to the sideboard and served herself another helping of eggs and a rasher of bacon. She added a couple of pieces of toast for good measure. She intended to hear the entire proceedings between Sir Anthony and Lucinda even if she had to chew at a snail's pace. Fortunately, food was plentiful, and she could have all the servings she would need to avail herself of every word.

Sauntering back to the table, Ginny said, "Sir Anthony was just about to leave us, were you not?"

"Oh, no! You mustn't!" Lucinda exclaimed.

"Well, I do have some business to attend to in London, but I suppose it could wait a while longer." Ginny wasn't sure if Sir Anthony's smile was for Lucinda or courtesy's sake. Surely he couldn't be attracted to the ninny!

"Oh, yeth, make it wait. I am so starved for company. Last month I broke out in itty-bitty spots all over my entire body. Oh, don't worry, the quarantine was over weekth ago, but it has taken forever for the silly spots to fade. I am mithing my very own London come-out because of it," Lucinda said with a wide-eyed look. "I am quite sure that no one hath ever endured such a tragic circumstance in the hithtory of the world."

"Oh, my!" was all Ginny could manage to say else darker thoughts would tumble off her tongue. Why, she seemed to feel herself the center of the universe!

"Enchanting," Sir Anthony murmured.

Suddenly, Ginny couldn't eat another bite. "I really should go check on Nan and see about sending for a doctor."

"Don't even worry about it for one itty-bitty minute. Mama hath theen to it and he should be arriving soon."

If Mrs. Barrington had taken it upon herself to send for a doctor, things must be serious. "Is Nan that sick then? I must see her right away."

"Oh, I wouldn't if I were you. Mama thays it looks like the chicken pox, same as I had. If it is, we shall all be quarantined in the house together. Isn't that marvelouth!"

Sir Anthony smiled at her, indulgently. "If that is to be the case, I can't think of two more charming ladies to help while away the time."

Amazing. Not only had Lucinda transformed Sir Anthony into his former polite self, but he was now extending his largesse to Ginny as well. Nevertheless, even a saint couldn't take a quarantine's worth of Lucinda Barrington. It was perfect! Sir Anthony was bound to show signs of strain in the interim, and Ginny just might find out what it was about him that didn't quite meet the eye. "I find I am looking forward to it as well," she said.

"Oh? And what of your roses? Can you turn your back on them so easily?" Sir Anthony drew his gaze from Lucinda to give her a cool smile.

"It would seem I have no choice. Besides, this proves to be most entertaining." While Ginny was concentrating on giving Sir Anthony her haughtiest look, the door opened to admit the most beautiful man she had ever seen.

A true Adonis, his hair was as gold as Lucinda's and rippled in waves to his snowy white cravat. His eyes were dark and soulful, fringed by lashes long enough to make any woman envious. His mode of dress was modeled after Beau Brummel and his voice after Byron, deep and musical.

"Miss Barrington!" he cried. "I thought I would never lay eyes on you again."

"Lord Avery," Lucinda squealed. "You have come at last! Mama said you might when she saw you in London." This last was said with a decidedly lispless air.

"Yes, I have come, my flower, and not a moment too soon. It seems almost a past lifetime since I last gazed into those limpid pools of blue."

"He means my eyes," Lucinda informed Ginny and Sir Anthony.

Lord Avery seemed to take notice of them for the first time. "My flower, who are these people?"

"Why, this is Sir Anthony Crenshaw, and that is Miss Delacourt."

Lord Avery forced his eyes from Lucinda's face to Ginny's. He must not have found it utterly odious for he lost no time in striding to her side. "Miss Delacourt." He took one of her hands and turning it palm up, he placed a light kiss on her wrist. "De*light*ed!"

"It is a pleasure to meet you, my lord." Ginny pulled her hand from Lord Avery's and smiled into her lap. Lord Avery did not take the hint. He hovered over her, formulating his next flowery phrase, no doubt.

Sir Anthony stood with a loud scraping of chair legs against the gleaming hardwood floor. "Lord Avery, a pleasure. Have you had your breakfast yet this morning? There is a very good kidney steak on the sideboard."

Lord Avery lifted his quizzing glass and considered Sir Anthony. "Yes, indeed. I could smell it, so aromatic, so rich, wafting down the hall."

"Ooh, would you like some?" Lucinda squealed. "Let me help you." She picked a plate off the sideboard and began piling it with generous servings from each dish. Lord Avery followed like a dog on a leash.

"Well," Ginny said when Sir Anthony had seated himself next to her. "He is remarkable."

"You think so?" Sir Anthony looked down the length of his nose at her. "I think he is a bit of a nodcock, myself."

"Miss Barrington seems to find him utterly charming. She must feel comfortable around him. Her lisp has made a most sudden departure."

"Really? I hadn't noticed."

"No doubt it is her other qualities which claim your notice." Such as Lucinda's fluttering eyelashes and well-designed décolletage.

"Um, yes. No doubt. Now about our change in plans . . ."

"Oh, had we a change, Sir Anthony? I had already made the decision to stay on. It is only yourself who will be inconvenienced by the quarantine."

"If indeed there is one, Miss Delacourt. We have yet to hear from a physician."

"You seemed quite willing to accept the possibility a moment ago. Indeed, you expressed yourself delighted by the prospect of being shut up in the house with two such charming ladies."

"One mustn't believe everything one hears, Miss Delacourt."

"Oh really? Poor Miss Barrington. I'm sure she believes you find her enchanting."

Sir Anthony glanced at Lucinda still fussing over Lord Avery's plate at the sideboard. "She is refreshingly different."

From whom? Ginny wanted to ask but wisely held her tongue.

"Though I cannot fathom what she sees in Avery."

"Perhaps the same things she sees in you, Sir Anthony."

Sir Anthony did not respond, but the way his cup clattered in its saucer led her to believe she had touched a chord.

After taking a last sip of chocolate and serenely wiping her fingers on her napkin, Ginny stood. "I think I shall just go see about Nan. It was a pleasure to meet you, Lord Avery. Miss Barrington, so lovely to renew our acquaintance." With a nod to Sir Anthony and a flip of her skirts, she walked out.

Ginny made her way to Nan's room with new determination. There was more than a little evidence to suggest Sir Anthony was a man of real emotion, perhaps even of passion. With Miss Lucinda Barrington and Lord Avery standing buffer, she thought she could now unleash the beast.

Chapter Five

"What do you mean the doctor will not come?" Ginny demanded of Mrs. Barrington cowering behind the door of the adjoining room. Through a crack in the door, Ginny glared at the one brown eye, large with distress, Mrs. Barrington dared to expose.

A pair of highly rouged lips replaced the eye. "I mean that Dr. Simms trusts my good sense. She looks just as my Lucinda did a month back."

Ginny cast a look of frustration at Nan. Her fever had passed, but she was now covered head to toe with spots. She was a picture of agony, writhing in pain, lying on her hands. Ginny knew the urge to scratch those spots was almost beyond her ability to withstand.

"If the doctor would just come and see her, I'm sure he would know what to do for her."

"It's the chicken pox, plain and simple," came Mrs. Barrington's voice through the door. "Poultices for the itching and laudanum to make her sleep is the best we can do." The crack in the door disappeared with a snap. There were the sounds of footsteps, another door opening, and Mrs. Barrington's capricious step down the hall to the stair.

Sir Anthony, reading the paper in the library, heard someone coming down the stairway. It could only be Lucinda. She had a light, unpredictable step, not a thing like Ginny's brisk, even stride. He tossed the newspaper onto a table, hoping to relieve his boredom with some conversation when she passed by the open door. He counted himself most fortunate when he spotted the matronly lace cap on a dark head of hair in time to duck his own into the hastily retrieved newspaper. He had no wish to converse with Mrs. Barrington. He hadn't made many points with her of late, and she had a way of letting him know it. A high-pitched, whining sort of way.

Too late. She had seen him. She tripped into the room like a battle ship in full gale. "Sir Anthony, is that you?"

Gad. Could that be a musical tone to her voice? He wondered what he had done to put her in such charity with him. He lowered the paper. "I've just been helping myself to the periodicals. It seems that the 'change has suffered a bit of a reverse."

"How unfortunate," Mrs. Barrington crooned. "My, you are looking very natty this morning, Sir Anthony."

He emerged from the society page and gave her a wary smile. "Yes, well, one can affect wonders with a good, bracing bath."

"Dear me. Was the water that cold, then?"

"Just a bit cooler than tepid, but I'm not wishful to complain. Your hospitality has been most abundant."

Mrs. Barrington blushed and twittered behind the hand she had put to her lips. He supposed it was to hide a row of sadly yellowed teeth.

"Well! I am most happy to hear you say so. I imagine you might have heard already. The doctor has ordered the house under a ten-day quarantine."

"There was a rumor bantered about at breakfast. Miss Delacourt and I are fortunate to have stumbled upon such a capable hostess."

"It is our good fortune that we have two handsome bachelors in our midst at such a time."

"Two?!" Sir Anthony prayed he wasn't being considered a potential mate for the Barrington's hen-witted daughter. "Ah, that is to say, Avery is staying? He can't have been exposed as of yet."

"Very true, but we mustn't let on. Our poor Lucinda has been confined to the house for the past month, and we could not let such a talented young man slip through our fingers. He is a poet, you know."

Sir Anthony tried to smile. "So I've heard."

"Yes, well, we shall convince him to stay. Actually," she added coyly. "It should not be very difficult to achieve. He has had his eye on Lucinda for quite some time."

"That is not surprising. Miss Barrington is a treasure." One to whom Lord Avery was more than welcome.

Mrs. Barrington perched on a burgundy leather chair across from Sir Anthony and launched into what proved to be a well-rehearsed report. "Our Lucinda has been trained in all the fine arts, as you yourself can plainly see. She is literate in French and the language of music. She plays, sings, dances, and paints the most exquisite watercolors! She has the manners and conversation of any young miss above her station, and though her lisp is a bit unusual, I hear they are considered quite exotic in London this season." Mrs. Barrington punctuated this last remark with an arch look and a meaningful nod.

"Yes, she is, to say the least, captivating. In turn, she seems quite captivated with Lord Avery. Is there an understanding between them?"

"Naughty, naughty, Sir Anthony." Mrs. Barrington wagged a jeweled finger at him. "It wouldn't do for you to show too much interest in my little darling." She affected a comely blush. "There is nothing to speak of as of yet. You can see that it wouldn't be proper to say anything further on the matter."

The woman certainly had a wily way about her. Sir Anthony inclined his head. "Consider the matter forgotten."

"You do have such pretty manners, Sir Anthony." Mrs. Barrington gave him a bright smile. "I must say, after clapping eyes on you last evening, I never dreamed you had turned into such a pleasant gentleman. I'm sure you have ever so many young ladies throwing their caps over the windmill after you."

"Would that it were so, Mrs. Barrington, but I am only a baronet. Pleasant manners are a poor substitute for nobility. I would even go so far as to say that there be certain ladies who will hold out for the highest title to which they can aspire."

Mrs. Barrington's smile faded and she t
hands together in her lap. "I daresay that is the case with
some ladies. Er . . . you must be bored to flinders in here
without any young people present to entertain you." She
stood. "I shall set about rectifying the situation!"

Sir Anthony lost no time in rising to his feet and
bowing Mrs. Barrington out the door. Her tone of voice
when pleased with him was nearly as strident as that
when she was not. He felt sympathy for the squire. It
must always be the high-pitched whine or that strident
falsetto for the rest of his days. Wouldn't it be much
more efficient if she simply said what she felt rather
than subjecting mankind to such unpleasantness?

Sir Anthony caught himself up short. He was beginning to sound like Ginny. He muttered an oath and tossed
the paper into the chair by the fire. He prowled the
room, restless to be away from matchmaking, both
Grandmama's and Mrs. Barrington's. It wasn't as if he
wanted to marry Lucinda . . . gad! But nor could he
stomach Lord Avery's being preferred as an eligible
parti simply because he had a higher title. He had a sudden memory of Ginny's smile when Avery had kissed
her hand and felt as if he had been kicked in the gut.

A rustle of silk outside the door caught his attention.
Surely this was Lucinda come at her mama's behest to
ease his boredom. He hoped he was safe in that quarter.
Surely her parents preferred the lord to the baronet. It
was always best to be courteous even so. He adopted
his most charming smile. "Miss Bar—"

"Oh, were you expecting Miss Barrington?" Ginny
quizzed as she came through the door. "The last I saw

her, she was playing chess with Lord Avery in the drawing room. You sent me a message?"

Sir Anthony didn't know what she could mean. He stood silent a moment too long, but it was a moment well spent, taking in the pleasing contrast of the dusky curls against her creamy skin and the way her long lashes swept just along the crest of her pink cheeks. "Message? I sent you a message?"

"Yes. Mrs. Barrington said you wished to see me."

Comprehension dawned. He had assumed she had gone in search of Lucinda, but it seemed he was expected to entertain Ginny while Lord Avery put the seal on his relationship with Miss Barrington. "Yes! Of course . . ." he said, but he could formulate no further reply.

"Sir Anthony, what is it? If you wish to discuss travel arrangements, I'm afraid it is impossible. We are all confined to the house for the better part of a fortnight."

"Thank you, I've been informed." He retrieved his paper and made himself comfortable. "In light of our situation, I thought we should make other arrangements." Of what sort, he wasn't sure. He was hoping Ginny would take the reins from there.

"Do you refer to informing Grandaunt Regina of our whereabouts? She won't be expecting to see me anytime soon, but I daresay she hoped I would send a note about her roses back to London with you. We really should write to her and explain our situation."

By Jove, the very thing. "Very good, Miss Delacourt. I thought perhaps you had better write it. You would know better than I how to appease her on the subject of her roses."

Ginny walked over to the escritoire and drew out some notepaper. "I don't know about that. I'm afraid nothing will serve short of my laying eyes on them." With a graceful swish of her skirts, she seated herself at the desk and tapped the tip of her nose with the quilled pen. "I suppose I shall just have to tell her the truth."

As she dipped her pen in the inkwell and began to write, he studied her profile. He was fascinated by the way her emotions were mirrored in her face. He knew just when she came to the part about their misfortune on the road by the way her eyes flashed and her chin raised a fraction. When she wrote why they must stay on at Rose Arbor, she bit her lip with empathy for Nan. Her little nose wrinkled in consternation, most likely when she wrote her apology for not sending a report on the roses.

She signed her name with a flourish and sanded the paper. "Do please read this and see if I left out anything important. I want to send a note to Dunsmere and have some of my clothes sent here. I can't get along with just this one gown."

Sir Anthony took the paper and perused it. "Naturally, you will want to look your best for Lord Avery."

Ginny looked at him in some surprise. "My only wish is to not offend my fellow housemates by appearing at dinner in the same soiled and crumpled gown night after night. I should think you of all people would understand."

To his surprise, he chuckled. "I think I shall never again take good grooming for granted. I would be most grateful if you would ask that my spare wardrobe I keep at Dunsmere be sent along, as well."

Ginny stared at him, wide-eyed. "Those clothes must be at least three years old."

"What of it?"

"Only that they won't be bang-up-to-the-mark such as what you have on presently."

"Ah, yes, Miss Delacourt, but as you said, they will provide relief for my companions."

Ginny scratched out the second note leaving him to read what she had written to Grandmama. It was well written and certainly factual until the end, where she had added a postscript, which read: "Sir Anthony wishes to send his apologies for failing to accomplish his task."

Failing to accomplish his task! That was outside of enough! He forced himself to remain calm. "Miss Delacourt, I believe you have made an error here in the postscript." He leaned over her and pointed to the offending phrase.

She studied the paper. "No, I don't think so. I can't see that I've misspelled anything."

He felt his back stiffen. "It is the entire postscript that is in error. I'm sure I don't recall having said anything along those lines."

"Oh, that! You know your grandmama. A few well-chosen words and she is much more amiable about things. I hope you aren't going to make me write it over."

That was exactly what he had in mind, but it wouldn't do to say so at this point. In fact there was very little he could say without revealing how annoyed he felt. He knew it was unjustified. If only he knew what accounted for it. Surely he didn't care if Ginny called him a failure! Did he?

Pulling himself together, he said, "Very well, Miss Delacourt. I concede to your wisdom. If you will be needing me in the near future—a circumstance I very much doubt—I will be in the drawing room with the others." He managed a very proper bow and a perfectly correct smile before he got himself out of the room as fast as he could, no mean feat considering his sore ankle and the nonchalant stroll at which he forced himself to proceed.

Perhaps Miss Delacourt had no need of him, but there was little doubt in his mind he could make himself useful to Lucinda Barrington. He should attempt to save her from the lily-faced Avery. It would give him a way to pass the time. Besides, she couldn't possibly look forward to a lifetime of listening to his insipid poetry. Then again, she was not a girl without resources. It seemed that lisping baby talk could be unsheathed at will. Twenty years of that could pall on a man of even Lord Avery's stamp.

How he was to deal with either of them for the duration of the quarantine was a more troubling question. By the time Sir Anthony pushed open the drawing room door, he had developed a headache and a ferocious frown.

"Why, Sir Anthony, whatever is the matter?" Mrs. Barrington's shrill cry shrieked in his pounding head.

Sir Anthony forced a smile. He had one for every occasion. This was the one he used for matchmaking mamas:

charming but aloof. When Mrs. Barrington gave him a queer look and rushed out the door mumbling something about dinner preparations, he relabeled it his how-to-get-rid-of-Mrs. Barrington smile and sat down.

"Lord Avery, I understand you are to be staying on with us. It is good of you to wish to entertain the young ladies, but not at all necessary. You have not been exposed, I assure you." He was assured he couldn't put up with Lord Avery's dramatics for a single evening, let alone weeks of them.

Lucinda and Lord Avery turned to him with a jerk and stared at him in consternation. Anyone could see they had plenty to be concerned about. They were so close on the sofa, practically touching.

"What concern is it of yours, pray tell?" Lord Avery took Lucinda's hand and drew it to his lips.

"Lord Avery . . ." Lucinda gasped, fluttering her eyelids. She withdrew her hand and turned to Sir Anthony. "We were just discussing how we should pass the time during our confinement. I must say, it is much more pleasant to have the company of you two, as well as that of Miss Delacourt. When I had the spots, there was no one to amuse me." Lucinda's lips pressed in a pretty little pout. "But now there are the two of you, and I daresay I shall be vastly entertained." She clapped her hands, which had the effect of clashing cymbals in Sir Anthony's throbbing head.

"But, my darling, I have waited so long to have you to myself." Lord Avery possessed himself once more of Lucinda's hand. "I have been in a fever to see you since last we met."

Lucinda had the grace to look a trifle uncomfortable. "Oh yeth, it was at the Woolthley-Smythe house. Sir Anthony, were you not invited to that do?"

Sir Anthony felt himself powerless to reply. The lisp had returned. Was she attempting to attract him with her fabricated town-bronze or drive him mad?

"Leave him be," Lord Avery demanded. "Perhaps he is fevering with the pox himself."

"His eyes have taken on a bit of a glassy look," Lucinda murmured.

"Dear heart, we must find a place where we can be alone. I cannot bear to have another man feast his eyes on your loveliness," Lord Avery said, daring a tiny kiss to one of Lucinda's fingers.

"Sir!" Lucinda cried. "Pray, remember yourself." She sprang to her feet and moved to a window. "Sir Anthony, Lord Avery and I have been playing cards. It has been such fun! Do you think Miss Delacourt would come and play too? We could have a game of whist or picquet."

"I think that is a well-informed idea, Miss Barrington. The sooner we learn to entertain ourselves, the better."

Lord Avery scowled, rose, and stationed himself at a mullioned window on the opposite side of the room from Lucinda. Sir Anthony couldn't help but notice Avery had chosen the window with the most amount of sunlight, creating a positive halo around his golden locks.

Lucinda gathered the skirts of her pretty blue muslin frock in her hands and headed for the door. "I'll go get her. Perhapth later we can play a game of hunt the slipper," she lisped. The sound of the door slamming behind her was like the hammering of nails in a coffin. Preferably, Lord Avery's.

Sir Anthony glared at the poet posed by the window. What right had he to mince about kissing the hands of all the ladies? However, it was the memory of the kiss on Ginny's wrist—the inside of it, no less—that caused him to grind his teeth. In fact, his teeth were so tightly clenched together, he found it difficult to put his tongue to words.

"Sir Anthony, what am I to do?" Lord Avery spun away from the window and cast himself into a chair. "I have waited all this time for nothing, nothing! She does not love me. Her heart has not waited for me as mine has waited, waited to be near her, to breathe her air, tune my heartbeat to hers!" Mercifully, the muffled cries that followed were lost on Sir Anthony as Lord Avery had stuffed his head under the chair cushions.

"Come, come, Avery." He pulled the lime-green cushion from Lord Avery's head and regarded the poor, sniveling sot, his nose red and dripping. "You mustn't let the ladies see you like this. I daresay they'll be through the door any moment now." He handed Lord Avery his handkerchief, which he prayed would not be returned.

"Thank you," Lord Avery gasped, mopping his eyes. "Quite right, you know. I would rather die than have Lucinda see me this way."

What a blessed relief! He hated to see a grown man cry, even Avery. "Think nothing of it. See, here come the ladies now." Lucinda and Ginny walked in, looking a bit bemused. Had they heard the sobs coming down the hall? Lucinda especially looked uneasy and launched her worst bit of lisping yet.

"I have brought Mith Delacourt with me. She thays she would very much like to play cards and tho we shall. Shan't we, Mith Delacourt?"

Ginny agreed and stepped over to the card table. "Sir Anthony, would the two of you help to bring the table over here? We can put more chairs around it if we pull it to the center of the room."

"Oh, yes, I quite agree, Mith Delacourt." Lucinda tripped across the room and took Sir Anthony's arm. "Would you be my partner? I am sure you are a most skilled player."

For a horrifying moment, Sir Anthony thought Lord Avery would burst into a fresh bout of tears. His chin quivered, and he bit his lower lip until the spasm passed. Sir Anthony breathed an inward sigh and seated Lucinda at the table. Lord Avery, managing to be both charming and petulant, escorted Ginny to the table and professed himself "de*light*ed" to be her partner.

"Oh, isn't this marvelouth!" Lucinda's eyes rolled into the back of her head, presumably in rapture.

By the end of the game, which he and Lucinda won, Sir Anthony was willing to admit it had been somewhat amusing. Avery was proper and circumspect in his attentions for once, Lucinda's lisp finally faded into oblivion, and Ginny hadn't taunted him even once.

Chapter Six

That night at dinner, Ginny sat and studied the faces around the table. She sensed some definite undercurrents. Squire Barrington, dressed in prime twig, was in a jovial mood. She had no doubt it was due to the wealthy bachelors seated at his table.

Lord Avery, seated to the squire's right, was a bit more difficult to read. He alternated between feverish good humor and morose despondency. He sported the largest diamond stickpin Ginny had ever seen. It winked with blue fire, drawing the color of his superfine coat into its breathtaking depths. She was not surprised to see the squire's covetous gaze rest on it often.

Surely Lucinda noticed it also. Seated next to Lord Avery, she had an eye-popping view of the decadent stickpin but seemed to make a point of not looking at it. In fact, she was giving the lion's share of her attention to Sir Anthony, seated across from her.

As it was perfectly acceptable to speak across the table in such an intimate setting, he lost no time in striking up an animated conversation with the pretty heiress. Ginny felt an uncomfortable burning whenever he turned his gaze to Lucinda, who looked like an angel in that gauzy ice-pink creation. It matched the color of her lips to perfection and enhanced the creamy white of her skin.

Perhaps he was simply being polite as always. Didn't he spend nearly as much time conversing with herself as well as Mrs. Barrington? Curse him! There was no reading his actions when he was so faultlessly correct.

Ginny looked down at the folds of her lilac silk. She had been so happy to have it arrive with the rest of her clothes, and just in time to dress for dinner too. She had pounced on it immediately as being the prettiest of the lot and had instructed Maren to fashion her hair in a new, more becoming style.

"Are you not hungry, Miss Delacourt?" Mrs. Barrington leaned toward her.

"Oh, yes. Very." Ginny picked up her fork and began to eat. Mrs. Barrington had been so kind. She did not wish to offend her, and, as the food was delectable, Ginny had no problem doing her duty. "Umm, delicious."

Lucinda giggled into her hand. "My, what an appetite, Miss Delacourt! I'm afraid I couldn't eat another bite. I always tell Mama that seven courses is plenty, but Papa insists on nine or ten."

Nine or ten! What course were they on now? Ginny replaced her fork, hoping the others could not see the burning she felt, oh too well, in her cheeks.

"Of course, of course," the squire insisted. "I must keep up my weight. It wouldn't do, no, wouldn't do at all to get too thin."

Too thin! Why, the man was likely to blow away in the next wind. Mrs. Barrington, on the other hand, could stand to skip a course or two. She was not precisely fat but tended to bulge in the wrong places. How Lucinda managed to curve with such appreciable effect was little less than a miracle.

From the way Sir Anthony's eyes seemed to glow when he looked at her, Ginny supposed he thought so too. Somehow he had always managed to cover his admiration for her with that fashionable sangfroid. She may as well admit it; Sir Anthony did not find her attractive. And no wonder; she had been a positive thorn in his side since they had set out days before.

Entering the drawing room after dinner, Mrs. Barrington took her daughter by the arm and led her to a shadowy corner, where they began a loudly whispered conversation. Ginny could not help but notice that the names of Sir Anthony and Lord Avery were being bandied about with alarming frequency, but that alone was not enough to tell who was currently in favor. The way Lucinda threw out lures to the both of them told her nothing either, except that she insisted the men be fawning over none but her, as always.

Presently the whispering ceased. Lucinda uttered a fierce "As you will, Mother!" and flounced away to find a seat next to Ginny.

Mrs. Barrington remained in the shadows. "You may

wonder what our little conversation was about, Miss Delacourt."

"Oh, no, I was lost in my own thoughts, I'm afraid." It was patently untrue, but Ginny owned that there were times a polite lie was better than the truth. Perhaps Sir Anthony was rubbing off on her.

"There are things that are private between a mother and her daughter," Mrs. Barrington continued. "I hope you can understand our little lapse in manners."

Ginny glanced at Lucinda and saw her mute agony. "Yes, of course, Mrs. Barrington. It has been years since I have had a mother, but I do have a greataunt. Unfortunately, she doesn't limit her words of guidance to my ears alone. I'm afraid the lower footmen are all very much aware of every scrape I've ever fallen into."

"Do you fall into very many scrapes, Miss Delacourt?" Lucinda asked. "You used to be so boring! This is the best, most famous quarantine ever!"

Ginny waited for the customary clapping of hands, but it did not come. Perhaps it was an artifice she reserved for the gentlemen. "Thank you, and since we shall all be getting to know one another better, it would be most pleasant if we availed one another of our Christian names."

Lucinda smiled her delight, her cheeks dimpling. No wonder men admired her. Indeed, the pitfalls of her nature must seem wondrously small compared with her beauty, not to mention that vast fortune looming in the distance.

The door opened and the gentlemen entered the room. Lucinda whirled around, clapped her hands, and cried, "Oh, just in time! Miss Delacourt and I have decided to dispense with the formalities. We are to be plain Lucinda and Ginny. Isn't that famous?"

"Lucinda!" Mrs. Barrington called from her corner of the room.

"Oh, yeth." Lucinda gathered her gauzy skirts and stationed herself in front of Lord Avery. She followed this with a deep curtsy and a modest sweep of her lashes before she folded prim hands in front of her. "Lord Avery, we are moth happy to have your prethenth here tonight."

So, Lord Avery was Mrs. Barrington's choice of husband for her daughter. Ginny hadn't truly expected otherwise, even though Sir Anthony was every bit as wealthy and a good deal more sensible. Not only that, but the Crenshaw family was as old and respectable as the monarchy itself. Lord Avery was only the second earl since the title was created.

"You may call me Eustace," Lord Avery said, looking deep into Lucinda's eyes.

Mrs. Barrington tensed and stared at the back of Lucinda's head.

"As you wish . . . Eustace."

Mrs. Barrington relaxed. "Very proper, Lucinda. Of course, there is no need to call Sir Anthony anything but that."

Sir Anthony inclined his head and found himself a seat on the opposite side of the room.

"As for myself," the squire announced, "you may all call me, yes, you may call me anything you like. Though

Squire suits me best." He then took up a seat next to his wife, and the two fell to whispering between themselves.

"Well," Ginny remarked. "It will be a long ten days if we don't find something to do with ourselves."

"Oh, yeth, let's make plans." Lucinda grabbed Lord Avery's hand and, with a glance in her mother's direction, ensconced him on the sofa next to her. She then proceeded to stare at Sir Anthony, who had taken up a chair on the other side of the fire from Ginny.

"Lucinda, since Rose Arbor is your home, perhaps you can offer some ideas of what there is to do here for entertainment," Ginny asked.

Lucinda furrowed her pretty brow. "Well, let's see. There's cards and spillikins. Oh, and this is a famous house for Hunt the Slipper!"

Lord Avery leaned forward in his seat. "There is a vast library with all the poets. I am told there is even a copy of Homer. Have you read Homer, Miss Delacourt?"

"Yes, I believe so. Isn't he the one who wrote about the Greeks?"

"One of the many. Were you aware, Miss Delacourt, that Helen of Troy was believed to have dark hair?" Lord Avery stared intently at her brown locks.

"Why, no, I was not," Ginny said faintly.

"I think what Miss Delacourt is after," Sir Anthony hastened to add, "is information regarding entertainment that is peculiar to Rose Arbor."

"Rose Arbor is *not* peculiar!" Lucinda said with a stamp of her foot.

"Not at all, Miss Barrington. Only, pray tell us, what is available to us here that might not be other places?"

"Yes, that's it exactly!" Ginny exclaimed.

"Well, we don't have any ghosts or hidden passages, if that is what you mean. It's just a boring old house." Lucinda lowered her voice to a whisper. "Not a single murder or lovelorn suicide."

"Lucinda, we can't hear what you are saying," Mrs. Barrington warned from her dark corner.

"Yes, Mama." Lucinda stared into her lap, looking miserable.

The fire crackled and popped in the grate, and everyone's gaze seemed to be fixed somewhere among the roses patterned in the carpet at their feet.

Ginny looked to Sir Anthony for guidance. Surely his wealth of protocol could somehow get them lightly over this particular spot of rough ground. "Might you have an idea or two for us, Sir Anthony?"

"Just the usual amusements one resorts to in this situation."

"Oh? Have you often found yourself in this situation, Sir Anthony?" Ginny was suddenly very interested in the other young ladies' homes in which he was obliged to pass the time. "What, pray tell, did you do to amuse yourself then?"

"Cards, games, play-acting. The usual house party fare."

"Play-acting. Of course!" Lord Avery was so gratified by the suggestion he actually favored Sir Anthony with a hard stare. "It must be none other than the Bard!

'Heaven is here, where Juliet lives, and every cat and dog and little mouse, every unworthy thing, live here in Heaven and may look on her, but Romeo may not.'" Unlike Romeo, Lord Avery was able to look at whomever he pleased. So why was he looking at her and not Lucinda?

Ginny was startled when Sir Anthony's deep voice continued the quote with, "'More validity, more honorable state, more courtship, lives in carrion flies than Romeo.'"

Lord Avery whirled on him and wrung each word that followed through lips twisted with grief. "'They may seize on the white wonder of dear Juliet's hand, and steal immortal blessing from her lips, who, even in pure and vestal modesty, still blush, as thinking their own kisses sin.'"

Sir Anthony rose, his hands curled into tight fists at his sides. "'But Romeo may not. He is banished!'"

Lord Avery's eyes flew open in surprise. "'This may flies do, but I from this must fly.'" With a little hop-skip, Lord Avery found refuge on the sofa.

Sir Anthony remained standing until the tension eased out of his flexed hands and his top lip uncurled from an especially lethal sneer. Ginny couldn't remember seeing Sir Anthony so impassioned. She hadn't believed it was possible and couldn't fathom what accounted for it.

Lucinda, who had been sitting entranced throughout, came to life, clapped, and shouted. "Bravo! Bravo, that was very well done." With her shining eyes turned on

Lord Avery for once, she sighed. "I could do this every evening. It is vastly entertaining."

Ginny hesitated to point out that Sir Anthony hadn't been acting, especially when she saw the liberating effect the little scene had on his self-possession. It would seem that the beast's head had been raised; perhaps an entire play would open the door to the cage. She racked her brain for just the right one. It must have murder and mayhem. Oh, and one mustn't forget love and romance. Let Lord Avery and Lucinda be his target for the first, but she was becoming more and more curious what Sir Anthony might be like when in the throes of romantic passion.

"I agree with Lucinda," Ginny said with a furtive glance at Sir Anthony through her eyelashes. "In fact, I have the perfect play. *Hamlet*."

"*Hamlet*! I have always wanted to be in *Hamlet*." Lucinda rose and kneeled at Ginny's knee, heedlessly crushing the pink gauze of her gown. "My dancing teacher, who was an acting teacher also, but only not for me because Mama frowns on it . . . and rightly so," she dutifully added, "*he* said that the female role in *Hamlet* is every actress's *dream*."

"Yes, I have heard that said."

"If we are to do *Hamlet,* I must insist on the lead," Lord Avery announced. He took Ginny's hand from where it rested on her knee. "Here I have found my fair Ophelia."

Ginny was aware of the renewed tension coming from Sir Anthony's corner of the room. He pursed his lips, then smoothly said, "I think Lucinda should play the lead.

She is so suited to the part, fair and slight and ethereal. Ophelia needs to look as if she needs protecting."

Unlike me, Ginny thought, *who defends herself with a heavily loaded reticule and a well-sharpened tongue.* It was a lowering thought. Perhaps there was something to Sir Anthony's code of politeness. With as much tact as possible, she slipped her hand from Lord Avery's grasp. "I am very much honored, but I am not a good actress. I would do much better with a more staid part, such as the queen."

"Hearken well to her words, Avery. Miss Delacourt has very little experience in emoting a sentiment she does not feel." Sir Anthony rose and took Lucinda's hand, raising her to her feet. "But Miss Barrington strikes me as being just the lady to perform a mad scene with great gusto."

Lucinda's eyes opened very wide. "Mad scene? Ophelia goes mad?"

"Yes, of course, just before she throws herself into the river."

"Oh, but she doesn't *die*, does she?" Lucinda, who had been looking quite starry-eyed, now grasped the lapels of Sir Anthony's immaculately tailored evening coat. "I couldn't possibly play a woman who drowns herself!"

Sir Anthony didn't reply. Instead, he gazed down at Lucinda's white hands gripping his coat, then back at her face.

Lucinda gasped exactly as if she had been given a good shake. "I *am* sorry. I shall play Ophelia if you wish it, Sir Anthony."

There came a loud *ahem* from the shadows across the way.

Lucinda jumped and whirled around to face Lord Avery. "Whom do *you* wish me to play, my lord, I mean, Eustace?"

"My flower, do you truly care what I think?" Lord Avery looked deeply into her eyes.

With a flutter of lashes, she stammered, "Of course, Eustace. I wish to be agreeable."

Ginny, finding all of this painful in the extreme, began to rethink the wisdom of the awakening of beasts. "Why don't we each choose our favorite Shakespeare soliloquy? There is no reason to do a whole play." At least, she *hoped* a clutch of soliloquys would do as well. "Besides, I don't think Shakespeare ever wrote a play that had only four parts."

Lucinda, who had been looking close to tears, brightened visibly. "That's a marvelous idea, Ginny! Why, I could be anyone I choose."

"I agree, your idea is a stroke of genius, Miss Delacourt." Lord Avery took to pacing the room. "Especially considering there is no one but ourselves and the good squire and his lady to serve as audience. We shall all be surprised with each other when we recite our lines."

He put a hand to his heart and raised the other to the level of his eyes. " 'Alas, poor Yorick! I knew him, Horatio . . . ' " He dropped his hands and exclaimed, "Yes, I think I shall choose a soliloquy from *Hamlet*."

"And I shall be Juliet," Lucinda revealed. "She kills herself too, I know, but at least she doesn't go mad first.

There's something so romantic about dying for true love, is there not, Sir Anthony?"

There came the sound of parting lips from the shadows.

"I mean, Eustace?" Lucinda quickly amended.

He looked down his very fine nose at her. "I wouldn't know, Miss Barrington."

Ginny decided to change the subject before Lucinda burst into tears. "And whom shall you depict, Sir Anthony?"

"I'm not sure. Perhaps Caesar, or maybe Lear. I shall have to study before I choose. Doubtless you have already decided on your subject."

"I? Not exactly. Why do you say so?"

Sir Anthony brushed a mote of dust from his coat sleeve. "I thought it would be an easy decision. I feel very sure you would make a splendid Kate."

All were frozen in a stunned silence until Lucinda asked, "Who is Kate?"

Lord Avery answered her in an uncharacteristically quiet voice. "Katherine. She is the heroine from *The Taming of the Shrew.*"

Ginny felt as if she had been struck. Tears sprang to her eyes, but she would not give Sir Anthony the satisfaction of seeing them spill down her cheeks.

Lucinda looked puzzled. "But Ginny is not the least bit shrewish. If she is not a good actress, I should think it would be difficult for her to play one."

Ginny could not resist seeing how Sir Anthony responded to that remark and was gratified to see a wash of color suffuse his face. The muscle around his jaw tensed, and a vein at his temple throbbed.

"You are quite right, Miss Barrington," he said huskily. "Pray forgive my error. I find Miss Delacourt to be quite the actress, after all." With that he made a deep bow to the company at large and walked out.

Ginny didn't know where to look. "I think I shall retire also. All this drama has left me most fatigued." Whisking tears from her face, she quit the room and went immediately to the library. It had been a long time since she had read *The Taming of the Shrew,* and she intended to freshen her memory as to exactly what was so shrewish about its heroine. She found the correct volume, and, after leafing through the pages, her eyes fell on a most enlightening verse. "Her only fault, and that is faults enough, is that she is intolerable curst and shrewd and forward, so beyond all measure that, were my state far worse than it is, I would not wed her for a mine of gold."

So, this was how he thought of her! She felt the hot sting of tears in her eyes and cursed herself for being a fool. What did she care what he thought? It wasn't as if she had attempted to engage his interest. Still, it didn't feel pleasant to be thought of in such a light, even if the poor opinion belonged to someone like Sir Anthony. Especially Sir Anthony. She might as well admit it: She cared. Very much so.

The tears came then in earnest. Ginny tucked the book under her arm and ran from the room. She managed to hold her sobs in check as she dashed upstairs to the upper hallway. Once in her own room she fully intended to sob her heart out.

Thoroughly blinded by tears, she ran down the hall and threw open the door. Just as she was about to launch herself onto the bed and give full vent to her perplexing feelings, she stopped short. There in front of her stood Sir Anthony, his cravat gone missing and his shirt unbuttoned to the waist, his eyes dancing with amusement.

Chapter Seven

"Have you gone mad?" Ginny cried. "Get out of my room this instant!"

"Ginny, I . . ." Sir Anthony spluttered. For the second time in as many days, Ginny Delacourt had robbed him of words. Hastily, he began doing up the buttons of his shirt.

Her face flushed a glorious rose, and she turned to face the door. "I will allow you time to . . . to . . . *then* you will leave."

He swallowed his laughter when he realized her mistake. "I would be most happy to oblige you, Miss Delacourt, but for one thing."

"What?" she demanded, whirling to face him again.

"This is *my* room."

"Your room?" Her gaze flew from the dark-paneled wainscot to the paintings of the hunt along the walls. When she saw the spare, masculine bed, the covers

92

turned down and sporting a bloodred satin bed jacket, she gave a little shriek and dropped her gaze to the floor. "I do beg your pardon, sir."

"It does not signify. It is not difficult to lose one's way in an unfamiliar house."

Curiously, her flush deepened and she clutched to her chest the book she gripped in her hands. Her agitation was palatable, and still she would not look at him. "I allow you have most likely been present at far more house parties than have I."

"I expect I have, but never one where I was so rude to a fellow houseguest as I was to you earlier downstairs. I'm sure I don't know what possessed me." And as long as he didn't allow himself to think about it for half a minute, he was sure to never find out. "Will you forgive me?"

"Yes, of course, if you can forgive me my shrewish outburst. You can't imagine what went through my mind when I thought you had let yourself into my room."

Sir Anthony rather thought he could and carefully schooled his features not to betray his wry amusement. "I see you have found a book. Have you decided on a character to portray?"

Her expression hardened a little. "No. I thought I would do some reading before I decide. Well"—she reached for the door handle—"I should be off. Good night."

"Of course. Allow me to see you to your room." He put on his bed jacket, and Ginny blushed. In adorable confusion, she cast about until she found the door handle, eager to leave, but he stayed her hand. "I shall just take a look into the hall to see if anyone is about." He peered around the door and spied Mrs. Barrington and Lucinda just emerging at the top of the stairs.

"But Mama," Lucinda was saying, "I think it monstrously unfair of you to force me when you know I haven't had even one ball thrown in my honor . . ."

Sir Anthony yanked his head inside and eased the door closed. He put his finger to his lips and whispered, "Lucinda and her mother. They should be gone soon."

She nodded and gazed up at him. Her eyes were larger than he had thought, fringed with impossibly long, dark lashes.

"I trust you won't tell Grandaunt Regina of this. She would have us wed in a hair's breadth," Ginny said.

"Would she?" Sir Anthony heard the hard edge in his voice. He hadn't forgotten his initial suspicions that Grandmama and Ginny were planning his wedding. But could the forthcoming, true-speaking Ginny be capable of such deceit? Her face was always so expressive of her feelings even when her words were not, and she had seemed most ill at ease with this situation from the beginning.

"Indeed she would," Ginny replied. "She may be eccentric, but she is terribly hard-nosed about certain proprieties. Rather like her grandson."

He gave her his most devastating smile, one he hadn't occasion to use in quite some time, and briskly said, "It signifies not what Grandmama would do. The question is, would you?"

"Would I what?"

"Would you marry me?"

The look of sheer astonishment that crossed Ginny's face convinced Sir Anthony she had no part in a plot to make them tenants for life. She was too artless, even ingenuous. How could he have been so cruel as to imply that her tears earlier that evening had been affected?

"Am I to take that as an offer for my hand in marriage?" she gasped.

"What if it was?" Sir Anthony knew he shouldn't tease her but found that he was enjoying such unguarded emotion, so rare among the lords and ladies of his set. He carried her hand to his lips. "Would it be a fate repugnant or one cherished?"

Her hand began to tremble in his, and she clutched her book tighter to her chest with the other. "I am sure the Barringtons must have passed by. It should be quite safe for me to go to my room."

He knew she should return to her chamber, but he was filled with an inexplicable desire to learn how she felt about him now that he knew her face could not lie. "Ah, but Ginny, you have not yet answered my question." He was surprised when she flicked her hand from his and her eyes flashed with anger.

"You are being impertinent, sir! I do not answer impertinent questions, nor do I consider the intentions of a man who has deemed me worthy of his notice for a mere two days to be motivated by any finer feeling."

Sir Anthony was taken aback. He had expected her to laugh, lecture him on his faults, let him down gently, or, though it was a stretch, fall into his arms in blissful adoration. Instead, she had given him a scathing set-down while betraying precious few clues as to how she might answer in more ideal circumstances. And just when he thought he had the key to her thoughts.

What a fool he must seem to her. For a moment he had made himself vulnerable, and with growing wonder he realized how very much it hurt. He gazed down into her face, her eyes sparkling with anger, her cheeks flushed, and felt a tide of emotion too precipitate to define. Finding he could look at nothing but her lips, he put a hand on her waist to draw her close and another to the back of her head to prevent her escape. The anticipation he felt had nothing to do with the silk of her hair where it trailed along his hand or the supple curves of her waist and back. No, all he wanted from this kiss was to know how she truly felt. He had never known a kiss to lie.

Suddenly there was a loud *thunk*. His already erratic heartbeat jumped to new heights until he remembered the book Ginny had been holding and was now hastily retrieving from the floor.

He stepped back and took a few deep breaths. How did he let the situation get so out of control? He must make an attempt at normalcy. "I recall that you planned to do a little reading before bed, Miss Delacourt. Don't let me keep you."

Ginny stood up, her eyes full of angry tears. "No, I shan't let you keep me, and if you think I would let you have me, you are like all the other men I have known, to my regret."

Sir Anthony felt that familiar imperturbability come over him, almost unbidden.

"I am most sorry if I have offended you. I haven't the faintest idea why I would do such a thing."

Ginny's eyes blazed with fury. "Perhaps this will help you remember," she said. Then she hurled the book at him.

He wasn't sure when Ginny actually left. He thought he heard the door slam, but it was difficult to tell with all the ringing in his head. The chit certainly had good aim. This time she had caught him without the protection of headgear, and there would be a good-size bruise on his forehead come morning.

He bent for the book and all the blood rushed to his head. He swore, long and competently. At least he knew what book she had chosen. *The Taming of the Shrew* wasn't exactly what he would have selected as a sleep tonic, but it was better than some. Not that he would need aid in seeking Morpheus tonight. He was exhausted from reining in every emotion known to man in one short evening.

He finished undressing and climbed into bed. It felt wondrously good to close his eyes and rest his aching head on a soft pillow. If only he could banish the memory of Ginny's tear-filled eyes from his mind, he could get the rest he longed for. He willed her from his head, from the house, and finally to Hades, but to no avail. She would not go.

He groaned and rolled over. Why couldn't he conjure up the image of Ginny throwing that book at him? Certainly it would not inspire the tender feelings raised by the memory of how she had felt in his arms. For a moment he had felt he could be happy holding her that way forever.

He rubbed the painful lump growing on his forehead. He had come to his senses just in time. Could he have actually come close to kissing her? T'was appalling. For some reason, when around her, he found it most difficult to adopt the mask of indifference that had been his longtime number one defense.

He would have to steer a wide path around her until he regained control of himself. The house was rather small and company thin, but still it should not be too difficult a task since Ginny was furious with him and no doubt would avoid him as much as possible. In the meantime, he would have to find a way to get to sleep. With a curse, he jumped out of bed, dressed, and slipped outside.

The night was soft and balmy, with a high moon, perfect for a little night riding. What sheer relief it would be to ride fast and furious through the countryside, far away from the house and everyone in it. He made his way to the stables. It was pitch black inside, and he wondered how he would find the stable boy until he tripped over him where he had made his bed in the straw.

"Owww, eee! Wot's yer lay, there?" the stable boy cried.

"Nothing nefarious, I assure you," Sir Anthony replied. If he were bent on villainy, he would have had no need to leave the house. "Just find me a light and you'll see you have nothing to fear."

There was a shuffling and scraping as the boy found his lantern and lighted it. Swinging the lantern high, he peered up at Sir Anthony, taking in his well-cut clothes and cloudy expression. "You must be one of them swells staying up at the house."

Sir Anthony sketched a bow, allowing a fraction of a smile to play about his lips. "Indeed I am, and I am in need of your services this night. Do you have a mount for me, one with a bit of a kick in his gallop?"

The stable boy led Sir Anthony down the row of stalls to the end. "This here's Challenger." The stable boy threw Sir Anthony an assessing glance. "You should be able to pull it off, though I've yet to see anyone do it."

"The very thing. Keep him primed for me each night and your lips tightly sealed and there will be something in it for you at the end of my stay here."

The boy's eyes grew round, eradicating every last trace of his former wariness. "Gor blimey, guv. I'll be waiting for you every night, jus' see if I ain't. And mum's the word." Then he opened the door and led Challenger out of his stall and into the night air.

Sir Anthony stepped up to the dark bay and wondered if he had taken leave of his senses. Challenger seemed much larger upon close inspection and definitely dangerous. How the petite stable boy managed to saddle the brute was anybody's guess, but he did so with calm efficiency.

Sir Anthony regarded the rolling eyes and tossing mane and knew a qualm. He glanced back at the house and found his bedchamber window. Maybe he had exerted himself enough for one night. His gaze slipped to the opposite side of the house to a window much like his own, only he fancied someone stood looking out.

An image of Ginny, her eyes sparkling and her cheeks flushed, filled his mind. He felt as if he had been hit in the chest and the wind knocked clean out of him. With a ragged breath, he filled his lungs and launched himself into the saddle.

Bucking about in rage, Challenger turned into a snorting, rearing, crazy-eyed piece of horseflesh. Laughing outright, Sir Anthony gave the horse his head. If he were fortunate, Challenger would give him the ride of his life, leaving him with little strength for anything.

From her bedchamber window Ginny watched Sir Anthony streak away from sight. At least she felt fairly sure it was him. She had heard his chamber door open and his firm, steady tread down the hall earlier. She had not heard him return.

Upon leaving Sir Anthony's room she had found her own with ridiculous ease. How she had ever managed to take a wrong turn in the first place was unclear. She was mortified, angry, and hurt. Surely she had invited Sir Anthony's improper advances with her own folly. She couldn't expect him to believe she had come to his room in error.

How he must have laughed when she left, thinking her an inexperienced, foolish little wanton. She turned away from the window and sat on the edge of her bed. Well, she wouldn't let that thought interfere with her having a good night's sleep. No indeed. If anything, it would be the feel of his strong arm around her waist and his warm breath fanning her cheek that kept her head turning on her pillow all the weary night long.

Chapter Eight

Come morning, Maren drew the curtains. A shaft of yellow light filled the room, flooding Ginny's rose-strewn counterpane. She had dreamed that she was not herself, in a place she had never been before. Now she remembered. Rose Arbor.

"Glory, I must have fallen asleep." Ginny stretched and sat up against the rose-embroidered pillows.

Maren shot her a startled look. "If you don't mind my saying so, miss, I daresay you fell asleep some time ago."

Ginny laughed. "And precisely how did you come by that bit of information, pray tell?"

"Beggin' your pardon, miss, but you spoke so in your sleep after such a long bout of tossin' and turnin' that I couldn't help but worry about you."

"I spoke in my sleep? I don't know that I have ever done so in the past." Ginny took the cup of steaming chocolate Maren handed her and sipped meditatively. "What did I say?"

Maren, warming up to her new mistress with each hour spent in her service, was bold enough to sit on the edge of Ginny's bed. "You spent a deal of time saying hows you're not Kate or some such thing."

Ginny choked on her chocolate. So that was where she had been all night, in Petruchio's country house. Only the master of this house was a dark, blue-eyed devil who had no business laughing in her dreams.

"Are you all right, miss? You look kind of queer, like." Maren felt the pot on the stand by Ginny's bed. "The water t'ain't too hot, is it?"

"No, Maren, it's perfect. Please see to it that my blue dimity gown is put out." She wanted to be sure she looked as young and fresh as springtime. She'd much rather comparisons be drawn between her and the new day than with Petruchio's jaded bride.

Ginny entered the breakfast room just as Sir Anthony was regaling its occupants with some anecdote or other, one most likely something having to do with last night if the guilt in his eyes when they met hers was any indication. It was difficult to determine the case, however, as he snapped his mouth shut upon her arrival.

Indeed, Lord Avery, the squire, and his wife glanced apprehensively at her when she greeted them. All except for Lucinda, who, chin in her hands and eyes sparkling, was staring at Sir Anthony with a devastated look in her eyes. "Do go on, Thur Anthony," she cooed. "Your story is ever so funny!"

Ginny added her own protestations. "Oh, yes, do finish your story. It would seem that it was vastly amusing. Wouldn't you say so, Lord Avery?" But it was Sir Anthony she stole a glance at from the corner of her eye. She was gratified by the deep flush that suffused his face from his collar right up to the nasty bruise on his forehead.

"Oh, yes, vastly amusing," Lord Avery echoed. "But pray, how are you this morning, Miss Delacourt? The last we saw of you, you were in flight like the Goddess Daphne ere she was turned into a tree."

It was a comparison Ginny had not anticipated, though it was more favorable than the others she had endured of late. Unfortunately, it defied response. Taking a deep breath, she turned again to Sir Anthony. "Pray, sir, do not refrain from your tale on my account. I shall just go to the sideboard and fill my plate."

"Wonderful idea," the squire announced. "The morning is a wonderful time, yes, a wonderful time to breakfast. Always have maintained it was so, haven't I, wife?"

"Yes, dear," that good woman replied. Ginny had it as a fact that Mrs. Barrington rarely took breakfast before noon. However, it seemed the presence of two eligible bachelors did wonders for her appetite. Funny, it served the opposite function for Ginny.

She returned to the table with very little more on her plate than when she took it from the sideboard, an occurrence that prompted Sir Anthony to part lips and make utterance for the first time since Ginny entered the room.

"Why, Miss Delacourt, may I persuade you to have a coddled egg or two with that slice of toast? You will need more sustenance than that will afford if you plan to make a habit of sitting up half the night reading."

"For your information, Sir Anthony, I did not do any reading last night. I choose to spend my nocturnal hours sleeping." At least when she was able. "I believe I heard you wandering about last night in the hall, however." And on the stairs, right out the front door to the stables.

Sir Anthony had the grace to look a trifle discomfited. "Yes, I had an intolerable headache and thought I would go down to the library to find something to read as well."

As this communication sent the entire company into whoops, Ginny felt it best to forsake her breakfast. She didn't really want it after having been so mortified. It was clear Sir Anthony had been humiliating her with the tale of how she had come to be in his room, the story no doubt riddled with liberal commentary on her manners, morals, and jolly good aim.

She retired to one of the trio of small sitting rooms, all of which were decorated in shades of rose. The mauve room was nearest at hand and most convenient to shedding the hot tears that scalded her eyes. Whatever else this quarantine brought after all that she had endured, she felt quite certain she would leave with a hearty distaste for pink.

"I believe I owe you an apology, Miss Delacourt." Sir Anthony stood framed in the doorway, his entire being evidence of his agitation. Even his usual carefully arranged expression betrayed a modicum of concern. She thought she could almost see it in his eyes.

"What you owe me is an explanation, sir. Whether or not an apology should be in order thereafter is yet to be determined."

He entered the room. "May I sit?"

Ginny swept her skirts from the brocade sofa and inched to the farthest edge. "Please."

Sir Anthony regarded the acres of distance between Ginny and the proffered seat and moved with great purpose to a delicate side chair. Placing it directly across from her, he sat. "There, that is much better."

Ginny turned up her nose and presented him with her profile. It was bad enough he had sought her out in her private moment, but for their knees to be touching was outside of enough.

He cleared his throat. "I think you will agree that I crossed the line of decorum last night."

Ginny sucked in her breath. She hadn't expected him to regard her feelings in such a matter. She looked down at her hands folded primly in her lap. "I do, more than you know."

"I realize you find my attentions distasteful. I wish you to be at ease. No such advances will be made in the future."

"I am happy to hear you say so." That wasn't precisely the truth, but how else to explain the mixture of relief and utter dejection now gripping her heart?

"Now I think you owe me an apology."

Ginny turned to stare at him. "Whatever for? Surely you don't believe that I came to your room intentionally!" Naturally, he did, but she had her pride to think of.

Sir Anthony, his eyes dancing, merely tapped his bruised forehead with exaggerated care.

Ginny could not suppress a smile. "Ah, yes, the book!"

He nodded. "And for believing I would divulge that interesting little tidbit to that crew in there."

"You mean you did not?" Ginny was astonished. "It seemed clear from all that was said they had the whole from you even as I came into the room."

"Well, er, I had to tell them some of the truth."

Ginny narrowed her eyes. "How much of it, pray tell?"

"Never fear. I did not cast aspersions on your honor, but I had to tell them how I came about my bruise."

"And need you bring me into it? For all I know you might have fallen off your horse."

Sir Anthony did not betray the surprise he must surely have felt. "You know I was out riding last night—and threaten me with it? That would not be wise considering that I did come by this bruise at your hand and they have yet to learn how."

"I find that difficult to believe in light of their mirth a few moments ago. Oh, what must they think of me?"

Sir Anthony leaned back in his chair so as to afford him a better view of the lovely picture she presented. Her pink cheeks and sky blue gown were pretty as a spring day. Perhaps he would allow her to blush a bit longer. Then again, perhaps not. The lady had suffered enough embarrassment at his hands.

"Come now, they think only that you are a trifle clumsy."

"Clumsy? Does such a fault explain how I came to be in your room or the manner in which I left it?"

"No at all. But it did explain my lump when I told them that we had met each other in the hallway and that you had dropped your book. We both bent to retrieve it and you struck me in the head with your chin in so doing."

Ginny drew a deep breath. "Oh, well done! That was very sensible of you." Her color was almost restored to its natural shade. "I must thank you for your presence of mind."

"It *was* rather clever of me." Then again, he had had most of the night to come up with the story. "In gratitude, would it be remiss of me to ask that you keep my secret?"

"That you spent the night riding? Yes, I suppose I could. That is, as long as you are not endangering anyone in doing so," she added.

"No. That is, unless, of course, horses are vulnerable to the chicken pox."

Ginny laughed. At last! It seemed he had waited an age for that laugh. So much for his late-night resolve to stay away from her, but something had to be done. He couldn't allow her to think he had sullied her good name. And at the breakfast table of their hosts, no less.

There was a rustling of silk skirts outside in the hall. Ginny's bright smile took on a look of unease. "I think it best if we rejoin the others. It wouldn't do to jeopardize my so recently regained reputation."

"Of course." He took her arm and walked her to the door. She fit into his side perfectly. He could become accustomed to that sensation. It really was too bad that he and marriage didn't fit.

At the door she paused and said, "Shall we be friends, then?" She looked up at him with such warmth and sincerity, his heart turned over.

"Yes, I think that would fit the bill nicely." Really too bad indeed, he thought.

Ginny went directly upstairs to see Nan. She found Mrs. Crandall, the housekeeper, applying poultices to the worst of the spots. "Thank you, Mrs. Crandall. I'll see to that." Ginny gently pried the last poultice from the startled housekeeper, who clucked in disbelief all the way to the door.

"I thought that woman would never let me be!" Nan cried.

"Has she been pestering you, love?" Ginny applied the poultice of oats dipped in milk to Nan's elbow, relieved to see the glint returned to her eye.

"Tormenting me is more like. She is worse than the spots, and *they* itch something fierce." Nan raised a hand to her face but Ginny deftly caught it and placed it under the bedclothes.

"You had best go, miss. I would hate for you to come by this 'cause of me. It's been two days, and I'm still getting new spots every hour."

"You will feel better soon." Ginny moved with speedy efficiency about the room, plumping pillows and opening windows. "I know, I had it when I was nine."

"Nine! However did they keep you from scratching the skin right off your bones?" Nan reached for a pox but remembered herself just in time.

"My mother often sat and read books or told stories. Would you like me to do so now? I see there is a volume of Sir Thomas Moore's *Irish Melodies* on the bed table."

Nan made a face. "Miss Barrington had that sent up. I suppose I should be grateful for the kindness, but it only served to blue-devil me."

"Why is that?" Ginny took the volume in hand and a paper fluttered out. It was covered by a flowery script, which read:

I had this of my papa when I was similarly afflicted, and it brought me much comfort to know the history behind one little poem. The poet wrote it for his wife when she contracted the pox and she was worried about having itty-bitty scars all over her body when the itty-bitty spots went away. I was ever so worried myself, but if a man who is the special friend of the Prince Regent and Byron could still love his wife after seeing her with spots, I'm sure I can find someone to love me too. I'm not so sure about you, seeing as you are an abigail and I have never seen you, with or without spots. I would, but Mama strictly forbids it. Yours, Lucinda.

"Well," Ginny said, replacing the note, "I cannot see why this should have you the least blue-deviled. If you had ever seen Lucinda, you would feel honored to have been so singled out by such as she." Not to mention amazed. Really, the girl meant well, but she was prodigiously dull-witted. How many abigails of her acquaintance could read? The fact that Nan could was beside the point.

"Is she very pretty?" Nan asked. "She must be to worry so about having her looks spoilt."

"Yes, very, and vain besides." Ginny drew a chair closer to the bed and sat. "She speaks just as she writes but with an abominable lisp."

"Truly? The poor dear!"

"Oh, you needn't feel sorry for her. It is an affectation. I hope she gives it up soon. It is vexing beyond anything!"

"And what does Sir Anthony think of her?" Nan asked. Ginny saw that she watched her closely for her reaction.

"You know I don't care two pins for what Sir Anthony thinks. I daresay he finds her well enough." She shrugged her nonchalance. "Anyway, it doesn't signify if he does favor her. Her parents have her practically promised to Lord Avery, a fine gentleman and very handsome."

"Never as handsome as Sir Anthony," Nan insisted.

"How could you possibly know that?"

"Why, no one would know how to be, that's how. Sir Anthony may be too caring of his clothes and he may pay his valet more than the Prince Regent spends on corsets, but that's no never mind. Sir Anthony has a natural attraction that any woman would find hard to resist."

"Why, Nan Plunkett, I am surprised at you! You're too young to know of which you speak."

"I'm a full year older than you when you received your first offer of marriage," Nan retorted. "And I was never so glad when you turned that cawker down flat! You would do much better to marry Sir Anthony. I knew as much the minute I laid eyes on him."

Ginny stood and hastily began tucking in bedsheets to hide her face. She had heard this diatribe regularly for three years, but it still served to raise a mighty blush in her cheeks. "I had best talk to Mrs. Crandall about making you a new poultice for that fever. Yours has gone to your brain, it seems."

"My fever is long gone and you know it. Do come back and tell me more of your goings on," Nan begged.

"I shall if you promise not to speak of Sir Anthony in such a way again," Ginny relented.

"I promise because you want me to, but truly you can't expect me to remember a thing I said once I'm over this horrid plague."

"I suppose I shall have to be content with that." Ginny smiled and left the room. Out in the hallway, her smile faded. If only Grandaunt Regina hadn't sent for Sir Anthony to be her escort, Nan would never have started harping on that old subject.

At least she had until the end of the quarantine to be assured Nan wouldn't pester her about Sir Anthony. It would never do for the abigail to guess how her mistress had passed the night, her eyes tightly closed against the memory of his smoldering eyes. She hoped agreeing to be his friend wouldn't prove to be her undoing.

Chapter Nine

Sir Anthony had spent the better part of the morning in the damask rose salon, gazing out the window. It was double-doored, looked out on the beginnings of what promised to be a monumental rose garden, was trimmed in rosewood, naturally, and had thirty-nine panes. He ought to know better than anyone; he had counted them at least sixty-seven times since he had grown bored watching Avery woo Lucinda and had taken himself off.

It was deuced difficult for one to amuse himself under the circumstances. Apparently, someone had let on that Lucinda favored that little Irish chap Sir Thomas Moore. If he had to hear how Avery's wishes "would entwine themselves verdantly, still" one more time, he would find it necessary to lose his breakfast through any number of those thirty-nine panes.

Worse yet, Lucinda was loving every minute, which meant nothing could induce Avery to cease and desist.

Certainly nothing Sir Anthony could possibly say would hold any water, but just as he was about to open his mouth in another vain attempt, Ginny entered the room.

He was gratified when she came directly to his side. "You were about to say something."

He smiled. "Yes, I was, but demme if I knew what it was. To what do I owe this unexpected pleasure?"

"What? Do you mean my joining you with full intention?"

He nodded. "You don't think I wish to make myself any part of that, do you?" He indicated the couple on the sofa discussing the advantages of the sonnet over the ballad. What one had to do with the other was beyond his wish to ever know.

"I think it best if we contrive to involve them in something else, wouldn't you agree, Miss Delacourt? Perhaps that game of Hunt the Slipper Lucinda referred to the other evening."

"La, sir! Don't be gulled into thinking myself unaware of your intentions!" Ginny exclaimed, her eyes twinkling. "A dark passage here, an innocent kiss there, and Lucinda shall be none the wiser, am I right?"

"Is that what you think of me, then? I will have you know my intentions toward Miss Barrington are most honorable." After all, what could be more honorable than his total disinterest?

Ginny's bright smile became a bit fixed. "In that case, sir, I think you ought to know that Lucinda's parents have chosen Lord Avery for their daughter. It wouldn't do to upset their plans."

"Not even for the sake of true love?" He had no intention of marrying the likes of Lucinda Barrington, but he enjoyed allowing Ginny to think he might.

"No, not even for that. I think the Barringtons put more value on other things." By which she meant a lofty title, he felt most sure. "Besides, they seem quite taken with the man." Ginny leaned back against the window and looked archly up at him. "I don't think you should be able to tear Lucinda away from him if you tried."

Why, the chit had some nerve! He felt a muscle twitch in his jaw. Unclenching his teeth, he said, "I believe she had eyes for only me at breakfast." He placed a hand against the window above Ginny's head and stared down at her. She gazed back at him. "You could take a lesson in the art of flirtation from such a one as she, I'll have you know."

He was never to hear what promised to be a most tart reply, for suddenly the window flew open and Ginny began to fall. Before she had time to scream, he had thrown his arms around her and jerked her away from danger.

Clutching her, he realized she felt much smaller than he had imagined, really just a tiny little thing. Her heart hammered against him through the soft curves of her breast, and she trembled. Time seemed, for a moment, to stop until gradually Sir Anthony became aware that one end of the ribbon so fetchingly laced through Ginny's dark curls was fluttering against his lips, a stiff breeze was coming through the still-open window, and his arms ached like the devil from holding her so tightly against his chest.

He loosened his grip and Ginny stepped out of his arms. It was as if the sun had stepped away into night. Bemused, he looked about the room and saw that Lucinda and Lord Avery stared at them in consternation. Clearly an explanation was in order. "Er, Miss Delacourt nearly fell out of the window."

Lucinda sprang from her seat and ran lightly to Ginny's side. "Oh, yes, we saw the whole thing." She turned to look out the window. "And we are so high up. If you had fallen all the way down, I believe it would have hurt prodigiously!"

Ginny gave a shaky laugh and lightly touched Sir Anthony on the arm. "It seems as if you are responsible for rescuing me once again. I was never so glad for your being by except, perhaps, when Seb and Dobbs chose to call."

He carried her hand from his arm up to his lips which he allowed to hover above her fingers a fraction longer than strictly proper. "It was my pleasure."

Ginny blushed and Lord Avery sauntered over to assess the situation. "What a narrow escape, sir," he expostulated. "However did you think so fast as to catch her right out of the window? It defies imagination!"

Sir Anthony glanced at Ginny and saw that she blushed, though her eyes danced with merriment. Gad, she looked a different girl from the one who had looked at him so coldly across Grandmama's desk. Tearing his eyes away from her, he bestirred himself to explain. "I was well aware of the danger as I had been studying the window for the past hour. I believe Miss Delacourt was about to suggest we do something to amuse ourselves.

Or would have, had she not been so rudely interrupted." He bowed, and allowed a slight smile to play about his lips.

Ginny looked momentarily nonplussed but made an admirable recovery. "Yes, I seem to recall something said about Hunt the Slipper."

"Oh, indeed yes, let us do so at once!" Lucinda cried with her customary urgency. "It will be famous! I haven't played in ever so long. Why, it must have been before I was laid so low with the spots. Come Eustace, let's ask Mama for a slipper."

Sir Anthony watched Avery trot off with Lucinda. The way he stayed glued to her side, he no doubt intended to find himself stuck with Lucinda in that dark little corner of which Ginny had spoken. He headed after the pair and noted Ginny followed companionably by his side. "Miss Delacourt," he inquired after a bit of thought. "Would you know where I could lay my hands on a copy of Moore?"

She looked up at him. "Whyever do you ask?"

Meeting her gaze, Sir Anthony felt something soft uncurl within him. "I had thought to find a poem rhapsodizing on the beauty of eyes." Grayish-green ones, of course.

"You can't be serious!" Ginny laughed and took his arm. She was looking forward to their game. Unlike Lucinda, it had been eons since Ginny had played Hunt the Slipper. Unlike Sir Anthony, she hadn't been quarantined during a house party either, and thereby hadn't mastered the finer points of the game. Notwithstanding, Ginny felt certain the object in pursuit was meant to be the slipper, not unprotected females. Even in the "dark walk" at Vauxhall Gardens she hadn't been attacked by so many groping hands.

Lucinda had no trouble convincing her parents to join in the game. Mrs. Barrington had scurried off to find a slipper, one embroidered by Lucinda's own hand, for the purpose, and the squire had gone to instruct the maids to close all the curtains, drapes, and blinds in the house. It was Mrs. Crandall who eventually did the hiding, and soon the six of them had gone their separate ways in the grand pursuit.

Ginny felt sure she had turned in the opposite direction of every man in the party only to throw herself into the pitch-black linen closet to begin a thorough investigation when she was accosted by a firm pair of arms. Next, she found herself being subjected to an unpleasantly moist, loudly smacking kiss.

When she was able to draw breath, Ginny let out a gasp and slapped her assailant on the cheek. "Unhand me, or I shall tell the squire of your villainy."

"I-I beg your pardon, yes, indeed I do," the squire's voice quavered. "Forgive me for believing you to be Mrs. Barrington."

Ginny went rigid with shock. "Squire Barrington!"

"Yes, well . . . yes. My lady wife and I always play Hunt the Slipper such. It ensures the young people of the prize. You mustn't, no you mustn't say a word to anyone. May I have your word of honor?"

"Why, yes, of course." There was certainly no soul living she chose to tell of this. Ginny groped her way to the door, unsure as to whether she should believe the squire's story, until she encountered Mrs. Barrington coming in. Ginny wished she could sink through the floor. What would her hostess think? "The slipper isn't here," she called gaily, though her voice cracked with tension.

"Don't you think I know that?" Mrs. Barrington snapped, cross as two sticks. She disappeared into the closet, her taffeta skirts rustling after her. Ginny thought she heard a tiny giggle once the door had closed but she really couldn't be sure. All she could think about was how it wasn't Sir Anthony who waited for her in that closet, wasn't Sir Anthony who closed his arms around her and kissed her breathless.

It was just as well. At least, she thought so until the next pair of arms caught hold of her. She was just gaining the upper hallway after being most careful not to trip on her skirts on the darkened stairway, when a figure darted from the shadows and crushed her in a viselike grip.

For one brief moment her heart fluttered wildly in her breast. She could almost hear Sir Anthony's voice saying, "Mere friendship is not enough for me, Lucinda."

Lucinda? It was another moment before she realized the voice had been real and it had not been Sir Anthony's. She peered into the darkness not realizing how close her captor was until her nose came in contact with something hard and sharp.

It was Lord Avery's enormous diamond stickpin and his voice saying, "I can scarce believe you dared to meet me, my flower."

Somehow Ginny was not surprised. No doubt Lucinda took after her parents in that respect. "If it is Lucinda you wait for, Lord Avery, I suggest you unhand me before she arrives. I do not think she will forgive you for starting without her."

Lord Avery's hands fell from her as if she were made of live coals. With a yowl he jumped back, colliding with a pedestal holding an urn. He made a noble effort to catch it before it hit the ground but, sadly, botched the job.

He had only time to replace what was left of the urn on the righted pedestal before Lucinda's light step was heard on the stair. "Eustace, is that you?"

Instantly, Ginny moved into the shadows to the left of the stairs, while Lord Avery hid behind the broken statuary. "Eustace," Lucinda whispered. "Where are you?"

For some reason Ginny could not fathom, Lord Avery made no response. She knew she ought to tiptoe down the hall to her room as fast as she silently could, but she did not like to be discovered hovering in the shadows a hair's breadth away. She would wait until Lucinda found him, leaving her free to slip away with relative ease.

To Ginny's horror, when Lucinda gained the top of the stairs, she turned left. "Eustace, what did you wish to talk to me about?" she implored, stretching forth her hands to steady herself. Before Lucinda made contact with Ginny's non-Averylike form, she spun on her heel and moved down the hall as quietly and quickly as possible.

Just as Ginny was about to turn the handle of her room, a hand shot out of the darkness and closed tightly about her wrist. "I wouldn't do that if I were you," a deep voice drawled.

"Oh, really! I have simply had enough of this. Why shouldn't I enter my own room?"

"Because I have already searched it for the slipper and it is not there."

Ginny gasped. "Do you mean to tell me, Sir Anthony, that you entered my room and searched it?"

"Hush—they mustn't hear us! Best to let nature take its course."

Ginny forgot her former question for a new one. "Do you not care if Lucinda is compromised by Lord Avery in a game of Hunt the Slipper?"

"Avery is a romantic. I doubt he knows what a golden opportunity is his just now. And Lucinda, I daresay she has no inclination of what his purpose is. She is very innocent."

"Innocent?" With that practiced lisp and plunging neckline? Ginny resisted the temptation to stamp on Sir Anthony's foot. "So, it does matter to you? What happens to Lucinda, I mean."

"It shall all turn out in the end, Miss Delacourt, never you fear."

"Fear? What have I to fear? It matters not to me how this all turns out!" she hissed.

"Doesn't it?" With his hand still gripping her arm, she could feel him move closer so his breath fanned her cheek. "What you have to fear is losing."

"Losing! To Lucinda?" How dared he!

"Naturally. If we don't hurry, they will find the slipper ere do we, and I had it of the housekeeper the prize is an entire blancmange."

Ginny felt unaccountably relieved. She choked on

the bubble of nervous laughter that welled up inside her. "In that case, we had best hurry and find it. I most especially love blancmange."

In the end, it was the squire who found the slipper under his own bed when he had gone up to take a snooze after his tryst with his lady in the linen closet. It seemed Mrs. Crandall thought it a great joke to lay the slipper in place of the master's own. To compensate for the difficulty of the task, she made a small blancmange for each participant.

"That was very well done of her," Ginny commented to Sir Anthony. He was seated to her right at the dinner table yet failed to hear her. He appeared to be wholly consumed with every detail of Lucinda's toilette. They were in silent communication, it seemed, for Lucinda had only to point to a certain aspect of her gown or jewelry for Sir Anthony to give a slight nod and the ghost of a smile in her direction.

It was positively disgusting and most shockingly rude, to say the least. And there was Lord Avery seeing all of it, looking as if he were about to water his blancmange with his tears.

"Lord Avery," she said hastily, not wishing to see Mrs. Crandall's efforts washed down the table. "Would you consider favoring us with some of your poetry tonight?" Even as she said it she wanted to bite her tongue. But what was done was done, and Lord Avery looked so pleased.

"Yes, my dear Miss Delacourt, it would be a pleasure beyond bearing." Indeed his face shone with an almost insupportable joy.

"That is," she amended, "if the others are of a like mind."

Murmurs of assent went all around the table. It was difficult to tell the genuine smiles from the forced, but Ginny suspected there were some of each.

Lord Avery jumped up from his chair. "Then it's settled! Let us forgo the port and have at it." Taking Ginny by the arm, he propelled her to her feet. "I would be delighted to escort you to the front-row seat, Miss Delacourt." He tucked her arm in his and hurried her out the door.

Ginny realized, with some trepidation, that Lord Avery was using her to make Lucinda jealous. If so, matters could only go from bad to worse.

Chapter Ten

The evening had taken a turn for the worse. Lord Avery's enthusiasm was hard to stomach, but his souful expression as he stood before them at the front of the music room was enough to turn one off one's food. Sir Anthony supposed the facial arrangement to be intentional but doubted the hangdog face of a professional mourner was the desired result.

"Oh, you look exactly like Lord Byron," Mrs. Barrington exclaimed.

"Yes, indeed." Lucinda clapped her hands. "You could be twins!"

Never mind that Lucinda had never laid eyes on Lord Byron, Sir Anthony thought, not to mention that Byron was dark of hair and eye.

Lord Avery seemed not to care for that little detail. "Ladies, you honor me." He bowed and drew a packet of papers from deep within his waistcoat and cleared his throat. "Light, if you please."

Mrs. Barrington twittered and hastened forth with a brace of candles. She placed them on the pianoforte next to where Lord Avery stood, his hand caressing the smooth cherry finish.

He once again peered at his papers and in a moment of great transparency moved the candles ever closer to his side. Lord Avery's pale locks flared into glorious gold tresses in this new proximity to the flickering flames. The poetry had not even begun and Sir Anthony could feel his stomach churning.

He stole a glance at Ginny, seated near the front of the room, from his preferred chair at the back where the light was dim and he could slip into slumber undetected. It also had the added advantage of providing him with an excellent view of Ginny's reaction. At the moment she was giving every indication of being eager to hear Lord Avery's drivel.

"Cornflower eyes, like dawn arise," Lord Avery intoned.

Sir Anthony had no trouble determining for whom this poem was written. Certainly there was no doubt as to who the author was though he wouldn't be surprised if Lord Avery had fallen prey to the temptation of plagiarism. Lord knows *he* would under such circumstances. The poem continued at agonizing length, delineating each and every charm Miss Barrington possessed. After listening to them described in Lord Avery's words, Sir Anthony was inclined to view even "dimpled cheeks, as well as elbows," in a bad light.

At length the poem ended. "Bravo!" Ginny cried, clapping her hands à la Lucinda.

The squire and Mrs. Barrington were equally impressed. "Can't think, no, can't think why we haven't had you read for us before now," the squire pronounced. His lady merely smiled and turned a coy look on her daughter, who sat blushing down at her hands in her lap.

Thank goodness it was over, at least. "Very fine, Avery." Sir Anthony began to rise from his chair but was stopped cold by the sound of Ginny's voice.

"Pray, do another," she begged.

Avery had the arrogance to look gratified and pulled a second sheaf of papers from his pocket. "The subject of this poem is quite a different one, as I am sure you will discover for yourself ere long." With a lingering glance at Ginny he took a deep breath and plunged into passionate recitation.

"Gray-eyed lady in the dark, can you hear my pounding heart? Still it, still it, with a kiss. Turn my fever to my bliss."

Sir Anthony had no wish to hear the words that followed and was mercifully spared from doing so by the incessant pounding of blood in his ears. How dared that dog write a poem about Ginny! What right did he have? What claim? If anyone were to write an ode to her gray eyes, it should be himself. The thought had certainly crossed his mind more than once.

In horrified fascination, Sir Anthony watched Lord Avery sway to and fro in the grips of poetic passion. The pounding in his ears increased, and he felt almost as if he were in a world far removed from the scene he watched: Lucinda pouting; the squire and Mrs. Barrington, puzzled smiles glued to their faces; Ginny, smiling through her tears; Lord Avery swaying, ever swaying, exposing his golden locks to the flicker of the candles.

Sir Anthony exploded from his chair just as Lord Avery's hair burst into flames. "Avery, watch out!" he cried. As he sprinted across the room, he heard a crash and a scream, but he hadn't time to reflect on its cause.

Ginny arrived at Lord Avery's side before him, a bowl of roses in her hands. Together they hefted the large bowl over Lord Avery's head and dumped the contents.

Lord Avery no longer swayed. With an acute disregard for his near disaster or the state of his clothing that Sir Anthony could only wonder at, Lord Avery fell to his knees at Ginny's feet. "My Goddess. My Benefactress. My Protectress. I am your servant, now and forever!"

Sir Anthony could not abide the fact that the blush rising in Ginny's cheeks was caused by someone other than himself. Since when could anyone but he cause her cheeks to turn so delightfully pink? Since Lord Avery, his hair scorched, dripping wet, and strewn with roses knelt at her feet, it would seem.

"There is no need, my lord." Ginny plucked at the roses cascading like water down Avery's length. "I did very little, really. It was Sir Anthony who first alerted us to what was happening, and besides, I could never have lifted that water over your head without his aid."

Sir Anthony turned his head from the sight of the blubbering Avery with distaste. Lucinda swooning on the floor was hardly a more cheerful prospect, but it restored his good humor to have something useful to which to apply himself.

"My poor darling girl." Mrs. Barrington patted Lucinda's hand while the squire attempted to ply his slender body to the task of lifting her.

Sir Anthony knelt by Lucinda. "Did she hit her head, do you know?"

The squire looked at him with alarm. "Oh, no, sir, no indeed. She fainted! The sight of Lord Avery in flames undid her."

"Then I daresay she will be all right presently. I shall be happy to carry her to her room for you. With your permission, of course."

"Of course, of course," the squire babbled.

Belatedly, Sir Anthony realized his coat was not tailored for such activities as scooping maidens from the floor. Lucinda was a bit heavier than he knew and his coat a bit tighter than he thought but he would worry about that slight tear in each armhole sometime after he had rid himself of Miss Barrington.

Ginny watched Sir Anthony leave the room, Miss Barrington cradled in his arms. The tenderness with which he shifted her about, so cognizant of her comfort, caused a curious deflation of her spirits. For some reason she did not care to examine, she wanted Sir Anthony to find her admirable beautiful, and charming, but it seemed little had happened to change Sir Anthony's opinion of her since that first conversation in

Grandaunt Regina's library. Was she still so distasteful to him?

There were moments when she thought not. There was a quickness of wit in their conversation and at times an intangible connection between them that bespoke a lively attraction. A look in his eye that was sometimes present . . . Could he be unaware there were moments when his social façade melted away to reveal glimpses of something much more?

Breakfast was more restrained than it had been the morning previous. Lucinda was still in her chamber when Ginny entered the breakfast room. Squire and Mrs. Barrington seemed greatly shaken. Sir Anthony was inscrutable as ever, his face a mask of indifference and very white, except where the brown and purple bruise spread along his forehead.

Lord Avery, his hair no longer curling in waves to his cravat, seemed more concerned with other matters than his shorn locks. "I must insist all the servants be questioned."

A pained expression crossed Mrs. Barrington's face. "We have already done so. They were much aghast at the loss of so valuable a piece."

"Loss? Loss you say? One does not lose a diamond of that size."

"Of course not," the squire assured him. "No doubt it was taken by somebody. Indeed, I had it of Mrs. Crandall that she found the kitchen door unbolted this morning, not to mention Grandmama's broken urn. We are very concerned about it, very concerned."

"Are you trying to say somebody entered the house, came to my room, and stole my diamond stickpin without so much as glancing at any of the other valuables in this house?"

"You forget the urn," Mrs. Barrington retorted.

Lord Avery blanched.

Ginny had to agree with Lord Avery. It seemed unlikely that someone from outside the house was the culprit. "I see Lord Avery's point. The door was most likely left unbolted by someone on the inside." Ginny hardly knew what she was saying until it was said. With a start, she remembered Sir Anthony's midnight rides and her promise not to reveal him.

Did he catch her slip? His dark head was bent and his gaze on his plate. Surely he wouldn't allow one of the servants to fall under suspicion for his own folly. Ginny waited for him to speak, but he did not.

"No." Mrs. Barrington shook her head. "Mrs. Crandall locks and bolts that door every night before she goes to bed. There is no need for anyone to use it after that. Ah, Lucinda," she said. "You have joined us at last."

"Yes, Mama." Lucinda quickly filled her plate and sat across from Lord Avery. She darted a venomous look at Ginny, which she could only credit to the fact that her beau had gone up in flames in her honor, so to speak. Life would certainly settle down when Lucinda decided that the love of one man was preferable to the attentions of all. Ginny hoped it would be soon.

"Oh, Eustace," Lucinda said, "I nearly forgot. I found this in my room this morning." She placed the diamond stickpin on the table. Then she picked up her fork and began to eat, blithely unaware how everyone stared aghast at the diamond. Even Sir Anthony betrayed a hint of surprise.

Mrs. Barrington, her eyes fastened on the stickpin and her breath coming in little gasps, found voice to rend the air with a screech.

"What is the meaning of this?" the squire demanded. "How did this, I say, how did this get in my daughter's room, my lord?"

Lord Avery began to blubber. "I-I don't kn-know. I haven't set foot in there."

"I should say not!" Mrs. Barrington cried.

"And for what reason would you have done so, my lord?" demanded the squire.

"How did your diamond come to be in my poor dear's room if you weren't with her?" Mrs. Barrington wailed. "Lucinda, do you have anything to say for yourself?"

"No, Mama. I don't know how it came to be in my room. It was simply there, and I'm ever so glad I didn't step on it. I almost did and I think it would have been very painful for I had on no shoes at the time."

Mrs. Barrington's eyes rolled up into her head. "Lucinda, how could you speak of such things? To your room at once!" She jumped to her feet and shooed Lucinda out the door. A silence fell on the room, pierced here and there by diminishing wails from Mrs. Barrington.

"Avery, you must marry my daughter!" The squire came to the point in a minimum of words. It was evidence of his great anger, as if the crimson face and bulging eyes weren't enough.

"Come, Miss Delacourt," Sir Anthony said. "I believe there is a splendid art gallery on the second floor you have not as yet seen." He held his hand out to her.

She allowed herself to be led from the room but not without a backward glance for poor Lord Avery. She felt sorry for him. It was bad enough to be shackled to Lucinda for life without the engagement occurring under such unsavory circumstances.

"Do you think they are guilty of wrongdoing, Sir Anthony?"

"Those two? Hardly. Innocent as two lambs."

"Yes, but, there comes a time when innocence ends. Who's to say the moment when it all occurs?"

Sir Anthony gazed down at her and shook his head. She could see he was amused. She was learning to discern the subtle clues. "Believe me, my dear," he drawled. "There are signs. If there was anything havey-cavey going on between them we should all be the wiser."

"Lucinda's parents seem to think there is reason to be alarmed. Surely he was in her room! How else would she have the pin? Lucinda may be a half-wit but she wouldn't steal it simply to return it. There is no sense in that."

Sir Anthony dismissed her comments with a wave of his hand. "There are a variety of ways it might have occurred. He could have unknowingly wandered into her room during Hunt the Slipper and dropped it, or better yet, it could have become tangled in her clothes when they were in the hallway."

"You see! There is reason for her parents to be alarmed. I would not wish my daughter to be embracing a man in a dark hall."

"Does that go for you, as well, or only your daughters? You're not bound to have many with that prudish attitude!"

"There are other ways to come about daughters, Sir Anthony. Proper ways."

Sir Anthony frowned. "And there are other ways to acquire a stickpin. We could try dancing."

"What does dancing have to do with anything?"

"Why, only that it allows close enough proximity to entangle a gentleman's stickpin in a lady's gown without precipitating an engagement."

Ginny considered. She supposed it was within the realms of possibility. "If we could prove how easily it could be done, Lucinda and Lord Avery would not fall under such suspicion."

"Done." Sir Anthony held out his hands. "You hum. A waltz, I think."

Ginny felt her heart begin to quicken in her breast. The gallery they had now entered was large enough for a couple to waltz in, though it hardly seemed proper.

"Come, come, Ginny. I promise, children cannot be produced through waltzing."

Ginny felt heat wash over her entire body. No one had ever discussed such intimate things with her. Despite her embarrassment she wanted to waltz with him. She wanted to feel his arms around her, wanted to hear him say her name again. But if she did he would feel the pounding of her heart.

She found she could not look at him and glanced down. "You aren't wearing a stickpin. Perhaps tonight." That would be safe enough with everyone present. "I daresay the Barringtons will not object. It would give us young people something to do."

"Very well. I shall be sure to wear one to dinner."

She felt her composure returning and dared to look at him. "Why? What reason could you possibly have for helping clear up this mess for Lucinda and Lord Avery?"

"Anything to make you happy, Miss Delacourt. Your servant, as always," he said with a sketch of a bow.

Ginny swallowed to ease her tightening throat. As usual, the dratted man was just being polite! She changed tack. "And if your theory is not so easily proven?"

Sir Anthony stroked his chin. "There are always the servants. Perhaps we could convince the Barringtons that one of them took it, then suffered pangs of guilt. It would be easy to drop it in Lucinda's room and hope for the best."

"Would you truly allow one of the servants to stand accused of something he or she has not done?" She saw that he opened his mouth to respond, but she charged ahead with a new accusation. "Which reminds me, why did you not speak up about the door? I think I am right in suspecting it was you who left it unlocked."

He inclined his head. "Yes. I went for a ride again last night."

"Under the circumstances I think it best if you inform the Barringtons."

"I almost spoke, but then Miss Barrington entered the room and made my confession wholly unnecessary."

"Still, it would ease their minds and perhaps save Mrs. Crandall a scolding."

Sir Anthony clenched his jaw and swept his gaze to the floor. "I would rather not."

"I think, sir, you have something to hide." Ginny was greatly agitated by his lack of response. "I think I should leave."

"Have I given you such a disgust of me then, Miss Delacourt?"

"Yes." Ginny wished she could recall the word, but it slipped out before she could stop it. "Unless, of course, you tell me what it is you so desperately wish no one to know."

He cocked his head. "I will if you tell me why you had tears in your eyes during Lord Avery's nauseating recitation."

"Why, I thought it a charming poem." The fact that her tears were the result of holding back her laughter was one she did not wish Sir Anthony to know. Poor Lord Avery deserved better. "I was . . . deeply touched." And so she had been, in a ridiculous sort of way.

Sir Anthony stepped closer and tilted her chin. "I do not think you are telling the truth, Miss Delacourt."

"What you mean to say is that you *hope* I am not telling the truth."

"Did I say that?"

"Of course not. You wouldn't. You don't care to reveal anything you feel." Ginny could hear her voice growing louder, almost shrill, but it didn't signify. "In fact, I begin to doubt you have feelings. You, Sir Anthony, are a man without feelings, emotions, or passions!"

Ginny only caught a glimpse of Sir Anthony's face, white with anger, before he jerked her into his arms and kissed her with searing hot lips. Under his demanding mouth she gasped in protest, but it only afforded him further opportunity to batter her defenses. She felt as if her body was melting into his despite her best efforts to remain rigid and inaccessible.

Sir Anthony chose the moment her breath came in shuddering gasps and her knees buckled beneath her to suddenly release her. Then he stepped back and regarded her with an expression of cool indifference. "You were saying?"

Chapter Eleven

Sir Anthony could not believe what he had done. With growing alarm he watched Ginny run out of the room and out of his life. Surely she would have nothing to do with him after the way he had treated her.

What had caused such madness? The blood that had been boiling in his veins since Avery had read that cursed poem took only a moment to bubble over into uncontrollable passion. What did it mean? He couldn't possibly be in love with that opinionated, headstrong, loose-tongued girl! It defied contemplation. Ah, but he had caused her pain, and it was as if the knife was buried in his own heart. With a groan he balled his fists together and pressed them to his forehead.

He willed calm to his pounding heart and strolled to the window at the end of the gallery. He must beg her forgiveness at the first opportunity. Even if she did her best to elude him for the rest of the day, she would have to afford him a moment after dinner. After all, she had promised him a dance.

The balance of the day was one of torment for Sir Anthony. He was unable to catch even a glimpse of Ginny, something he found more irritating than surprising. Where she could be hiding was a mystery. He knew she wasn't with Lucinda, who had closeted herself in her room ever since her engagement to Avery over the eggs and kippers. Mrs. Barrington sailed between him and Lucinda's locked door every half hour, hoping to soothe ruffled feathers.

"Lord Avery," she cooed for the twelfth time. "Won't you go and try to talk some sense into the girl?"

Avery, pale and drawn, turned tragic eyes on his hostess. "It is all too clear she does not wish to be my wife. I have offered for her, under duress I might add, and she has accepted. That she is unhappy about it is a matter beyond my control."

"Don't be silly, my lord. Sir Anthony, pray tell him! All she needs is a few words of romance."

"Perhaps, Mrs. Barrington," Sir Anthony replied, "your daughter is in need of some time to reflect. There will be opportunity enough for romance this evening, am I right, Avery?" He inflicted Avery with a hard stare, and Avery gave a nearly imperceptible nod in return.

"There, you see, Mrs. Barrington, all shall be well. I can see it now, a little champagne to announce the joyous event, some music to stir the blood, maybe some dancing . . ."

"Dancing! Just the thing! I shall go straight up to my poor darling and have her try on her ball gowns. She has been so downcast, having missed her coming-out, you know." Mrs. Barrington sailed out of the room at full clip.

"My thanks, Crenshaw," Avery mumbled. "I thought I'd never be rid of the old warship."

Sir Anthony winced. He certainly didn't envy Avery his future mother-in-law. The afternoon dragged on in similar fashion until, with much relief, Sir Anthony escaped to his room to dress for dinner, mercifully far from Avery's morbid natterings. Faith, the man had gone on all day every bit as white and dense as a wall. He would never ensure Lucinda's interest that way.

Sir Anthony caught his reflection in the mirror and scowled. Only three days into this dratted quarantine and everything had gone wrong. His hopes for an amusing time for the remaining week had been dashed, he had made mice feet of his vow to avoid his Grandmama's choice of bride for him at all costs, and now his blasted neckcloth chose to be recalcitrant. How could he dance with Ginny under the pretense of passing along his stickpin if he couldn't get the misbegotten thing tied in the first place?

When had everything begun to go wrong? He wanted to say it was all that Avery chap's fault, but none of this, not one of the misfortunes that had befallen him these past few days would have occurred if Miss Ginerva Delacourt had decided to remain in her room one fateful morning.

There. He had tied it. His valet, whom he was rarely without under ordinary circumstances, would never let him out the door with such a contraption under his chin, but no matter. Next, the stickpin. Sir Anthony perused the contents of Avery's borrowed jewel box until he found just what he was looking for. If the two-carat emerald-cut black ruby couldn't find its way into a ladies' gown, no stickpin could hope to do better.

Sir Anthony surveyed the results. He looked rather like a man who had been swallowed by a billowing white fish, its one staring eye turned black in its head. Sir Anthony shuddered. Gad, he looked nervous as a deb and about as attractive. He consigned the mirror to eternal hellfire and made his way to the drawing room.

Ginny was already seated when he walked through the door. She was wearing a delightful green confection with a white lace overdress. She must have forgotten how angry she was with him earlier, for she turned to him the moment he entered the room. Devil take it, she was beautiful!

"Ah, here he is at last, at last." The squire rose to his feet and offered his arm to Mrs. Barrington, resplendent in gold silk. "I believe we may now go in to dinner. Cook rang the bell this past quarter hour." He cast Sir Anthony a deprecating glance.

He hastened to offer Ginny his arm and take their place at the end of the line.

"Squire Barrington seems a trifle put out by your tardiness," she said in a cool voice.

"Yes, well, one must be understanding in cases such as the squire's." Sir Anthony leaned down to whisper in her ear. "The man is so thin he no doubt hasn't enough fat to live off of between meals." He thought he saw the beginnings of a smile, but it disappeared.

"You are horrible."

"Yes, and I need to speak with you about that."

Ginny looked at him in surprise. "Do you? It seems you are always wishing a private word with me over some matter or another. Whatever you wish to say you can say here."

Sir Anthony looked around the dining room they had just entered and ran a mental finger along his collar. She wasn't going to make this any easier for him but it was imperative he apologize to her. When the footman pulled out Ginny's chair, Sir Anthony whisked a napkin to the floor. As he bent to retrieve it, he had just enough time to whisper in her ear, "My apologies."

If only the footman had not been so fastidious in his duty their heads would not have met with such a re-sounding thump that Ginny's reply was lost to him. To make matters worse, the cursed footman beat Sir An-thony to his objective, presenting the napkin to her with a flourish.

"Thank you." The wide smile she gave him was one usually reserved for butlers and the like, not the never-to-be-acknowledged lowly footman. It made Sir An-thony's blood boil. Blindly he groped for his chair, but the footman once again was there before him.

"Look here, boy," Sir Anthony hissed, "I can pull out my own chair, thank you." He sat and glanced at the ex-pressions of shock and unease on the faces around him. "What? What is it?" Was it his cravat? Did he have smut on his nose? Merciful Zeus! He should have stayed upstairs.

Ginny, seated next to him, said in a low voice, "I believe they are not accustomed to Sir Anthony, the man of passions and emotions."

"Is that so? In that case, I shall do my best to reform."

"La, sir, after only one day?" She gave him a saucy grin. "I was just coming to terms with the reformation of this morning."

Sir Anthony felt himself consumed with guilt. Now she was casting out lures and all because of his act of corruption. He leaned to whisper in her ear. "The last time I saw you, Miss Delacourt, you were more than a little angry. I find I cannot blame you. It will never happen again."

"Won't it?"

Was that a note of regret he heard in her voice? He scanned her face for further signs, but her attention was diverted by Mrs. Barrington.

"Our Lucinda and Lord Avery have a very interesting announcement to make after dinner. To honor the occasion, there will be champagne and dancing in the drawing room."

Lord Avery stared at the wall in moody silence, and Lucinda twisted her hands in her lap.

"How lovely," Ginny said. "I was hoping there might be dancing."

"May I take that as a compliment, Miss Delacourt?" Sir Anthony whispered.

"No, you may not. I only wish to dance with you to save those two from their misery. Look at them!"

Sir Anthony regarded her intently. "Do you consider impending marriage a misery?"

"Don't be a goose! They are unhappy because of the circumstances surrounding their engagement. I daresay Lucinda had visions of a tumultuous London season chock full of offers of marriage from every eligible bachelor in the land! After which nothing but a most spectacularly romantic, and need I say dramatic, proposal on the part of Lord Avery would have done. Clearly, he does not understand the cause for her unhappiness. He is taking it so personally, poor dear."

"Well, you can't hope to help matters in that gown."

"I beg your pardon!"

"What I mean to say is, how am I to drop this stickpin down your gown with all that lace? It's practically got its hands around your throat."

"That is precisely the reason I wore it. I have no desire to spend the evening with a lump like that swimming about somewhere in my décolletage. Besides, you aren't to drop it on me! Somehow I am to attach it. I thought lace a much better prospect than satin in that pursuit."

Sir Anthony felt his mood lighten. "I daresay this stickpin will look a sight better on you than it does on me."

"Oh, I don't know," Ginny mused. "I feel sure I couldn't carry off a third eye nearly so well."

Ginny knew that last barb was too cruel, but really he deserved to be set down a peg or two. She was no serving girl to be so ruthlessly kissed! On the other hand, she had goaded him into the outpouring of emotion that had resulted in that heady kiss, had been goading him to unleash his emotions since they had set out for Dunsmere. So why did she feel so miserable?

The tinkling of glasses filled the room while the squire led Lord Avery and Lucinda to the front. "I propose a toast to Lord Avery and my daughter, Lucinda, on the happy event of their engagement." The squire raised his champagne in the air and quaffed it in a gulp.

Ginny noticed Sir Anthony hesitated to drink his until the happy couple did the same. To her chagrin Lucinda set her glass on the mantel, untouched, while Lord Avery held his stiffly in front of him as if it were a bouquet of flowers.

Mrs. Barrington's strident voice rushed in to fill the silence. "Dancing! We must have music. Squire, why don't you play so the young people can dance?"

She rustled over to Lucinda and Lord Avery, who stood side by side, as lively as two parasols propped in the corner. Taking each by the elbow, she said, "You two happy lovebirds should dance with each other first." Somehow she managed to get the pair facing each other, then their arms fashioned in waltzing form.

The squire smiled his content and began to play.

"No doubt you know how to waltz, Miss Delacourt?" Sir Anthony said.

"Actually, I was tolerably good at it. That is one of the things I enjoyed during my time in London."

Sir Anthony held out his arms. "Shall we then?"

Ginny was surprised by her own willingness to be close to Sir Anthony. Indeed, the prospect of being held in his arms sent a positive shiver of delight down her spine. He looked so very handsome in his dark evening suit in spite of that hideous cravat. It looked as if he had tied it with his thumbs. And that stickpin!

It took only a moment for her to realize the futility of their plan. Sir Anthony was a good head taller than she and his stickpin was almost level with her eyes. How in the world was she to catch it on her gown? Several possible courses of action occurred to her, but her cheeks grew hot to think of them.

"You're blushing, Miss Delacourt." He smiled down at her. "Was it something I said?"

A gasp of laughter escaped her. "Now you are teasing me. You haven't said a thing and you know it." She couldn't seem to resist smiling into his eyes.

"You are right. I haven't." He returned her smile, and it seemed as if he were seeing into her soul. "Forgive me. I was otherwise preoccupied."

"Doing what?" Ginny asked, a little breathlessly.

"Why, drinking in your beauty, minx."

"Oh," Ginny said and looked down, feeling herself grow warm all over. Then she glanced over at Lucinda and Lord Avery, their steps dragging and their heads turned at right angles to their bodies. How sad they looked. She must do something to help them.

"Sir Anthony, I have been considering our options."

Sir Anthony looked a bit startled. "Have you? Aren't you being a bit precipitate?"

"I don't see how. Careful planning is always called for in these matters. Now, I have thought and thought but I cannot think how it can be done. I think it would be best if you were to get down on your knees and pretend you are looking for something."

"Must I? Is there no other way? I know I shouldn't have but it was only a kiss, after all."

"What do you mean, only a kiss? Really, you are being most obtuse. I think I will dance this next with Lord Avery and tell him of our decision. I hope it will alleviate his megrims a bit."

Sir Anthony looked confused. "Why should our engagement cheer him when his own has not?"

"Engagement? Us? Don't be ridiculous. I was speaking of our plan to prove his innocence. You dance with Lucinda next and tell her as well. Then, we shall dance again. That's when you pretend to be looking for something on the floor and I catch your stickpin on my lace overskirt."

Sir Anthony did not reply. She was startled to see that he had turned crimson from his neck all the way to the roots of his hair, and when he finally spoke, his voice was cold and aloof. "As you wish, Miss Delacourt. Please let me know if there is something else I can do to be of service to you." He sketched her a brief bow and strode over to Lucinda.

Lord Avery lost no time in asking her for the next dance. She would have to puzzle over Sir Anthony's reaction later. "Lord Avery, I can't help but notice how very unhappy you are. Don't you wish to marry Lucinda?"

"I thought I did, but she clearly doesn't want to marry me! Look at her, so dull and lifeless."

"Come now, Lucinda is very fond of you!" Ginny glanced over at Lucinda where she was slowly coming to life under Sir Anthony's glaring smile. She swallowed the lump in her throat. "See, she is smiling."

"Smiling, yes, at Sir Anthony. She doesn't want anything to do with me."

"Now, that is only because she feels she has been robbed of all the excitement of falling in love and being offered for in the proper way."

"Is that my fault? I would have done it differently had I been given the opportunity!"

"Perhaps, Lord Avery, it is not too late. Sir Anthony and I have been thinking." Ginny proceeded to outline their plan to him. "So, you see, as soon as Lucinda's parents understand, you can release Lucinda from the engagement or convince her of your undying love and devotion. Isn't it famous?"

"I suppose so," Lord Avery said, listless as ever. "You truly are very clever, Miss Delacourt."

"Why, thank you, Lord Avery," Ginny said. "Now, go to her."

Lord Avery shuffled over to Lucinda who turned once more into a statue upon finding herself in his arms. Sir Anthony, almost as stiff, claimed Ginny for the next dance and said, "Does the man know nothing but waltz music?"

Ginny blinked back tears. What had she said to make him so cold? Putting on a brave smile, she said, "I believe he is trying to set a romantic mood for the engaged couple."

Sir Anthony only grunted in response. He said even less for the next half of the song at which point Ginny finally found the courage to request he proceed with the plan. "Would it be too much to ask? In light of your current ill humor and all."

"Ill humor? I, in an ill humor?" Sir Anthony favored her with a grimace. "Why, I am the happiest of men.

Let me prove it to you. I will now go down on my knees to allow you to catch my stickpin in your gown, interrupting the engagement of Lord Avery to Lucinda so you may win him for yourself."

Ginny frowned. "Lord Avery and me? No, that's not it at all." But Sir Anthony was already on the floor, out of hearing distance of her frantic whispers. Apparently he did not hear her warning cries either, else he might have had time to move out of the path of Lord Avery and Lucinda who were once again gazing at the ceiling.

There was a screech and a cry and a quantity of muffled oaths before the tangle of arms, legs, and frothy skirts came to rest in a heap on the ground. To Ginny's immense surprise Lucinda was the first to jump to her feet, entirely unaided. "You buffoon!" she cried. "I shall never marry you." Then she burst into tears and ran from the room.

Chapter Twelve

The house party had come to an end. The quarantine, however, was still in effect. Since the night of her great humiliation, Lucinda had once again barricaded herself in her room while Squire and Mrs. Barrington attempted to keep their male guests from bolting. Ginny had also retreated, spending most of the last four days in either Nan's room or her own, where she whiled away the time reading.

For the fiftieth time she picked up a copy of *The Taming of the Shrew*. She was determined to find some evidence that Katherine had been misjudged. The poor thing was simply young and . . . impetuous. She drew a deep breath and had the lowering feeling she was reading more into the character of Katherine than Shakespeare intended.

Suddenly the words began to swim along the page in the most alarming fashion. She must have strained her eyes with all the reading, there could be no other explanation; shrews didn't cry. Ginny shut the book with a snap and paced the room.

It had been somewhere between Petruchio's words of "Kiss me, Kate" and "We will marry o' Sunday," that she stumbled upon the truth: Sir Anthony was much like Katherine's tolerant and long-suffering suitor. Gradually it had occurred to her that Sir Anthony didn't feign a politeness he did not feel only because it was fashionable, but because he did not care to wound her. On the other side of the coin, he hid behind his alter ego as a means of protecting himself from hurt.

Oh, how she had misjudged him! She knew now that he was everything she thought he could never be, a man who felt passion, pain, humiliation, and injured pride. And she had caused him to feel every one of them! She knew he must also be a man capable of deep love, tenderness, joy, and happiness and yearned to be the cause of those emotions, but it was too late.

Twice he had asked if she would marry him. Not for one second did she believe he was serious on either occasion, but she was sure to never hear him propose to her again. She had rejected him, whether intentionally or not; she had accused him, scolded him—in short, she had been a shrew. No wonder he protected himself behind his infernal code of etiquette!

The knowledge that she had hurt him, that he could not possibly want her, caused a pain much deeper than one she had ever known. There could be only one explanation: she loved him.

Finally, she concluded that time spent alone in her room, though enlightening, solved nothing. Opening her door, she checked to make sure Sir Anthony was nowhere about, as she could not bear to face him just yet. She paused to consider if it were a safe time of day to make her way to Nan's room without being spotted when she heard what sounded like muffled weeping.

Having followed the sound to the upper floor, she decided it must be coming from even higher. Finding the stairs to the attic, she took them up to the door, which sprang open to her touch. The sobbing was very loud now. Sure enough, the light from a beveled glass window revealed a pale and drawn Lucinda curled up at the foot of a trunk.

"Why, Lucinda, dear, whatever is the matter?" Ginny, heedless of the the danger to her skirts, sat on the dusty ground and brushed the hair from Lucinda's eyes.

"N-n-nothing," Lucinda replied in great gasping sobs.

"My dear, you can hardly expect me to believe that! Here." She offered Lucinda her handkerchief. "Is it Lord Avery?"

Nodding, Lucinda took the scrap of linen and blotted her eyes. "He-he-he does not love me," she gasped and dissolved into another bout of tears.

"You know that is not true. Lord Avery is forever going on about your lovely eyes and rosy complexion, but if you don't stop weeping you will soon look quite haggard."

"Oh!" Lucinda sucked in her breath and sat bolt upright. "I daresay you are right," she stammered, twisting the handkerchief in her hands. "I can become quite splotchy when I cry, and it hasn't been so very long since my complexion has cleared from the pox."

"It would be well if you kept that in mind," Ginny warned. Somehow, seeing Lucinda suffer only made her own heart ache all the more. "You mustn't go down to dinner looking as if you were sickening with a fever."

"Oh no, I shouldn't want that. Only I daresay I shall have dinner brought up on a tray as I have ever since, since . . . ."

Ginny anticipated a fresh bout of tears, an event that could prove disastrous to her already soaking handkerchief. She jumped to her feet, hands on her hips. "Come now, Lucinda. Red, puffy eyes do not look well with pink-spotted silk. Not only that, but your behavior is most unbecoming in a young lady of your years."

Wide-eyed, Lucinda swallowed her sobs and rose to her feet. "I must admit, I have been a bit peevish, but do you blame me? I missed my own coming-out, there hasn't been a single morning after a ball when I awake to find the parlor full of flowers from my admirers, I am engaged without having had a single London season, and not one rich young man has come to call to ask my papa for my hand in marriage! You must see how monstrously unfair life has been to me!"

Ginny felt a good shake was called for but feared it would only bring on another fit of weeping. "Well then, we shall have to see how we can change things."

"Yes, but how? It all seems so impossible!"

Ginny felt Lucinda's troubles were nothing compared to hers. At least Lucinda was actually engaged to Lord Avery. Still, Ginny felt determined not to allow two people in love to marry under such a cloud of doubt and unhappiness.

Ginny looked Lucinda square in the eye. "You *do* love Lord Avery?"

Lucinda, struck dumb with the intensity of her emotions, nodded, her lower lip trembling.

"And I am convinced he loves you! Only, you have been locked in your room for so long he may have forgotten why. Never fear, you must remind him."

"I don't know what you mean."

Ginny glanced at Lucinda's woebegone face and groaned. It was Lucinda's lively vivaciousness Lord Avery was missing. How to bring the color back into her cheeks? "I know! Let's have a ball!"

"A ball? With only the four of us? It wouldn't be much different than the other night."

Lucinda's lip was once again trembling. Ginny glanced around the room for inspiration, her gaze falling on a trunk full of old gowns. She pulled a gold brocade dress from a long-gone era off the top of the pile. "Yes, this is exactly what we need. A masquerade ball! Wouldn't that be lovely, Lucinda?"

"Yes . . ." She hesitated. "But won't it be a trifle odd? Even if I wear a mask, everyone shall know right off who I am."

Ginny was encouraged by the self-indulgent tone creeping back into Lucinda's voice. "It would take some of the fun out of it, I suppose. Oh, but Lucinda, look! This blue velvet would look stunning on you. What a quantity of lace there is at the sleeves!"

"It is beautiful," Lucinda breathed. "And just the color of my eyes."

Actually, the shade of blue was closer to Sir Anthony's brilliant orbs. No doubt he would notice how lovely Lucinda would look in that gown, and she wouldn't blame him. Still, Lucinda needed to be seen in it and admired. It was just the thing to bring her back to herself.

"I have had the most famous idea, Lucinda! The quarantine is over on the fifteenth. Let's have our ball on the sixteenth and invite the county!"

Life sprang into Lucinda's slight form. "Oh, yes!" she cried and clapped her hands. "I should love that above all things."

Ginny felt almost giddy with success. "We shall have so much to do to get ready. Invitations, menus, our costumes, oh, and we must ask your parents for their permission."

"They never say no," Lucinda said, skipping about the room. "Oh, won't it be glorious? I shall dance with all the men, even the fat ones, and Eustace will be so jealous!"

"If you can only be so joyous until then, I think you will have your Eustace in the palm of your hand long before the ball."

Lucinda turned up her perfect nose. "We shall see. Perhaps I shan't want him."

Ginny stifled a gasp of annoyance. Really! The girl should be horsewhipped! Hoping to distract her, she asked, "Where did these gowns come from?"

"I don't know, exactly." Lucinda tripped over to the trunk and sunk her hands into the sumptuous silks and satins. "Some ancestor, I suppose. They have been here forever. I used them to play dress-up when I was a little girl. Ooh! I know just the one for you!" Lucinda held up a board-chested gown with panniers in a most alarming shade of orange.

Ginny wrinkled her nose. "I don't think so."

"Oh, I am convinced it would look famous on you. You have the coloring to carry it off."

Ginny rather doubted anyone had the coloring to carry off such a gown and pitied the poor woman for whom it was made. "Let us see if there is something else. I would rather not look like a squash."

"Well, why not this one, then? It should fit you."

Ginny eyed the black bombazine with distaste. It was the sort of gown still favored by maiden aunts and elderly widows. "Really, I could almost think you wish me to look a dowd."

"No, of course not," Lucinda said in a faint voice, delving once again into the depths. She emerged with another panniered gown, this one in rose and silver.

"This one might do," Ginny murmured, holding the heavily embroidered taffeta gown against her. It was a lovely shade of rose with embroidered leaves forming the panniers and accenting the low, square-necked bodice. The whole was frosted with a fine web of silver net that shimmered in the light.

"It will look beautiful on you," Lucinda said in a wistful voice. "I am sure all the men will find you irresistible."

Ginny felt a pang of remorse. "If you like, I shan't wear it."

"Oh, no. With your gray-green eyes and pink complexion this gown was made for you. You will look exactly like a rose. I know! You shall go as the spirit of Rose Arbor. They all might admire you, but they won't know who you are. Mama has a wig that will go perfectly with that dress, and if you were to wear a mask I should be quite content."

"But won't the others be looking for me? I mean, it is only a matter of time before they realize it is I."

"Pshaw," Lucinda said with a shrug. "You look just like any number of girls in the village, dark hair, medium height, average figure. Any one of them could be mistaken for you."

Ginny felt a hot retort spring to her lips but held back. The restored Lucinda was certainly a trial but a sight better than the downcast, unhappy girl she had found sometime before. Now if only nothing happened to mar Lucinda's newfound glow, all would be well between her and Lord Avery.

When Ginny left the attic, Sir Anthony was waiting at the bottom of the stairs. She was nearly in his arms before she realized he was there. She sprang back, startled, her eyes wary, but Sir Anthony thought her smile seemed purely spontaneous. The last time they had spoken, she had wounded him deeply, more than he cared to admit. That notwithstanding, he wanted to see her more with each passing hour. What he felt had no language known to him, and he needed her to supply the words.

Taking a deep breath, he willed himself to speak. "Miss Delacourt, it is good to see that you are feeling more the thing." She had already started moving away but glanced up at him from the corner of her eye. Encouraged, he followed her down the hall while casting about for a reason to prolong the encounter. "Er, having been away from things, so to speak, for so long, I daresay you haven't heard." His breath froze in his lungs with anticipation.

"Oh?" she asked. "Nothing dreadful, I hope."

He felt the knot in his chest relax a bit. "Ah, yes, well it seems that someone found the kitchen door unlocked again."

Ginny stopped and turned to look at him. "And you think it was I who let out your secret?"

"No!" He had made her defensive and he cursed himself for a fool. "I merely thought you would find it amusing. Mrs. Barrington is persuaded that someone has been sneaking out. So last night she set someone to lie in wait."

"Oh, dear! You weren't caught out, were you?"

Sir Anthony felt the constriction in his chest disappear in spite of his anxiety about being discovered as the culprit. "No, the lad was asleep when I chanced upon him and knew nothing of my coming and going."

"You really shouldn't risk it!" Ginny exclaimed, her lip catching adorably between her teeth. "Mrs. Barrington takes the quarantine very seriously. Not only that, but she is very strict with the servants. She allows no fraternizing between the kitchen maids and the stable hands. Or perhaps it is the squire she fears is slipping out," she said, laughing.

To see her after four long days, merry and laughing, was like happening upon an oasis in the middle of the desert. He drank in her cool beauty, her shapely form gowned in lavender sprig, the ribbon threaded through her hair accentuating the gray-green of her eyes. Eyes one could drown in . . . .

"Sir Anthony, are you quite all right?" Ginny asked, her expression puzzled.

Realizing that he had been staring at her, he wondered what they had been discussing. "Yes! Oh, yes, of course. I was only thinking on how to avoid such a situation in the future. If I were caught outside, I daresay my only hope to escape Mrs. Barrington's wrath would be nothing less than an actual outbreak of pox."

"I daresay you are right," Ginny replied. "Well, I need to go see Nan. She is bored to flinders, poor dear." Then she disappeared into the servant's quarters.

He thought the encounter went rather well, even if it was far too short. She had spoken to him and had shown concern for his welfare, both of which were promising. He wasn't sure where he stood with her, but after four days without her, there was no doubt in his mind that he wanted to be standing right next to her for the rest of his life. Four nights ago, when she had so dashed his feelings, he had been humiliated, angry, and hugely infatuated. Today, as he watched her walk down the attic steps, he knew what he felt for her could only be love.

He had a ways to go if he was to win her love in return. He knew she would never marry for less than genuine affection. An image of Ginny, eyes flashing and pert little nose in the air, entered his mind. It would not do to push her. She would only rebel, passionate little shrew that she was. The steps he would take to aid in her full capitulation were clear enough, but unlike Petruchio, he would not try to change his beloved. Before he spoke any words of love or marriage, Sir Anthony knew he must mend his own ways.

Chapter Thirteen

Sir Anthony's daydream was rudely interrupted by a tap on the shoulder. Reluctantly, he turned to find Lord Avery, his chin wobbling. "Come, now, Avery," he said, putting his arm around his shoulder and steering him toward the stairs, "you really mustn't. With those red, glassy eyes, Mrs. Barrington will have you in tea and poultices in a trice."

When they reached the salon, Avery slumped into a chair and put his head in his hands.

"What is it? Miss Barrington hasn't fallen into a decline or some such thing?"

Lord Avery rocked his head in his hands. "No, nothing like that. In fact, she seems quite gay."

Sir Anthony felt a stab of annoyance. "Well, what is it then? You're not still pining over her, are you?"

Lord Avery raised his head. "And why should I not be? Wouldn't you if your intended called you a buffoon

159

and announced to the world her intention of never marrying you?"

"I hardly think the occupants of this house constitute the world!"

Lord Avery shot from his chair. "And then for her to be suddenly so gay and merry when I thought she was every bit as miserable as I. It is beyond bearing!"

Sir Anthony was confounded. "Have you seen her? She has been least-in-sight for days now."

"I just ran into her in the dining room. She was eating! Eating, I say! When I commented on her restored health, she launched into a monologue about a ball she plans to give when the quarantine is over. All she could talk about was how lovely her gown will be and with whom she will dance and how many. She is in raptures, while my heart is in shreds and I despair of ever knowing happiness again!" Once more, his chin began to wobble and tears sprang to his eyes.

Sir Anthony felt something akin to panic. Anything but the tears! "Come now, Avery, it can't be that bad. Surely the girl just needs a good talking to!"

The look of hope that sprung to Lord Avery's eyes was too sudden, swift, and sure for comfort. "You would talk to her, for me?"

It wasn't precisely what Sir Anthony had in mind. He proceeded with caution. "If there is something I can do or say that would ease your woes—within reason, that is—then I am happy to oblige."

"Oh, bless you!" Lord Avery cried, his tears all but disappeared. "Talk to her! Find out what her game is.

Does she still wish to marry me? What am I to do to win her heart? I must know!"

"Calm down, there is plenty of time left," Sir Anthony soothed, leading Avery back to his chair. "We have nearly three or four more days of this quarantine still to get through. Perhaps if you brightened up a bit, a moratorium of sorts on the tears, et cetera. In fact, you haven't seemed any happier about the engagement than she."

"I was unhappy about it but only because of the way it came about." Dejected once more, Lord Avery hid his face in a handkerchief. "I came to this house with the intention of asking her to be my wife. I could wait no longer!" he cried. "But if she doesn't make it clear that I am her choice, then I will look elsewhere. There are other fish in the pond!" His head jerked up. "Ones perhaps not so very golden but beautiful nonetheless."

The panic was back. "You don't mean Miss Delacourt?"

"Certainly I do. Why not? She has given me no reason to think she feels adversely toward me. Besides, I am a lord. She would be a fool not to want me. In return, I think she would make a very comfortable wife."

"If you think that, then you have never kissed her," Sir Anthony mumbled, feeling savage.

Lord Avery drew himself up in a posture of hauteur. "Naturally, I have not. And I have not been alone with Lucinda in her bedchamber as everyone seems to believe."

"I think perhaps you should concentrate on one thing at a time," Sir Anthony replied with as much calm as he could muster. He doubted Ginny cared for a title or the men who bore them, but Avery wasn't exactly the sort of noble she despised either. Perhaps Avery's habit of saying everything he felt was exactly what Ginny wished for in a mate.

The sooner Avery had Lucinda safely hooked, the safer Sir Anthony would feel. He mustered up some enthusiasm. "Why, you and Lucinda were made for each other! In fact, Ginny said Lucinda has been blue-deviled over being robbed of her coming-out. She certainly enjoys being courted. It stands to reason that the way this engagement came about is causing all the trouble!"

"I suppose you're right," Lord Avery agreed, pacing the room. "Yes, yes, of course! It's not me at all! Oh, why didn't I think of it before!" he cried, his eyes growing wide and his face pink with excitement. "It's perfect!" He turned glowing eyes on Sir Anthony. "So, you'll do it then?"

"Do what?" Sir Anthony didn't like the direction this conversation was taking.

"Court Lucinda, of course!"

"What?!" It was Sir Anthony's turn to shoot out of his chair.

"Not for keeps, of course! If what you say is true, and I daresay it is veritable fact, Lucinda wants romantic drama and plenty of it!"

"Yes, but shouldn't it be you who supplies the drama, not I?" Besides which, how was he to further his romance with Ginny while courting Lucinda? It defied all reason.

"Oh, I will, never fear! It is simple; tonight at dinner, flatter her until she is putty in your hands. My Lucinda has but one flaw, she becomes putty far too easily," Avery mused.

"Er, yes, I see. Putty," Sir Anthony murmured, amazed by this new side of Lord Avery.

"Second, insist that she meet you in your room after everyone else has retired."

"Oh, no, I don't think that would be at all . . ."

Lord Avery seemed not to hear. "That is when I arrive on the scene!" he said with growing excitement, one finger in the air, the other hand clenched in a fist. "I rescue Lucinda from your clutches and bear her away to the safety of her parents. Suddenly, I am a hero, our engagement will no longer be under a cloud of suspicion, and Lucinda will happily settle down in her new role as my intended bride."

Sir Anthony was impressed. The plan in its entirety made some sense. In fact, it could actually work. Of course, if the intended target were anyone else, it was an utter piece of folly, but one could not deny the phenomenon that was Lucinda. Sir Anthony began to pace.

"You must promise to rescue me, er, *her* right away," Sir Anthony asked with a firm shake of his finger in Lord Avery's direction.

"Yes, oh yes!" Lord Avery agreed, his head bobbing up and down.

"You must promise that no word of this gets out to anyone whatsoever!" If Ginny stayed in her room for dinner just has she had for the past three nights, she need never know about it until it was all done. Surely by then he would have had a chance to explain the ruse.

"Yes, yes indeed, anything you say," Avery promised, head continuing to bob.

Certainly Ginny would understand, even approve. Hadn't she come up with her own plan to bring Avery and Lucinda together? Then why did he feel a growing presentiment of disaster? "I suppose it *could* be worth the risk . . ." Sir Anthony began but was struck speechless by Lord Avery's hurling himself at his feet in an attitude of supplication.

"Please, oh, please, I beg of you. It is my only hope!"

Sir Anthony sensed tears in Avery's future. "All right, all right, if you insist, yes, I will do it."

Avery jumped to his feet. "Perfect! Time to start dressing for dinner! No, never mind, it's early days yet, but you, you should get started. You will need all the time there is left if you hope to outshine me tonight!"

Avery left the room a changed man. Hope had sprung eternal in his heart. Sir Anthony couldn't help but feel more hopeful toward his own romance as a result, but first he would have to get Avery and Lucinda smelling thoroughly of April and May.

Ginny was beginning to suspect Sir Anthony to be a man in love. He appeared in the drawing room before dinner in a state of agitation heretofore unknown to her. His eyes were a bit too bright, and his usual fluid grace was replaced by sharp and hurried movements. The dinner bell was rung before she had a chance to reflect long on the change in him.

The meal, consisting of mutton, partridge pie, braised ham, and various vegetables, was nothing out of the common way, but Sir Anthony's actions were. When he leaned over the table to whisper a few words to Lucinda, Ginny told herself he was merely being polite. When he gazed at Lucinda steadily throughout the main course, Ginny decided he must have a pressing reason to do so. It wasn't until the fruit and cheese were placed on the table and Sir Anthony likened Lucinda's lips to the plums on her plate that Ginny began to grow concerned.

It would seem Lord Avery agreed. "You go too far," he hissed, punctuating his remark with a kick to Sir Anthony's leg under the table. Ginny could only speculate as to Sir Anthony's reply as it was inaudible. The fact that it so effectively placated Lord Avery aroused her curiosity further.

Sir Anthony then turned once again to Lucinda and said, "It would seem your fiancé takes exception to my admiration of you. But when one is promised to such a beautiful girl as yourself one must become accustomed to the efforts of other men to win your heart, isn't that right, Avery?"

To Ginny's surprise Lord Avery's only response was to glower into his plate. Lucinda, for once speechless, gauged her betrothed's reaction from beneath a sweep of lashes. Squire Barrington and his wife exchanged looks of astonishment. Ginny's fork clattered to the floor. A footman attempted to restore it to her, but she was incapable of any action except that of staring in horror at the scene before her.

Mrs. Barrington rose to her feet. "I think it is time the ladies withdrew." Lucinda wasted no time in following her mama out the door, indulging her curiosity only once to confirm that Sir Anthony's gaze did indeed trail her progress from the room.

When she had gone, his gaze swung back to Ginny, guilt written all over his face. His admission of guilt only strengthened her sense of betrayal. Quickly, she hurried away before she was blinded by the tears she knew were coming.

The faces that greeted Sir Anthony when he entered the drawing room were all curiously blank of expression. As no one spoke, it would seem their brains were equally devoid of thought, but he didn't fool himself on that score. Everyone that mattered must think him a thorough cad. He hated what he had to do, but he could hardly pull out now.

Avery came in right behind him and, without even a glance at his betrothed, took up a seat next to Ginny, a clever ploy that would leave Sir Anthony a clear path to Lucinda. Hurrying across the room to where she sat by the fire, he lowered himself into a position beside her where his words would go unheard by the others. "Miss Barrington. Allow me to apologize for that uncomfortable scene earlier."

Lucinda frowned. "You said those pretty things to make me uncomfortable?"

"No," though he had certainly been uncomfortable saying them. "It's only that I should not have been so bold with so many others about. We wouldn't want to upset Lord Avery, would we?"

Lucinda made a moue. "We wouldn't? I had rather thought it to be a very good idea."

"Why is that?" It was not the reply he was expecting. Maybe this would be easier than he feared. "You must tell me, Miss Barrington."

"If I were to tell you, would you promise not to tell Eustace?"

"You have my word of honor. My only wish is to stand your true friend."

Lucinda gazed at him, wide-eyed. "My friend? You are not in love with me, then?"

"No, my dear, I am not. Did you wish me to be?"

"Yes, of course! Oh, pray, do not misunderstand. It is only that I am most hopelessly in love with him but ever since our engagement, he no longer seems to be in love with me. That is why *you* need to be in love with me!"

"I'm sorry, but I'm afraid I do misunderstand!"

"It is very simple. Ginny persuaded me that if I acted happy and cheerful, Eustace would remember that he loves me. It hasn't worked." She looked anxiously at Avery and Ginny seated together across the room. "It was my own idea to look as fetching as possible at the ball and dance with everyone who asks me, even the fat ones." She sighed.

Sir Anthony struggled to maintain his sobriety. "I begin to see your dilemma."

"Oh, I am so glad! I was afraid no one knew how much I would despise having to do that. And you mustn't tell me that no fat men will ask me to dance, because I know Jem Feddleswank intends to. He is forever asking me to stand up at the local balls."

"And you are afraid you will have to do him the honor."

Lucinda nodded. "It is not so much that he is fat, it is that, well, he creaks."

"He creaks, Miss Barrington?"

"On account of his corset. And he . . ." She hesitated and leaned so close to Sir Anthony, he thought her mother, seated not three feet away, would be carried off in a fit of apoplexy. He tried not to think about how Ginny was reacting at the moment.

"Miss Barrington, whatever could be so horrible? I trust he does not take liberties . . ."

"Oh, no, nothing like that. It is much worse. He . . . he sweats."

Sir Anthony could not restrain the fit of laughter that escaped him.

"Miss Barrington, that is a fate to be avoided at all costs. However, I do believe I have a solution to your problem."

Lucinda clapped her hands. "How wonderful! What is our plan?"

"Avery is meeting me in my room tonight directly after we all retire. You must be there first."

Lucinda frowned. "I will ask my mother. I can't think she will approve, however. She may even say we must get married."

Sir Anthony knew a spasm of alarm. "No! We shan't tell your mother. No one shall know anything about it but Lord Avery. Don't you see?"

"No, I don't." Lucinda looked as if she were about to weep.

"Come, Lucinda, what do you think Avery would do if he thought I were about to ravish you?"

"Is that what you are planning to do? Because I don't think I would like it much," she said with a pout. "And I don't think Lord Avery would like it much either."

Sir Anthony ground his teeth. "We won't *want* him to like it. He will see that you are in danger, remove you from my clutches, and declare his undying love. For you!"

"Yes, oh yes, now I see! It will all be so romantic! He will drag me into his arms"—she cried, her eyes shining—"then, perhaps, throw you out of the window or some such thing. It will be marvelous!"

Sir Anthony didn't know whether to laugh or cry.

Sir Anthony didn't know whether to laugh or cry. He was holding a beautiful girl in his arms, who, no matter how lovely, was not the object of his affections but more valuable still in that she was to pave smoother the road to his true love. She was a tantalizing armful, though not precisely tempting when his memories of the more womanly Ginny filled the very same space.

Ginny! He hadn't expected her to show up for dinner and never had a chance to explain the ruse to her. Just after his conversation with Lucinda, Mrs. Barrington had tired of the mismatched liaisons, he and Lucinda in one corner, Ginny and Avery in the other, and set up a card table where she could keep everyone under her eagle eye. It was an agonizing evening, to say the least. And now he was standing in his bedchamber, his arms full of Lucinda.

She was gazing up at him, her eyes pools of uncertainty. "Are you certain this is how it is done, Sir Anthony? You are holding me so stiffly and not at all close. I don't know that Lord Avery would find anything exceptionable in it at all."

"My apologies, Miss Barrington." He shifted her in his arms and attempted to draw her closer without any part of them touching. As he pulled her this way and that, Lucinda gasped but remained impassive in his embrace until finally he had to admit his was an impossible endeavor. There were simply too many parts at too many angles to take all of them into account.

Just when he concluded that touch they must, steps were heard in the hall.

"Oh, do hurry, sir," Lucinda cried.

Panicked, he yanked her full against every part he possessed.

"Yes, just like that," Lucinda said, her voice ecstatic and loud enough to be heard by whomever lurked on the other side of the door.

"Lucinda! What are you doing in there?!" a voice from the hall demanded.

Sir Anthony made a move to bolt the door, but Lucinda was too caught up in her role to realize the voice did not belong to Lord Avery. She flung her arms around his neck causing him to drag her dead weight across the floor. "Save me, save me!" she cried loud enough to wake the household.

He did not make it in time. The door flew open and there stood Ginny, the person dearest to his heart and least welcome in his bedchamber.

"Whatever in the world are you doing?" Ginny winced. It was quite clear what it was they were doing. Hadn't she found herself in just the same position, in just this same room, in just those same arms? Somehow the recollection only increased her confusion.

"Dancing lessons." Sir Anthony tugged at Lucinda's hands clasped tight about his neck. "We were attempting to dance, were we not, Miss Barrington?" Lucinda only gazed at him, a look of acute incomprehension on her face. "For the ball."

"Oh please, Sir Anthony, you don't truly expect me to believe Lucinda came to you for dancing lessons? I have seen her dance at more than one local assembly, quite creditably I might add, though I have never before witnessed a version of the waltz so warmly performed."

Ginny noted the startled look that leaped into his eyes. Then his face adopted his familiar shuttered look. "It is I who cannot dance, Miss Delacourt. Miss Barrington was good enough to take a moment to show me a step or two."

Ginny stared, bewildered that he could utter such a bald-faced lie. After all, he had waltzed with her in his arms only four nights ago.

"Ginny." He spread his hands in supplication and took a stumbling step toward her, the unyielding Lucinda still clutching him round the neck. "There is more to this than you think. That is, less has happened than you suppose."

"Exactly what is it I have supposed to have happened?" Ginny never received an answer, for just then a door was heard to open down the hall.

Sir Anthony and Lucinda shot each other an intense look. "Avery!" Sir Anthony said, renewing his efforts to put some distance between himself and Lucinda.

"Eustace!" Lucinda cried, pressing her cheek to Sir Anthony's and locking her arms behind his neck at the elbows.

Ginny slammed shut the door and went to head off Lord Avery.

"Miss Delacourt," he said, "what are you doing here? Ah, that is, at this time of night. Thought you were sleeping."

Miserable, Ginny tried to ignore the sounds of a struggle coming through the door. "Yes, but I woke up. There was a noise, cats fighting, I think."

Lord Avery was having none of it. "Cats! In Crenshaw's room?" Then he flung open the door, allowing him a full view of Lucinda and Sir Anthony clutched in each other's arms.

Ginny followed as Lord Avery charged into the room. "Sir Anthony! I insist you unhand her at once!"

Sir Anthony ignored him and looked imploringly at Ginny instead. "This wasn't meant to happen. Let me explain!"

"Yes," Lucinda spoke for the first time, "let him tell you. We are in love!"

"Crenshaw!" Lord Avery shouted. "You weren't meant to make her fall in love with you!"

"Well, I am," Lucinda said in a shrill voice, reminiscent of her mother's, "and he loves me, only he won't stop trying to get away," she said, clutching him tighter around the neck.

"Avery, no!" Sir Anthony shouted back. "She loves *you*! Get on with it, already!"

Lord Avery rallied. "I say, unhand him! I mean, her, unhand *her*!" He charged up to the pair, his hands clenched in fists. "I can't account for my actions if you don't do so this very minute!" He made a manful attempt to punch Sir Anthony, but Lucinda wouldn't let him have a clear shot.

Ginny began to have the feeling that matters were not what they seemed. She watched in rapt fascination as events continued to unfold.

"Miss Barrington, it's over," Sir Anthony hissed, "you must let go!"

"No!" she shouted, stomping her foot and landing it on Sir Anthony's recently healed ankle. "I shan't. You must at least hit him first!"

Ginny was unclear as to whom Lucinda was addressing with her last request. It would seem Sir Anthony and Lord Avery were equally nonplussed as no punches were thrown. Instead, Sir Anthony clutched his hair in both hands, Lord Avery sank to the floor, and Ginny began to laugh.

Lucinda, crestfallen and bewildered, asked, "But what about going through the window? You said . . ." She was stopped from saying more by Sir Anthony's finger on her lips.

"Go through the window?" a voice behind Ginny bellowed. "Were you planning, I say, were you planning to elope or just run away together?"

Chapter Fourteen

"Papa!" Lucinda cried, allowing her arms to slide from Sir Anthony's neck to her side where they drooped like petals on a wilted flower.

"Lucinda!" Mrs. Barrington cried.

Sir Anthony groaned, and from Lord Avery's spot on the floor came the sound of weeping.

"Come with me this instant, young lady!" Mrs Barrington snapped. She stalked over to Lucinda and, taking her firmly by the hand, drew her out of the room. "You too, Miss Delacourt!" she said with a snap of her fingers.

Ginny felt it best to comply and followed the other women down the hall, Mrs. Barrington ranting all the way to Lucinda's room.

"I declare, if I knew we were housing two such serpents in our midst, I would have sent them packing as soon as I clapped eyes on them, pox or no pox!"

Lucinda was hustled into her room, changed into her night rail, and tucked into bed, all without a word in her own defense. Ginny had often thought of Lucinda as witless, but she never seemed more so than she did now, lying in her bed like an expressionless doll.

Mrs. Barrington tucked the covers around her daughter, then blew out the candle. "We will discuss this further in the morning!" she said, then marched Ginny out the door and into the hall.

"Go straight to your room and be sure to lock your door!"

"Yes, Mrs. Barrington. But if I could only make a suggestion . . ."

"In the morning!" Mrs. Barrington shouted, then stomped down the hall to her own room, slamming the door behind her.

Now that all the shouting had stopped, things seemed very quiet. Too quiet. Sir Anthony's door lay between Lucinda's and her own, and she doubted she could pass by unnoticed. She knew Sir Anthony had much to say to her, and she wanted to hear it, every word. She wasn't sure how to feel about what had just transpired, but clearly things were not as they had appeared when she first walked into his room, and she knew she would not sleep until she had heard the whole truth. She also knew Mrs. Barrington most likely had her ear pressed up to her bedroom door.

She would have to walk by as quietly as possible and hope he had the sense to wait until morning for explanations. This proved to be a dangerous course of action. The arm that snaked out behind Sir Anthony's door and wrapped itself around her waist came as a profound shock, and she very nearly gave a shriek. Deciding she was safer from Mrs. Barrington's wrath, at this point, to capitulate, Ginny allowed herself to be pulled across the threshold.

While being clasped in Sir Anthony's arms and soundly kissed, it occurred to Ginny that she was wrong about oh so many things. She had thought she knew him so well, could interpret every look, every action, every mask he chose to wear, but she was finding it harder and harder to predict what he would do. She found she rather liked it. She was wrong too about herself. Four days ago she had reason to hope he loved her. Forty minutes ago she was convinced he wanted none but Lucinda. Most of all, only four seconds ago she had truly believed that she would have resisted such an assault.

Instead, she melted with a fervent heat, and there was a singing deep within her that filled her with wonderment. There came sensations, even sounds, she barely recognized as belonging to her and only gradually did she realize that the rustling and murmuring were coming from elsewhere.

"The Barringtons," she murmured against Sir Anthony's lips. "They must have heard me come in here."

"No, it is I," Lord Avery said from his corner on the floor.

Ginny gasped and pushed Sir Anthony away. "What is he doing here? What were you thinking?!"

"Oh, him! I forgot he was here. You! Out!" he said, helping Lord Avery off the floor and out the door. "And you, my dear Miss Delacourt," he said, indicating a chair, "must sit."

Drawing up a chair across from her, he sat down and took a deep breath.

Ginny threw up a hand. "Don't. It's not necessary. I think I have it all sorted out."

"You do? You mean, you aren't going to read me a lecture or break bottles over my head?"

"No! I'm not angry. I see what you were trying to do, both you and Lord Avery as well as you and Lucinda. Why two plots on the same night I am at a loss to explain, but with Lucinda, most anything is possible. Perhaps you should fill me in on the details tomorrow—one engagement under a cloud of suspicion is quite enough."

"Yes," he said, relief washing across his face. "I believe you do understand," he said very quietly.

Something was wrong. Something was very, very wrong. "What do you mean? What do I understand so well?"

"Ginny, don't you see? The Barringtons insisted Lord Avery marry their daughter when they merely suspected they had been together in her room. I was caught redhanded."

"You mean . . . you can't mean they . . . No! Why should they break off her engagement with Lord Avery only to marry her off to you? As long as she marries one of you, her reputation is in no danger whatsoever!" she cried, as panic started to make its way up her lungs into her throat. "Why shouldn't it be Lord Avery?"

"Ginny," he said softly, taking her hands in his, "I hope you are right. I pray that it is so. All we can do is wait and see."

"Wait and see? Wait and see! You would marry Lucinda?"

"No! Not if I could help it. I will do everything in my power to avoid it, if it comes to that. But if Lucinda doesn't get over her petulance for Sir Avery, if he loses patience with her and sees me as a way out, I might have no choice!"

Ginny was aghast. "What do you mean, no choice? Just say no!" The panic took over and welled up in her eyes and down her cheeks.

"Ginny, there's still time to avert disaster. The quarantine isn't over for three whole days. What difference does it make if they insist we are betrothed if we are the only people to hear of it?" He tilted up her chin and brushed at her tears. "Do not despair."

She nodded and dragged herself to her feet. It was silly to be so distraught over something that hadn't even happened. Yet Ginny had a foreboding that the Barringtons would insist on marriage between Lucinda and Sir Anthony. She suspected he thought so as well. If word of it got out, it was as good as done. For a man to cry off from an engagement was strictly taboo, even among the less scrupulous.

And Sir Anthony was always polite.

With unseeing eyes and leaden feet she found her way to her room. Somehow she managed to undress and fall into bed.

A few rooms down the hall, Sir Anthony sat at his desk and tried to think. Only a few more days left of this ghastly quarantine. How much more damage could he do in the days remaining? How much damage could he manage to undo?

Laying his head on his arms, he closed his eyes. He awoke to the singing of birds and the sun shining. He groaned. Who gave the day permission to be so bright? His mood did not match the day. There was nothing to look forward to. He could hardly woo Ginny with an engagement to Lucinda hanging over his head. He didn't know if the Barringtons could be made to understand what had happened, or if it even mattered. Worst of all, that meant no more kissing Ginny. How had he let himself get so out of hand in the first place? Grandmama would comb his hair with a footstool if she knew how he had made such a muddle of things, not to mention precipitating so many acts of impropriety with her grandniece.

As he began to dress, the day did not improve. He wished, for the hundredth time, that he had Conti, his valet, with him. And for the hundred and first time when he nicked himself shaving. And for the hundred and second time when he was barely able to struggle into his jacket, his neck and shoulder muscles sore from his night at the desk. No doubt having a grown woman hanging from his neck like a barnacle off a ship was to blame. Eventually, however, he felt able to face the consequences of his actions and headed downstairs, where he encountered Lucinda about to enter the breakfast room.

"Good morning, Miss Barrington."

Lucinda tossed her curls and flounced away. Things were looking up.

Following her into the breakfast room, he was almost knocked over by Lord Avery storming out.

"Good morning, Avery."

Lord Avery looked him up and down. "The moment I am able I will send for my seconds. They will be calling on you here, so do not think to escape."

This was not a good sign. Sir Anthony inclined his head but was too puzzled to make a reply. As he pushed open the breakfast-room door, he noted that Lucinda and Ginny were seated on the farthest ends of the table from each other. He nodded politely to each and took a seat next to Mrs. Barrington, who pressed a well-used handkerchief to her nose and rushed from the room.

"Well, I am not in good odor today, am I?" Sir Anthony poured himself a cup of coffee and looked around the table.

"It is a sad state of affairs, a sad state of affairs, indeed," the squire said with a tragic smile. "It seems we could all do with some cheering up. Miss Delacourt?"

"Yes?" Ginny gave the squire a bright smile. Sir Anthony thought it a trifle too bright.

"Would you like to go for a stroll through my rose garden? Perhaps you could advise me on some additions I wish to make. I believe your Grandaunt Regina has some varieties that would look well, oh, very well indeed, with those I have already."

This time Sir Anthony thought Ginny's smile looked painted on. "Of course, squire. Only, do you think it wise? Your wife has me convinced my eyes should fall from my head if exposed to the sun during the quarantine."

"We shall just have to take the risk, then, shan't we?" the squire replied.

Sir Anthony watched Ginny leave on the squire's arm, his heart aching.

"You will have to learn to get over her when we are married," Lucinda said.

Sir Anthony choked on his coffee. "I'm sorry?"

"I could not like it if you were to be in love with her when we are married, that is all."

Sir Anthony bit his tongue and counted to ten. He certainly hadn't expected Lucinda to be the one to broach the subject of marriage. "Is this your parents' idea, or have you decided this on your own?" He scrubbed at the coffee stain spreading over his neck-cloth. Conti . . . one hundred and three.

"Mama and Papa and I have been discussing it all morning. Seeing as Eustace and I are no longer engaged, they think it would be a good idea if I married you. After all, it is your fault everything went wrong! Eustace didn't declare his love, he didn't hit you or even throw you out of the window. And you said he would!"

Sir Anthony choked again. It was worse than he feared. Two Barringtons were a respectable challenge, but the three aligned together were nearly insurmountable. "But you love Avery! Why would you cry off?"

"I do love him, but this is all so much more romantic, don't you see?"

"No, I don't see."

"Well, it hardly matters now because my parents insist that since you besmirched me, you must marry me."

Sir Anthony choked, coughed, and choked again. "Besmirched? Lucinda! Didn't you tell your parents the truth?"

"But of course! I told them you were making love to me in your room and Eustace didn't try to stop you!"

Sir Anthony put down his cup and resolved never to drink coffee again. "Lucinda, you know that isn't true. I was not making love to you, and Avery did try to save you." There was something wrong about that statement, but he would have to consider just what at a later time. "Lastly, you don't want to marry me."

"But he didn't try hard enough," Lucinda whined, her nose in the air. "I might as well marry you as anyone else if Eustace won't have me. You're rich, titled, and handsome. And besides, if we are already engaged I won't have to dance with sweaty, creaky old Jem Feddleswank at my ball."

"No, of course not," Sir Anthony murmured, looking down to note the coffee spreading along his snow-white cravat onto his shirt. "Excuse me, I think I have had too much to drink."

"I do hope you will take better care of your clothes when we are married!" Lucinda snipped.

"Miss Barrington, you leave me with very little to say." With that, he fled the vicinity and retreated to his room to lick his wounds and plot his escape.

Chapter Fifteen

"It is a lovely, yes, a lovely day for a walk in the garden, is it not, Miss Delacourt?" The squire squeezed Ginny's hand where it lay on his arm. He chuckled. "In spite of all the romantic turmoil, eh, what?"

Ginny stifled her annoyance. The squire could not possibly know how her own heart roiled. "So there is to be no wedding between your daughter and Lord Avery. I shall always consider it a sad misfortune, as they seem very fond of one another."

Squire Barrington sighed and sighed again. "Lucinda assures me it is as she wishes. I don't know when it happened, but it seems she has developed quite a tendre, quite a tendre indeed, for Sir Anthony. Of course, he is not the catch Lord Avery was, but here now, you would not tell him I said so, would you?"

"Of course not," Ginny said. Besides, she didn't in the least agree. "Then it is all settled," she said in a dull voice. "Lucinda is to marry Sir Anthony?"

The squire paused to admire a rose before answering. "Well, there has been no formal offer, but we expect nothing less, nothing less, found as they were together in his room. My Lucinda is a vastly pretty girl, oh, vastly pretty. Still, I am not so sure what it is that inspires gentleman to exhibit such wanton conduct in her presence." He leaned close to whisper in Ginny's ear. "Beauty is not everything, and my Lucinda is sadly lacking in other minor areas."

Ginny cast about for an appropriate reply and, finding none, hid her confusion in the petals of the nearest rose. She certainly was mellowing. There was a time when she would have told the squire precisely what she thought of his rag-mannered daughter and her latest engagement.

"You do not recognize that rose?" the squire asked. "It is a very rare one indeed. Only your guardian, the dowager duchess, and I possess such a rose in all, yes, all the county. I endured great pains to secure that, I tell you."

Ginny wasn't sure she wanted to hear the details. In fact, the subject of roses was one she did her best to avoid with the squire. The conversation seemed always to make its way to a request for clippings from her Grandaunt's precious collection, something she would never allow. Ginny endeavored to say as little as possible when they happened upon a newly dug bed of rich brown earth crying out to be filled with roses. Grandaunt's roses.

"Well, whatever do we have here?" the squire bellowed. "My gardener has been hard, yes, hard at work, it seems. Is it not splendid?"

Ginny gazed at the dirt at her feet. "Marvelous." Flowers were glorious, but digging in the soil with her bare hands was not. Nevertheless, the new bed was significant. Undoubtedly the squire was about to renew his request for specimens. The knot of misery that had been forming in her stomach since the previous night tightened with a painful jerk.

"Miss Delacourt . . ." the squire began, but Ginny would not allow him to continue.

"Why, Squire Barrington, is that not a Rosa Gallica Agatha just the other side of that arch? It is one of my favorites. They say that Josephine Bonaparte had one in her garden."

"Well, I daresay she did," the squire blustered in confusion. "She had one of everything. A sad waste when her collection was destroyed, a sad waste indeed." The squire mourned, allowing himself to be pulled along the path to the Gallica rosebush.

Ginny refrained from mentioning the fact that Grandaunt Regina disdained such a common rose and refused to have one in her garden. It was enough she had turned the squire's thoughts to coveting Josephine's roses rather than those at Dunsmere. It was a pity the man spent so much time lusting after what he did not have instead of appreciating the truly impressive collection he had already acquired.

It was shocking to walk under the archway groaning under the weight of a vigorous climbing rose only to emerge into a peaceful little courtyard alive with the sounds of bees humming, water rippling, and Mrs. Barrington's secauters clicking away with frightening regularity. At her feet lay a pile of luscious pink blooms at their peak of glory.

"My precious life, what are you doing?" the squire wailed.

Mrs. Barrington turned unseeing eyes upon him. "I am pruning the roses, my husband," she said. The insatiable clicking resumed.

"But, my love, why? Why?" The squire remained rooted to the spot.

"Perhaps she is not feeling quite the thing," Ginny suggested. In fact, she looked a bit mad, chopping away at the perfect roses with such calm fortitude.

It was when the newly formed buds began to fall to the blade that the squire was spurred into action, running across the courtyard through the man-made pond to the other side, where he gripped his wife's wrists against further violence to his roses.

"It is all your doing!" Mrs. Barrington struggled for control of the secauters, bursting into tears when her husband won the battle. "All you care for are your roses, and look what it has gained you! Lucinda is to marry a mere baronet instead of an earl, and we are shut up in the house for days on end because you insisted on picking up your fellow rose lover!" She cast a venomous glance on Ginny. "And someone," she screamed, "someone continues to make themselves free in our home in the middle of the night! Have you nothing to say for yourself, sir?"

The squire put an arm around his sobbing wife's shoulders and turned to Ginny. "The kitchen door was found to be unlocked again this morning. I believe it has all been too much for her. I shall just take her to her room."

"Of course," Ginny replied. She retrieved the secauters from where the squire had dropped them on the ground and surveyed the damage. With judicious pruning she hoped the bush could be coaxed into blooming again before autumn.

It was a miracle she did not inadvertently clip away the two remaining buds, just opened, that lay deep within the center of the bush. With shaking fingers Ginny drew the perfectly formed buds closer. Their stems were entwined almost as if they had their arms about one another, protecting each other from the disaster that befell their fellows.

If only she could stand with Sir Anthony's arms around her, thus.

"Miss Delacourt?"

Ginny whirled about to find Lord Avery standing in wait, his arm outstretched. She felt her face fall and hoped the disappointment did not show. "Lord Avery. What can I do for you?"

"I have come to escort you back to the house. The squire regrets that he left you so abruptly and feared you may be suffering from shock, considering the circumstances."

Ginny took Lord Avery's arm and turned with him toward the house. "I am surprised he said so much on the subject. It doesn't seem fair to Mrs. Barrington, poor woman."

"Oh, all of us in the downstairs part of the house could not be prevented from hearing every detail. Mrs. Barrington has such a lively voice, so full of clarity and . . . volume."

Ginny felt worried by the restraint in his reply. "I hope you do not blame yourself too much, Lord Avery! It is not only your broken engagement that troubles her. She is very upset about the intruder." Pensive, Ginny bit her lip. She hadn't thought Sir Anthony had left the house last night, but she had slept with such profound exhaustion, no doubt she would not have heard him leave even if he had.

"Yes, I had it of the squire. Once again the door was found unlatched, but nothing was missing." Lord Avery spoke without his accustomed flair, a thoughtful expression on his face. Ginny hoped he was not putting any pieces together with regard to Sir Anthony's nocturnal activities and was relieved when his next comment was unrelated.

"It is such a fine day, let us talk of something else. When I learned you were without companionship, I was most gratified by the opportunity to speak with you privately."

Ginny no longer felt relieved. Lord Avery's tone was too serious, too formal. "I'm not sure I understand your meaning, my lord."

"You have spoken of my broken engagement." Lord Avery averted his face to hide a trembling chin.

Ginny knew a moment of hope. Surely he still wanted Lucinda. How could she convince him to pursue her? "Yes, I feel it is a very sad case."

"Then, you feel for my emotions, you understand my plight?"

"Yes, I think perhaps I do." How could she not when his sweetheart was now engaged to her own?

"I cannot say that I am totally sorry things have happened the way they did."

"No? But you love her!"

He sighed. "I must make the best of things. There are other ladies whom I greatly admire."

Ginny glanced away. Could he be courting her? She mustn't encourage that! How to get him thinking of Lucinda? "There is one who has greatly admired you as well, my lord!"

"Truly? In what way?" Lord Avery's face fairly glowed, breathless for her answer.

Ginny thought back to the comments Lucinda had made about Lord Avery in the past. "Well, there is your shining hair. And your beautiful eyes." Had Lucinda nothing to say about his character? The closest she could come to a trait of that kind was when Lucinda had gloried in his ability to rhapsodize on her various features. "Oh, yes, and you are a man of many well-phrased observations."

Ginny had expected Lord Avery to be pleased but was much taken aback when he fell to his knees on the cobbled path and clutched her hands in his.

"Miss Delacourt, you do not know how happy you have made me. It was too much to hope my regard could be so reciprocated."

"Well," she hesitated. "It has been." Which was in keeping with the truth even if that regard had shifted.

"Then fly with me this very night. Oh, Ginny, Ginny," he said with a groan, turning her hands palm up and burying his face in them. "Say that you will."

Amazed and speechless, Ginny found the only thought she could formulate was a hope that Lord Avery did not begin sniveling when her hands remained so close to his nose.

"I have my traveling coach with me," he mumbled, almost inaudible. "It would be no difficulty at all to have it readied in a trice. I would be most happy to journey as far out of the way as Dunsmere if you wish to retrieve more suitable clothing."

Ginny glanced down at the green-sprigged muslin gown Nan had helped her into this morning. It had been quite suitable before Lord Avery had clutched several folds of it in his hands and wrung it tight without mercy. Had everyone suddenly run mad?

She forced herself to reply. "I . . . I don't know what to say," she murmured, snatching her hands away in anticipation of tears. "I will have to think on it." She dared not refuse him outright. The man was clearly unbalanced, and there was no telling what he might do.

He tipped his head back and gazed up at her. "You need only say the word. I shall be ready every night. Only make it soon." A shadow crossed his face. "There is a matter of business I must attend to. A matter of honor. It could cause a delay for us. You would not mind, would you, dearest?"

Ginny shook her head, afraid to say anything that might set him off. The man was a loon! It was with a feeling of gratitude that she achieved the house and could confine herself to her room. But first, she rapped on Lucinda's door.

"Come in," Lucinda called, sounding gay and carefree. Ginny entered the room and found her seated at the dressing table, brushing out her long golden curls.

"I thought you might be worried about your mother," Ginny snipped. She was finding it more and more difficult to be civil to the girl. If Sir Anthony was unable to find a way out of this coil, she was likely to become his wife, and for that she could not forgive her.

"Don't you have a care for your mama?"

"Oh, Mama is all right." Lucinda made a moue in the mirror and admired the result. "It seems the door was unlatched because that little maid of yours, Maren, ran away last night."

"Maren ran away? Are you sure?" Ginny's heart broke for the girl. She had been so happy with her lot as Ginny's abigail. Yet she found she could not blame her for not wanting to return to being the water girl, carrying those hot, heavy cans over those too-thin shoulders.

"Of course I'm sure. They say she is nowhere to be found. Besides, all of her things are gone." Lucinda shrugged into the mirror. "She was just a servant girl. Don't forget, we are to do our soliloquies tonight. Have you decided on one?"

In truth, Ginny had forgotten all about it. "No, I haven't. Do the others remember, do you think?" Could the others possibly care?

Lucinda looked struck. "Perhaps not. I shall run and tell Sir Anthony now." She tripped over to Ginny by the door. "We are to be married, you know."

Ginny quelled the pain she felt at Lucinda's words and forced herself to smile. "I have been expecting it. I wish you much happiness."

"Thank you," Lucinda chirped, then pranced down the hall to Sir Anthony's bedroom door. Could she really be so happy at the prospect of marrying him? What of Lord Avery? There was something here that did not quite meet the eye.

Full of confounding thoughts, Ginny hurried to her room. She must begin now to find the perfect soliloquy before tonight, one that would put Sir Anthony in no doubt of how she felt about him, how much she loved him. She tried not to think what might happen if he was unable to stop the engagement from being made public. It would be very difficult to cry off once that happened, nearly impossible. In the meantime, she would have to trust him.

Sir Anthony heard Lucinda's tripping gait traveling from her room to his. He had hoped she was only heading for the stairs and forced himself to be very still, afraid to make a noise in case she was seeking him. When she knocked a second time and called, "Sir Anthony, I know you are in there," he realized the futility of his actions and opened the door.

"Yes, Miss Barrington, what is it?"

"You must call me Lucinda now that we are to be married."

Sir Anthony closed his eyes. "You might recall that I have not offered for you as of yet, Miss Barrington."

"But you will," she insisted. "You know you will.

You said, 'as of yet,' which means that your offer is forthcoming."

"I regret my choice of words." Oh, did he ever regret them! No doubt she would cause him to regret every word he had ever uttered in her presence. How such an empty-headed creature could be so clever was beyond his scope of comprehension.

"Well, anyway," she continued. "I came to remind you about the soliloquies. You do have yours prepared?" She smiled, overtaxing her once-enchanting dimples. "I trust it is something . . . suitably romantic?"

"It will be something suitable, all right." Actually, he had clean forgotten about the whole thing and wondered that she had not. Nevertheless, somewhere there had to be a passage that would say for him all that he wanted and needed to say. Something that would make Ginny know how he felt and who he truly wanted, regardless of to whom he might find himself engaged.

"In exchange, you must do something for me, Miss, er, Lucinda."

She smiled prettily up at him. "But of course! What is it?"

"Promise me that you won't allow your mother to put the announcement of our engagement in the papers."

"See!" she cried with the maddening clapping of the hands. "I knew it was just a matter of time before you offered for me!"

"Er, yes. I thought it would be far more romantic to wait until the ball, don't you agree?"

"Oooooooh, yes! Yes! Whyever didn't I think of that? I shall go and tell Father right away. Mother is feeling poorly. Good-bye, my darling," she called, and pranced down the hall to the stairs.

Sir Anthony shut the door and thanked his maker. He had dodged a bullet. True, he had agreed to be Lucinda's intended, but in exchange he had won the agreement not to put the announcement in the paper. Feeling the battle half won, his thoughts moved to his choice of soliloquy. Ginny would not be best pleased when she heard from Lucinda that he had actually "proposed," no matter how negligently, but after tonight no one would be in any doubt as to who it was who held his heart.

Chapter Sixteen

Sir Anthony entered the music room and found a comfortable chair. He longed to sit by Ginny, knew he was expected to sit by Lucinda, and so opted for a well-padded seat by the door where he could make a quick escape in case the room erupted into fainting, flailing, or flames, as it had been wont to do in the past.

He noted that, with the exception of Mrs. Barrington who was looking a trifle wan, the occupants of the room were fairly bristling with suppressed excitement. It was a wonder what a period of total confinement could do for one's sensibilities.

Sir Anthony found he was greatly anticipating the evening as well. For once in his life, he was going to say what was on his mind. He was going to say it hiding behind a mask of Shakespeare's making, but at least it was not one of his own this time.

Squire Barrington made his way to the front of the room, his buttons bursting with pride. "For tonight's entertainment we shall have to devise a means by which to determine who should go first, and so on and so forth. Does anyone, anyone at all, have a suggestion?"

Lucinda waved her hand in the air. "I do, oh, I do."

"Yes, my dear?"

"We should pull straws from the housekeeper's broom and make each smaller than the next. The one who picks the shortest shall go first. Or is it the one who picks the longest?" She pouted, rolling her round blue eyes in indecision.

The party at large adopted the suggestion with great gusto, almost as if it were the work of genius. No doubt it was the manner in which the Barringtons settled all their little disputes.

The squire pulled the aforementioned straws from his coat pocket. "Now," he said, "Whoever pulls the shortest straw shall go first, and so forth. Lucinda, you shall be first to draw." He held the little bundle of straws out to her.

Lucinda clapped her hands and squealed with delight. Sir Anthony wondered how she could be so happy in light of her engagement to himself when it was Avery she loved. With a coy glance around the room, Lucinda closed her eyes and tugged at the straws. "I have the short one!" she cried.

The squire cleared his throat. "We shall have to see, have to see. Someone else's could be shorter, my dear."

"Oh," Lucinda said.

Sir Anthony groaned. How could he possibly endure being leg-shackled to such obtuseness for the remainder of his days? Ginny might sometimes seem a shrew, but she had a lively mind and a sharp wit, and he loved her for it. Before the night was out he intended for her to know just that.

Ginny was next to pull a straw, then Avery, and finally Sir Anthony. As it turned out, Lucinda's was indeed the shortest straw, followed by Avery, Ginny, and himself.

Lucinda scampered to the front of the room. She arranged the skirts of her pale blue gown, laced her fingers together, and adopted an expression of supreme misery. "I am Juliet," she said in sepulchral tones and launched into her memorized speech. "Oh, bid me leap, rather than marry Paris, from off the battlements of yonder tower . . ."

Sir Anthony felt his heart complete a leap of its own, but the sensation of joy was short-lived. The look of pure contempt she radiated at Avery made it clear to whom she was addressing this diatribe. The fact that she had to turn her head to glare at him over her shoulder diluted the impact not one whit.

"Or walk in thievish ways," she continued. "Or bid me lurk where serpents are; chain me with roaring bears . . ."

He closed his eyes and entertained a vivid image of Lucinda chained to a cage in the royal menagerie at the Tower of London, her eyes brimming over with tears, gazing in terror at the moldy old bear kept captive there.

"Or shut me nightly in a charnel house, O'ercover'd quite with dead men's rattling bones, With reeky shanks and yellow chapless skulls; Or bid me go into a new-made grave . . ."

Now there was an idea . . .

"And hide me with a dead man in his shroud—Things that to hear them told have made me tremble—And I will do it without fear or doubt, To live an unstained wife to my"—she paused to turn a brilliant smile on Sir Anthony—"sweet love."

Lucinda smiled and curtsied as if the room had burst into applause after her performance. In reality, the squire was the only one who had the presence of mind to applaud his daughter. Mrs. Barrington was too occupied with dabbing at her tear-filled eyes to clap, and Avery seemed to have eyes only for Ginny.

Sir Anthony mechanically brought his hands together and glanced at Ginny. She sat like a statue with the same look of polite interest she had worn since Lucinda began. When had she learned to do that? He felt sure she was laboring under the influence of some strong emotion, and it was not like her to keep her feelings from at least surfacing across her expressive features.

She must have felt his gaze upon her, for she turned in his direction, allowing him to see the wealth of sadness lingering in her magnificent eyes. A moment later, she was clapping and had turned to Lord Avery.

"I believe you are next, my lord," she said with a sincere smile.

Lord Avery rose to his feet with obvious reluctance. It was difficult to fathom that such as he could ever regret the opportunity to wax eloquent. Perhaps he had something against Shakespeare. No doubt if Avery were expected to read his own words, he would show greater enthusiasm. For one terrifying moment Sir Anthony felt sure Avery would do just that, for he slipped a slim volume from his inner coat pocket.

"Ladies and gentlemen," Avery said with a slight bow. "I bring to you tonight a pair of sonnets from the revered William Shakespeare." He made a great show of clearing his throat, fixed his ardent gaze upon Ginny, and began. "Being your slave, what should I do but tend, Upon the hours and times of your desire?"

Sir Anthony, very interested in Ginny's reaction to Avery's words, saw her stiffen. True, Avery glanced at her whenever he could manage between lines, but the words were simply the lines of a sonnet. There could not be any significant meaning, could there?

"I have no precious time at all to spend, Nor services to do, till you require. Nor dare I chide the world-without-end hour, Whilst I, my sovereign, watch the clock for you."

Sir Anthony began to feel a trifle uncomfortable. Avery's words and manner were so intense. It was clear they held some deeper meaning for him. He darted a swift glance at Ginny who sat very still, her eyes fixed on her hands held rigid in her lap. At least she was not blushing. That he could not have abided. He was so absorbed in his thoughts, he did not hear the remainder of the sonnet until the closing couplet.

"So true a fool is love that in your will, Though you do any thing, he thinks no ill."

Sir Anthony felt the blood run from his face. Those were certainly the words of a lover. Now that Lucinda was betrothed to another, Avery was free to pursue anyone he chose. It seemed his intentions were now all for Ginny—*his* Ginny!

The next sonnet was very much the same, though with a more impatient, fervent quality. Again, the closing couplet claimed Sir Anthony's unwilling attention.

"I am to wait, though waiting be hell, Not blame your pleasure, be it ill or well."

What was it Avery was waiting for? Some word or sign from Ginny? He tried to keep his head from jerking in her direction, to no avail. She looked to be in an agony of indecision, her fingers twisting together, her thick lashes veiling her eyes. What could prove to be so difficult for her? Unless, of course, she had some feelings for him.

Sir Anthony forgot to applaud this time. It hardly mattered. Everyone else was clapping wildly, even Ginny. His applause would not be missed.

"Miss Delacourt," he shouted above the din. "Pray, do not keep us waiting."

"I hope that you will all find my selection pleasing," she replied without looking up.

With a calm Sir Anthony was sure she did not feel, Ginny took her place at the front of the room. She opened her mouth but snapped it shut again when her eyes met his.

Drawing a deep breath as if to brace herself for a great ordeal, she said, "I have taken my selection from *The Taming of the Shrew*."

There was an audible gasp from Lucinda and Avery, and from someone else Sir Anthony suspected might have been himself. Ginny colored to the roots of her delicate brown curls. No wonder the girl found her lot so difficult. Her audience's reaction was to be expected, but surely, she was not to play the shrew after those times he had accused her of being one?

"Ah, *The Taming of the Shrew, the Shrew*," the squire said with delight. "One of my favorites." He settled back into his chair, dodging a glare of admonition from his dearest wife.

Ginny smiled. "I am glad to hear you say so, squire." The knowledge seemed to give her courage for the smile remained, and she proceeded without any sign of a doubt or qualm.

"Thy husband is thy lord, thy life, thy keeper, Thy head, thy sovereign, one that cares for thee, And for thy maintenance commits his body To painful labor both by sea and land, To watch the night in storms, the day in cold, Whilst thou liest warm at home, secure, and safe; And craves no other tribute at thy hands But love, fair looks and true obedience, Too little payment for so great a debt . . ."

Ginny bowed her head and curtsied, illustrating her words, then flashed Sir Anthony a look so arch, so coy, that he was cast into confusion. Surely she could not be employing sarcasm; it was not like Ginny to veil her words. Then again, he could not believe for one second that she meant a word of what she was saying. Fascinated, he gave her his full attention.

"Such duty as the subject owes the price Even such a woman oweth to her husband, And when she is forward, peevish, sullen, sour, And not obedient to his honest will, What is she but a foul contending rebel And graceless traitor to her loving lord?"

This was new. Could she be apologizing for past offenses? He reached up to touch the still-purple bruise from the binding of that book.

"I am ashamed that women are so simple To offer war where they should kneel for peace, Or seek for rule, supremacy, and sway, When they are bound to serve, love, and obey. Why are our bodies soft and weak and smooth, Unapt to toil and trouble in the work, But that our soft conditions and our hearts Should well agree with our external parts?"

Sir Anthony restrained himself from leaping to his feet. This was not the Ginny he knew at all. She might be a dab hand at battering gentlemen with books and reticules, but there was little more about her he would wish to change. The thought of a weak and vaporish Ginny, who mindlessly obeyed and always said what was acceptable in spite of her own thoughts made Sir Anthony's stomach turn. Worse, the thought that he had somehow been responsible for the creation of this submissive attitude reduced him to a state of intense sorrow.

"But now I see our lances are but straws," she continued, "Our strength as weak, our weakness past compare,

That seeming to be most which we indeed least are. Then vail your stomachs, for it is not boot, And place your hands below your husband's foot In token of which duty, if he please, My hand is ready, may it do him ease."

She finished with a flourish of her arms, extending the said hand to . . . Avery? He seemed to think so, for he leaped to his feet and, taking the hand in his, kissed it.

As Avery led Ginny to her seat, she gave Sir Anthony the most heartfelt look of mingled hope and sorrow to which he had ever been subjected. Sir Anthony stared after her, puzzled, unsure what to make of it. Did she think she must somehow change in order to win his love? If that were the case, he knew the words he had chosen to speak tonight were all the right ones. Unlike Ginny's presentation, however, his would leave her in little doubt of the exact state of his heart.

Ginny took her seat and attempted to persuade her heart from pounding out of her chest. She had never done anything so daring in all her life. She rarely had trouble expressing her thoughts and emotions, but she had never before worn her heart on her sleeve in such a daring fashion. She had not been sure she could go through with it. She had not been sure Sir Anthony would understand either. All she could do was hope.

As she prepared herself for his recitation she attempted to feel as poised and calm as she hoped she appeared. Surely whatever Sir Anthony had chosen for his presentation, it would be dull and unremarkable like the *Hamlet* soliloquy or some prosy sonnet. Nevertheless, if he turned to Lucinda and asked if he should compare her to a summer's day, she would scream!

Ginny stole a glance at Lucinda and thought she looked as if she expected some great words of love and romance from her Sir Anthony. She would do well to remember the words, "rough winds do shake the darling buds of May."

Sir Anthony stepped to the front of the room. Lucinda preened and tossed her curls, gazing at him in great expectation. Sir Anthony smiled at her and said, "I have chosen a few words from *The Tempest*. Mine is not a soliloquy but a stringing together of some choice words out of the mouth of Caliban. I hope that is acceptable to you all?" He glanced from one face to another for their approval before he began.

To Ginny's amazement he used no text or notes and was able to give his full attention to his audience. No doubt he would quote some words of admiration Caliban said of the beautiful Miranda but to whom would he look? Ginny was gratified when he turned his dark blue eyes on her. She looked down into her lap, unable to meet that unwavering gaze, and was unprepared for the intensity of his voice, the meaning behind his words.

"This island's mine," he said, thumping his chest. "By Sycorax my mother, Which thou takest from me. When thou camest first, Thou strokedst me, and madest much of me, wouldst give me Water with berries in't. And teach me how To name the bigger light, and how the less, That burn by day and night . . ."

Enthralled by the pleading in his voice, Ginny could not help but look up, only to encounter such tenderness in his expression that she thought she could not bear it. Even so, she was not prepared for his next words. Or were they only those of Caliban?

"And then I loved thee . . ."

Ginny's heart leapt into her throat.

"And showed thee all the qualities o'th'isle, The fresh springs, brine pits, barren place and fertile. Cursed be I that did so! All the charms Of Sycorax, toads, beetles, bats, light on you!"

Startled by his change in tone, Ginny glanced again at his face. She expected to see his mouth twisted in a sneer appropriate to his words, but he was looking at the ground, and his expression was one of great sadness.

"For I am all the subjects that you have, Which first was mine own king. And here you sty me In this hard rock whiles you do keep from me The rest o'th'island. Oh ho, oh ho! Would't had been done! Thou didst prevent me. I had peopled else This isle with Calibans."

Ginny was shocked. This blatant reference to progeny was embarrassing to say the least. A tide of scarlet washed over her at the thought of her producing little Sir Anthonys as well as his implication, in front of the entire household, that there had been opportunity for her to do so. At least he admitted she had prevented him.

Then again, perhaps it was her prevention of his "seducing" of Lucinda to which he alluded. Could he, pehaps, be begging her parents pardon? How did it help to get him out of his engagement to Lucinda?

Ginny tried to catch his eye, but he continued to look away until the end of his recitation. "You taught me language, and my profit on't Is I know how to curse. The red plague rid you For learning me your language . . ."

Her language. Had her self-serving plan to teach him true speaking succeeded so well? Surely it had not caused him as much pain as it had the imprisoned Caliban?

"Bravo, bravo, Sir Anthony." The squire rose from his seat and pounded Sir Anthony on the back. "I deem myself proud, proud indeed to have such a talent about to make himself a member of the family."

Ginny wanted to cut the squire's tongue out. She had heard all she wished with regard to his daughter's impending marriage to Sir Anthony. He had said he loved her, looked right at her when he said it; she would hold onto that for as long as it took. But how long would it take the perfectly proper Sir Anthony to jilt his intended?

Lucinda appeared to have as many questions. "Why, Sir Anthony," she said, "that was most romantic." She wrinkled her brow. "That is, some of it was. The rest of it seemed rather nasty and I didn't understand much of it, by half, but I am sure it was meant to be most complimentary."

Sir Anthony took the hand Lucinda extended to him. "I pray that you not reflect too much upon it, Miss Barrington. I meant you no slight."

Lucinda gave him a perfunctory smile, her eyes glazing over. Clearly the poor thing was just as confused as ever.

"Well, that certainly was enlightening, Sir Anthony."
Lord Avery had risen to his feet. "Need I remind you of
that appointment I spoke of earlier? I hope to meet with
you soon."

"I can think of nothing that would give me greater
pleasure," Sir Anthony replied.

"I knew it!" Lucinda cried, clapping. "You are to duel.
How very romantic! And to think, it is all over me!"

Lord Avery and Sir Anthony both turned to Ginny in
alarm. Through a haze of shock she saw Sir Anthony's
mouth open, saw him say something to her, but the
blood was drumming so in her ears that she could not
hear what is was he said. Sir Anthony to duel with Lord
Avery over Lucinda! The thought made her sick to her
stomach. What if Sir Anthony were to be hurt or even
killed? As if in a dream Ginny held her hand out to him,
saw him turn his head to her and ever so slowly walk in
her direction. She must say something to dissuade him.
He would listen to her. He had said he loved her, once.

The room began to spin with Sir Anthony always in
the middle, moving ever closer.

Off to one side was Lucinda dancing about the room,
crying, "A duel, a duel!" She was ecstatic. "There's to
be a duel!"

To the other side was the squire standing on a table,
his hand waving in the air. "Friends, Romans, country-
men, lend me your ears!"

In between, Lord Avery was consoling a wailing
Mrs. Barrington. Had they all gone mad?

All except Sir Anthony. He was taking a long time in
doing so, but he was still moving toward her, frowning,

his hand held out to her. Why didn't he hurry? Her knees felt weak and she was trembling. And why was he frowning so? She had said nothing, done nothing. He was the one who had been so cruel by saying that he loved her then cursed her for it.

The man was an enigma. If she could only sit down. Surely there was a chair there nearby. With relief, Ginny bent her trembling knees and descended into darkness.

Chapter Seventeen

Ginny opened her eyes to find Sir Anthony on his knees by her side. He was still frowning. She lifted her hand and touched the corner of his mouth. "What has happened?"

"She's awake!" a voice cried. It was Lord Avery. His face appeared next to Sir Anthony's, jostling for position. Sir Anthony's faded from view but not before Ginny saw his expression change to one of intense relief.

Ginny's heart twisting in her breast felt as if it were made of knives.

"Ginny, my darling, shall I lift you?"

"No!" Ginny struggled to control her sense of outrage at the thought of Lord Avery holding her in his arms. "If you would only lend me assistance in standing." She glanced up and saw that the three Barringtons had clustered about her like so many grapes on a vine.

Sir Anthony was standing beyond them, his back to her, contemplating his fingernails.

Ginny stood with Lord Avery's assistance. Sir Anthony moved over to the mantel, seemingly very intent on the porcelain shepherdess thereon.

Ginny took her courage in her hands. She had not forgotten about the duel—she must find some way to stop it! "Perhaps someone could take my elbow to assist me up the stairs?" she suggested with a hopeful look in Sir Anthony's direction.

"Of course, of course, my dear Miss Delacourt," the squire gushed.

"It would be my privilege to see to your comfort," Lord Avery pronounced.

There was a loud snap as the porcelain shepherdess broke in two under the pressure of Sir Anthony's clenched fingers.

Mrs. Barrington jumped, stole a glance over her shoulder, and bit her lip. "Why don't you do that, Lord Avery? She doesn't look at all well. I daresay she is sickening with the pox."

"Thank you," Ginny gasped, unable to find a way out of her dilemma. She laid her arm on Lord Avery's and allowed herself to be led from the room. The drumming of Sir Anthony's fingers grinding the pieces of the poor shepherdess into the mantelpiece followed her out the door.

"I am very sorry to have caused so much trouble," Ginny said to Mrs. Barrington, who hovered close by. The squire and Lucinda trailed behind.

"No trouble at all, my dear. You must know by now

that we are quite accustomed to nursing pox victims here at Rose Arbor."

"I have had the chicken pox," Ginny said in her firmest tones.

"Yes, of course you have, my dear." Mrs. Barrington took her other arm and gave Ginny a smug smile. "We shall have you up and about in no time."

Having arrived at the bottom of the stairs, Lord Avery reasserted his position. "Excuse me, madam, but I believe there is only room for two abreast on this staircase. If you would kindly step aside."

"Naturally, naturally," the squire said, pulling his reluctant wife from Ginny's arm. "We must give the two of them a moment, dearest," he murmured in his wife's ear with a glance at Lucinda.

Mrs. Barrington's reply was obliterated by the sound of the hall door being thrust open to reveal a white-lipped Sir Anthony filling the frame.

"I shall escort Miss Delacourt," he announced. "As the grandson of her legal guardian, I would be remiss to do otherwise." Bringing his second-best quizzing glass to his eye, he regarded the assemblage through it as if daring them to argue.

"But of course, of course," the squire sputtered. Mrs. Barrington snapped her mouth shut and allowed her husband to drag her well away from the coming fray. Sir Anthony advanced, but Lord Avery and Lucinda stood their ground.

"I don't think I should allow you to go to her room," Lucinda said in a shrill voice.

"Nor I," Lord Avery expostulated.

"On what grounds?" Sir Anthony's voice was now calm and poised to perfection.

"Why, on the . . . on the grounds of . . ." Lord Avery gave Ginny a pleading look. She dropped her gaze and stared at a fiber slub in the rose-red carpet. She dared not let their eyes meet, else he might misinterpret it as cooperation. She had not forgotten his proposal of marriage earlier that afternoon. How could she?

Lord Avery made a noise of exasperation. "Very well," he said, thrusting Ginny's arm from him. It was enough to make Ginny once again unsteady, and she swayed.

"Stand back," Sir Anthony barked, giving Lord Avery a rough push to the side. With a tenderness Ginny did not expect from a man so discomposed, Sir Anthony took her arm and led her, shaking, up the first step, then with a growl deep in his throat, swept her into his arms and carried her up the stairs with breathless speed.

Ginny forced herself not to react to her first shock of surprise and curled willingly into his arms and chest. He slowed a little and gripped her tighter to him with a convulsive jerk so that she could smell the mixture of cologne, starch, and skin where her face lay against his neck.

"Curse them all to the devil," he said, his voice ragged with passion, lack of breath, or both.

"Does that wish extend even to your fiancé?" Ginny asked, berating herself even before the words were out for having said it.

Ginny could not see his face so was unable to see his reaction. His only response was to say, "I suppose

I should put you down now. We are almost to your door."

"Yes, I suppose you should," she replied, but he didn't, nor did she expect him to.

He fumbled with the latch, managing to undo it despite his burden, and kicked the door open. In a moment he had lain her on the bed. "Do you need anything? Where is Nan—is she still ill?"

"No, she is quite recovered, but I don't know where she is."

Sir Anthony sank to his knees. "I shall find her for you, then." Instead, he stroked the hair from her face with such a tender expression in his eyes, Ginny thought she might melt.

It seemed at this moment he would do anything for her. "Anthony," she said, "you must call off the duel! I do not think I could bear it if anything were to happen to you." She felt her chin tremble and hot tears prick her eyes.

Sir Anthony dropped his hand from her face. "I can't do that, Ginny. It's a matter of honor."

"The same honor that won't allow you out of your obligations to Lucinda?"

"You mean the same engagement I am at such pains to break?" He smiled and took her hand in both of his. "Have I not proven that my honor does not come before you? I am guilty of more than one ungentlemanly act in your presence. In point of fact, it would seem your very presence precipitates the most alarming desire to throw all caution to the winds!"

Ginny had to laugh. "I would cry innocence only I know I am guilty, not only by chance but by design. I had to know if there was anyone behind all that pomp and circumstance that I could love."

"My little shrew!" he said, kissing her hand. He looked searchingly into her eyes. "But now that you have let Caliban out of his cage, is he all you hoped for? Or is he to be a prisoner of his broken heart forever?"

Ginny reclaimed her hand and laid it to his cheek. "You are far more than I had dreamed. But are you sure I am what you want? Wouldn't you rather have the reformed Kate of my soliloquy?" She smiled into his eyes. "I fear I shan't make you a very comfortable wife."

"That is what I am counting on! I find that I relish your brand of discomfort," he said with a most alarmingly wicked smile. "Oh, I can do without the flying objects—in fact, I will have to insist upon that, but I wouldn't change any other moment I have spent with you."

Ginny felt her cheeks grow warm. It was a most improper conversation, part of a most improper evening. Sir Anthony was right; he had behaved ungentlemanly in the name of love, over and over and over again.

"Anthony, if you are so willing to smudge your honor for me, then why continue on with this false engagement? And the duel! Why that?"

"Ah!" he said, standing up and brushing the dust from his pantaloons. "Because one is my solution to the other. If we duel and he wins . . ."

Ginny sat bolt upright. "He wins?!"

"Never fear, I haven't quite decided which will work best in our favor. As I said, if he wins, he will look the hero to Lucinda and she, I pray, will tell her parents the truth about last night. That should do nicely for letting me out of the predicament in which I find myself. If I win, Lucinda won't be able to hide her distress for Avery and will be forced to drop this play-acting of hers. Once again, she tells her parents the truth."

Ginny was aghast. "You can't be serious! Either way, doesn't someone have to get shot? The best I can hope for is that you are killed or must flee the country as a murderer?"

"Tut, tut!" he said with a smile. "Have you so little faith? I am known to be somewhat of a crack shot and plan to aim for injury, not death. Nothing drastic, just enough to make him the object of interest and fascination throughout the county. That should give Lucinda all the romance and drama she has been craving. Why, she will be the most fortunate girl she ever knew. Having a duel fought over you is a sight better than a coming-out, any day."

"Yes, I can see the truth in that. However, what of *his* skills? Does he have any?"

"By that do you mean skills with anything other than poetry, drama, and tears? I can't say. He has no reputation with pistols whatsoever. However, he is sure to see it the same as I. He no doubt has no more desire to flee the continent than do I."

Ginny had to agree, but wasn't it just this afternoon Lord Avery had spoken to Ginny about fleeing somewhere? She wasn't sure she could count on Lord Avery's motivations, but she knew she could trust Sir Anthony now that she could see the man behind the mask.

Come morning, Sir Anthony sat alone in the breakfast parlor, contemplating his fate. Matters most certainly had changed since the day he had first laid eyes on his intended, a lady he had grown to know and to dislike intensely. What great irony existed in the world, for the woman to whom he had lost his heart was the same he could not abide little more than a week ago.

He stabbed a sausage off his plate with his fork and scrutinized it. No, the answer wasn't there either. Hours pacing the floor in his room hadn't revealed a way out of his predicament nor had cudgeling his brain or riding Champion hell-bent-for-leather all through the night.

The sweetest part of it all and the most painful as well was that Ginny loved him. He knew that now. There had been no shrinking away from him when he carried her in his arms, no flying objects coming at his head. Then again, he had not tried to kiss her. He hoped she would be more amenable to his kisses on their wedding night—if he could manage such. He smiled. It would probably be wisest to have all easily-thrown objects removed from the room—just in case.

But first there was Lucinda to deal with. And Lord Avery. For some reason he was casting out lures for Ginny. Perhaps he should just put a bullet in Avery at the duel and be done with it. He would have to leave the country, but that would not be so dull if Ginny fled with him. That would take care of his difficulty with Lucinda as well. He felt sure her parents would not insist the marriage go forth after he had killed a peer of the realm.

He was smiling grimly to himself, thinking his plan not half bad, when Ginny appeared in the doorway looking more beautiful than he had ever seen her. Breathless at the sight of her, he took a moment to confine the image to his memory.

Her glossy chestnut curls were bound with a ribbon of pale apricot to match the soft folds of her gown, and a sash of emerald green, accentuating her trim waist, lit an emerald fire in her gray-green eyes. He thought she looked older and a bit wiser than she had a week ago. There was a radiance about her, a warm glow that he had never noted in her face before.

"Good morning," he managed to say. "You look . . . exquisite."

As he said the words, Ginny stepped into the room followed closely by Lucinda. He wondered if she would assume his words were for her.

She did. "Why, Sir Anthony, thank you. It must be all the excitement. Today is the last day of our confinement, and I declare, it hasn't come soon enough."

"Yes, at least we have our costumes for the ball to keep us busy today," Ginny said with a distracted air.

"Oh yes! Sir Anthony, you should see the gown I am to wear. It is—"

"Lucinda," Ginny interrupted. "We wouldn't want to spoil the surprise, now would we? If we are to get anything done today, we should hurry with our breakfast and be on our way."

"All right, but there should be time for Sir Anthony to at least guess the color I will be wearing. I am such a slow eater."

"You are too generous," Sir Anthony replied. In fact, it shouldn't take any time at all to guess. He couldn't imagine Lucinda wearing anything but blue, her best color, for such a momentous occasion.

"Ah, here you are, Sir Anthony." Mrs. Barrington bustled into the room and took a seat at the table. Waving away the pot of coffee Lucinda proffered, she said, "No thank you, my dear. I have already eaten. No, I come to speak to you about the intruder, who once again darkened our door last night."

Sir Anthony's gaze flew to meet Ginny's. Gone was the recrimination he expected to see, and he breathed a sigh of relief.

"The squire refuses to do anything about it," Mrs. Barrington complained. "He feels sure it is one of the servants sneaking out for some kind of tryst. We shall see." She sniffed. "I intend to set a trap, the nature of which I will keep to myself. I trust you all will do the same and not repeat what I have said to anyone? Especially the squire."

Sir Anthony gave his word, as did the others. Satisfied, Mrs. Barrington left the room, but within moments Lord Avery took up her chair.

"Miss Delacourt, Miss Barrington," he said with a nod to each of the ladies. Turning to Sir Anthony, he said, "I would like to have a few words with you in private, if I may."

"Certainly." Sir Anthony wiped his mouth and tossed his napkin to the table. It was an interview he had been looking forward to most eagerly. "Shall we, then?"

He led Avery into the hall, noting how wretched Ginny looked in comparison to Lucinda, whose eyes shone in anticipation. The chit was a monster of depravity!

Someone should take her over his knee and give her bottom the paddling of her life. Only, it wouldn't be him. He had already tamed his shrew.

Lord Avery was succinct and to the point. "I have heard from my seconds. They will meet us tomorrow at dawn. I would have been most happy to make it today, but what with the quarantine not quite over, I did not wish to risk anyone harm by exposure to the sun."

"No, indeed," Sir Anthony said gravely. "We wouldn't want to hurt anyone."

"Naturally," Avery snapped. A frown creased his brow for a moment, then was gone. "That is, except for you . . . you . . . ignorant pup."

"Ignorant pup? Avery, surely you could do better than that."

Avery turned scarlet, then turned on his heel and hurried away.

It would be good putting a bullet into him, even just an arm or a leg. He supposed he would have to be satisfied with a graze to the shoulder. The sooner Avery was over his injury, the sooner he would get down to the business of taking Lucinda off the marriage market. He returned to the breakfast parlor feeling lighter of heart with enough appetite to demolish that sausage.

Lucinda was on her way out as he entered, which meant he had Ginny once more all to himself. "Well, it is settled. The duel is set for dawn."

"Oh, Anthony, I still can't like it! What if he is good with a gun and he hurts you? Or what if he isn't and he accidentally kills you?"

"My darling, upon my honor, I swear to do my best to keep all in one piece."

"Truly? Because if you don't, I will die an old maid, Sir Anthony Crenshaw, and I shall lay all the fault in your dish!" She gazed up at him, her eyes shining.

How he had longed for this evidence of her adoration. "Yes, truly," he said, considering the wisdom of kissing her breathless and keeping a wary eye on the silverplate. "Everything is going to be all right." He wasn't going to let down this woman, whose capacity to love was rivaled only by his fear of being loved wholly for himself.

Chapter Eighteen

Ginny left the breakfast room feeling much lighter of heart than she had since she took up a seat across from Sir Anthony in Grandaunt Regina's coach. She supposed her situation might appear hopeless to another. The man she loved, who incidentally was engaged to another, was about to fight a duel that could decide their future happiness. It was a coil, to be sure, but somehow, some way, she knew Sir Anthony would set things to rights.

Love was truly a wondrous thing. Perhaps she was being blind to reason, but the thought only made her happier. Wasn't it said that love was blind? And she was most certainly in love. She hugged the thought to her, wrapped it about her like a velvet cloak. She felt different in this guise, almost like a confection in gay papers or a princess in her grandest gown.

Come the night of the ball she would look the part as well. How Sir Anthony's eyes would shine when he saw her in the pink panniered gown she had chosen to wear. Mrs. Barrington had found her an old, pale pink wig, the curls piled high on top with one or two ringlets escaping to hang down in coquettish abandon. There was no need for jewels; the trim of emerald green leaves embroidered around the neckline and hem and the silver netted overlay were adornment enough.

Feeling most content, Ginny went upstairs to join Lucinda in the continuing preparations for the ball. "Do you think we should wear masks?" she asked upon entering her room. "It would add to the fun, but I can't think we could possibly go unrecognized."

Lucinda only sniffed and, tossing her curls, returned to her book.

"What is that you are reading? It must be very compelling, else you would be all-consumed with the ball preparations."

"If you must know, it is a copy of Shakespeare's sonnets."

"Oh, have you not read them before?"

Lucinda shut the book with a snap. "No, I have not, and if you had read them for yourself instead of just hearing those few Eustace quoted, you would know they are much more interesting than some silly old ball!"

Ginny resisted the urge to rush to Lucinda's side and check her head for injuries. "You seem a bit out of sorts this morning. Is something wrong?" Surely being engaged to the wrong man must seem nearly as unbearable to Lucinda as it did Ginny.

"Yes. No! What I mean is, it is rather hard to be married so young when there are still so many men in the world who haven't as yet had the chance to admire me. Why, it hardly seems fair!" Lucinda said, moving to the mirror and touching up her curls.

"It is a hard thing you have been asked to bear, I'm sure," Ginny said dryly. "But you are luckier than most girls in that you have been engaged to not one but two men before you have even come out." It was time to educate this girl on the meaning of "fair."

Lucinda's face brightened. "That is true! I suppose I will be famous for that after I am married." She said the word "married" as if it carried the same meaning as "confined." Did the girl wish to be married to more than one man at a time as well? "But I truly do love him, so I suppose I shall be terribly happy."

"You do?" Ginny could believe that Lucinda might marry Sir Anthony to satisfy her own sense of drama, but she would never believe she loved him the way she loved Lord Avery. "I felt sure it was Lord Avery you preferred."

"Of course!" Lucinda said, indignant, then her face crumpled in confusion. "Uh, that is, I did. Now I love Sir Anthony. Ask anyone. I mean to marry him." Then she cocked her head as if listening to some unheard voice. "Did I say that right? Yes, I believe I did."

Throwing up her hands, Ginny left the room. She would rather pay a visit to the tooth puller than continue to attempt sensible conversation with Lucinda in her current state. As much as she hated that Lucinda was engaged to Sir Anthony, she could feel a measure of empathy for her. What kind of marriage could she hope for when they each loved someone else?

Ginny awoke the next morning, alarmed and confused. She had not intended to sleep, in fact believed it impossible to do so with her mind in such turmoil. She had lain herself on her bed fully dressed only to rest for a moment! However, she had been so very tired, what with putting the finishing touches on her costume, cutting and arranging bowl after bowl of redolent roses, and bustling back and forth from the ballroom to the servant's hall to relay instructions.

She had not seen Sir Anthony through the course of the day, though she thought she had once or twice heard the murmur of his voice coming from another room. She wondered how he was spending his time on the cusp of such momentous events.

Now it was morning and the angle of the sun suggested that the duel must already be in progress. Blessing the fact that she was gowned, Ginny hurried into the hall and down the stairs. The house was very quiet. Surely if someone had been hurt, the household would be in an uproar. Ginny moved to the kitchen, certain news would walk through the door there first, be it good or bad.

She was surprised to find Mrs. Barrington and Lucinda up, dressed, and in the kitchen before her. Of course, Lucinda would be eager for news as well, but Ginny hoped Mrs. Barrington had been kept completely unaware of the duel whatsoever. Clearly it was too late. She braced herself to deal with a hysterical Lucinda and her prostrate mother.

"I have found him out!" Mrs. Barrington cried upon spying Ginny. Her eyes were wild and her manner alive with energy, taking Ginny aback. "I lay in wake all night long, and now I know the truth."

Confused, Ginny looked to Lucinda. "Mama thinks Papa is the one who has been sneaking out of the house. She has been hiding here all night and says that three men left the house before daybreak."

"Separately," Mrs. Barrington hissed, as if the word were damning evidence.

"What reason would the squire have for sneaking out of his own home?" Ginny asked. "Besides, as surely as two of those men were Sir Anthony and Lord Avery, the squire was only going along."

"Yes, of course, Mama! If I were a man, I would have loved to go and watch the duel. I wish they would hurry back." Lucinda threw a look of apprehensive excitement at the door.

Mrs. Barrington did not appear to be mollified.

"You do not say in what order they left the house," Ginny pointed out. "Perhaps the squire was acting as Sir Anthony's second and went on ahead."

Lucinda nodded. "Yes. That must have been it, for though Eustace's, er, Lord Avery's friends have been staying in town since yesterday, Sir Anthony has had no time to find someone to act for him. Papa would have no choice. He would have to be Sir Anthony's second, because it would be very rude not to when Sir Anthony is his guest."

"As well as his future son-in-law," Ginny reminded her.

"Oh! That too."

Lucinda was as buffle-headed as ever but was clearly enjoying the drama of the day. Ginny turned her attention to her hostess. "I am sure Lucinda has come to the correct conclusion, Mrs. Barrington." It was a miracle that she had, but her reasoning could not be denied, especially since Ginny knew it was Sir Anthony who had been leaving the door unlocked behind him. Lucinda's could be the only logical solution for Mrs. Barrington having seen three men leave the house by the kitchen door.

"Do you really think so?" Mrs. Barrington, unsure, allowed Ginny to lead her to a chair. "I was so convinced he was seeing another woman."

"You will see, everything will be explained to your satisfaction, I am sure." Ginny's heart went out to her despite her uncertainty. She took the cup of tea the cook handed her and gave it to Mrs. Barrington. Cook brought a cup for Ginny and Lucinda as well, and with great trepidation Ginny sat down to wait.

Before very long there came the sound of footsteps on the other side of the door. Though Ginny felt sure they belonged to a man, she found it was impossible to determine who. Strange, she had thought she would know Sir Anthony's tread anywhere. This time she thought her heart would stop before the door opened. In a way, it was almost a relief when neither duelist stepped through the door.

"Conti! Whatever are you doing here?"

"Who is this person?" Mrs. Barrington demanded. "Isn't he aware this house is under quarantine?"

"This is Conti, Sir Anthony's valet." Ginny turned to the man she had met at Dunsmere on numerous occasions during his raids to the closet Sir Anthony kept there. "If you have come to act as Sir Anthony's second, I fear it is too late."

"A duelo!" Conti rapped out. "I knew eet. A man does not serve as a gentleman's gentleman without learning a thing or two. No!" He threw his finger in her face. "Do not tell me. Eet is over a woman, I can feel eet in my bones."

"However did you guess?" Lucinda hopped up with delight. "It is famous! And I am the woman!"

Conti gave Lucinda a disparaging glance. "Surely you jest! I would have bet my eye teeth eet is on account of the duchess' great-niece." Ginny thought she noted a hint of approval in his eyes.

"I am glad you are here, at any rate," Ginny said. "It is possible Sir Anthony will have need of you before long."

Conti froze her with a haughty stare. "I sincerely doubt that, Mees Delacourt. Sir Anthony is a crack shot!"

Ginny could not help but notice the intense distress that suffused Lucinda's face but could not give it further thought. Her attention was arrested by a new diversion.

"Conti, you fool! What are you doing here?"

Merciful heavens, it was Grandaunt Regina!

Mrs. Barrington scurried to her feet. "Your Grace, we are honored."

The dowager duchess fixed Mrs. Barrington with a basilisk stare. "If you were honored you would have seen fit to send someone to answer your bell. My servant has been ringing for the past ten minutes."

"Ohhh," Mrs. Barrington moaned, sinking into her chair.

"As for you," the duchess said, advancing into the room. "I have a few choice words for you as well."

It seemed that Conti had not been forgotten. It was pitiful to see the proud man reduced to a state of knee-knocking terror when faced with the full force of her grace's wrath.

"I repeat, what are you doing here?"

"I . . . I had a letter from Sir Anthony expressing hees wishfulness for me to come. I read between the lines. I knew there were troubles of the heart. Eet was my duty to come."

"I see." Grandaunt Regina brushed the valet aside as if he were a gnat, and she a woman of more than five feet, two inches tall.

"I should like to be seen to my room, and after that, I will require an audience with my grandniece. Is that understood?" She glared at Mrs. Barrington until that lady had the presence of mind to instruct Mrs. Crandall to prepare a room, any room.

Ginny bit her lip. What had she done to displease her aunt this time? "Grandaunt, perhaps you would like some tea while you wait?"

"I will not," she snapped. "It is an ungodly hour of the morning for tea. I shall have hot chocolate." She planted herself on the nearest chair.

Mrs. Barrington's eyes filled slowly with tears. "Yes, of course. Cook, do see if there is any hot chocolate in the house."

"Grandaunt," Ginny hissed. "What are you doing here? You should be in London, enjoying the rest of the season."

"And so should you. The truth is, I have been growing concerned for my roses. What with you trapped here and the squire out of my sight, I thought I had better see to matters myself."

She knew how her grandaunt was about her roses. Still, it did not explain why she was in such high dudgeon. "Why? Has something happened to the roses?"

But her grace was not attending. She was staring at the door, her face white with rage. "Thomas Barrington! How dare you!"

The squire stood transfixed like a fox caught in his lair. Even if he could have, it would have done the squire no good to run, for the evidence of his guilt was in full view. His hands were full of rose cuttings.

Mrs. Barrington slithered to the floor. Squire Barrington tossed the roses into the air and rushed to his lady's side. Ginny hurried to the sink to get a wet cloth when a cry from Lucinda filled the air. "He has returned!"

Ginny closed her eyes and prayed.

It was Lord Avery.

Perhaps God had not heard her through all of the chaos. At least Lord Avery was not hurt. He was trembling, disheveled, and crying like a stuck pig, but from what Ginny could see, there was no blood.

Mrs. Barrington had rallied upon Lord Avery's return and was hovering about him with her husband and daughter. Conti was attempting to call him to task for dueling with his master, and Grandaunt was still complaining about her roses. Ginny was finding it difficult to claim Lord Avery's attention.

"Please, please, just tell me if he is all right," she pleaded.

"Oh, I daresay he will get over it in time," came a voice from behind her.

Ginny whirled around. "Sir Anthony! You're here!"

"Somebody had to see the poor sot home."

"But the duel! What happened?"

Sir Anthony leaned his shoulder against the wall and sighed. "The guns weren't loaded."

Ginny was too stunned to reply.

"It's really very simple. As the challenged in this duel—did I say *this* duel? That implies there are more than one, and I can assure you this was my first. As a man about to enjoy the bliss of matrimony, I intend to make every effort to ensure it is my last as well."

Ginny blushed and looked down at her hands.

"Delightful girl," he murmured. "Ah, I digress. As the challenged it was up to me to select the weapons. I chose pistols as I knew the squire has a very fine pair in the library. It was his duty to check them, load them, etcetera, but it seems he was oblivious to anything but roses. The man actually loped off before the actual proceedings to pillage Grandmama's garden, leaving Avery lying low."

"Lying low?" Ginny was utterly confused. "Was Lord Avery hurt?"

Sir Anthony fingered his quizzing glass. "Not at all. Only his pride. He pulled the trigger, then fainted dead away. Poor fellow. I believe he has had rather a nasty time of it."

Ginny smiled through her tears. "Thank you. You said I had nothing to fear, and you have made it so."

"It was nothing," he said. "I only hope that all of your requests are as easily carried out." He gave her a look of such depth and meaning that it took her breath away.

"I daresay some of them will be," she replied, hoping he saw the same burning emotion in her eyes that she saw in his. She smiled and held her hand out to him.

He snatched it to his chest more quickly than she thought possible, and she heard his breath catch in his throat. "You can start by saving a dance for me at the ball."

"I shall be pleased to save them all for you, sir."

"And I should be more pleased to have you do so, but I fear there are others who might demand the same," he said with a playful air, but his gaze moved to Lucinda and his eyes were troubled. "I am afraid things haven't gone quite as planned," he said in a low voice. "Avery fainting dead away at a duel does not cut nearly the romantic picture as the same Avery wounded in a duel. We shall have to hope that matters between those two improves between now and the ball."

He brought her hand to his lips and kissed it. "Until then."

Chapter Nineteen

Sir Anthony was astounded. Dressing for a formal occasion was suddenly much easier than it had been since he had arrived at Rose Arbor. His hands did not shake with nerves, and he seemed to be possessed of the traditional number of fingers and thumbs. Could it be love that accounted for this feeling? Could it be the knowledge that his love was returned in such a way that he felt no nervousness, no qualms?

"I believe eet is due to the presence of your valet, sir."

Sir Anthony jumped. He was not aware he had spoken aloud. "You will be pleased to keep your opinions to yourself in future, Conti."

"Yes, sir," Conti replied, with an air that implied his master was making a huge mistake.

His master regarded himself in the mirror and tried to ignore the sheepish look in the eyes staring back at him. True, Conti was of considerable help in these matters, and he did seem to have a second sense when it came to matters of the heart. Hadn't he advised him three years ago to keep a sharp eye out for Miss Delacourt, as she promised to become a woman of rare qualities? He should have paid the valet's words more heed.

Of course Grandmama had said the very same thing on numerous occasions, but surely one could not blame him for not putting much stock in her opinions at the time.

"You had best mind what her grace has to say to you tonight. She's waiting for you in her boudoir." Conti treated his master's coat sleeve to a final swish of his brush.

"Do you read minds as well, Conti?"

Conti managed to look surprised and injured at the same time. "No, sir. That is, unless you insist on speaking your mind aloud."

Sir Anthony ignored the valet and checked the mirror for the fit of his black evening coat. It was worn over a waistcoat of pink cabbage roses on green stripes. Conti claimed it would complement Miss Delacourt's gown to perfection. How the man knew to bring it with him from town would forever remain a mystery.

"I can't think what Grandmama could possibly have to say to me two minutes before dinner and a ball."

"Your grandmama is never at a loss for words, sir," Conti said with a shudder. Then he bowed and handed Sir Anthony his mask and black domino.

Grandmama did not often require his presence, but when she did, she usually had something of great significance to impart. He supposed she might not approve of his lingering engagement to Lucinda, which was just as well. Neither did he. He relished the thought of telling her so.

"You are looking well tonight," he said upon being ushered into his grandmama's room. "I have long admired you in just that shade of purple."

"You have had little opportunity to do otherwise, Anthony. I have worn this color for decades."

Sir Anthony repressed a smile. "I see you are not got up in costume. It is to be a masquerade, you know."

"Naturally I have been made aware of that fact, but even had I brought something suitable along, I hardly think I would so indulge myself in such childish fancies." She eyed her grandson with an unapologetic air. "I see such reticence runs in the family."

Sir Anthony glanced down at his perfectly correct evening attire. "Yes, well, I have donned a domino. I haven't decided whether or not to wear the mask. I haven't had much time to procure myself a proper costume."

Grandmama sniffed. "I should say not. You have been here less than a fortnight and already you have managed to get yourself engaged to an empty-headed peagoose, fought an equally mindless duel, and wreaked havoc on my heart."

Her heart? "A pretty impressive list for someone you deemed useful only as an escort to Miss Delacourt in taking a look in on your roses."

"Precisely what Ginerva said when I had my interview with her this morning. The part about you being useful as well as impressive, that is. Do not fear, I allowed her to think my displeasure was entirely for your failure in that one endeavor."

"And for this I suppose I owe you my thanks." Sir Anthony folded his arms across his chest and regarded his grandmama unflinchingly. Somehow the old termagant seemed less threatening than before. He supposed it had something to do with Ginny's armed assaults on his person, which made his grandmother seem to pale in comparison. Zeus, it was going to be an exciting life!

"You may thank me later if you are so inclined. There is something I must tell you first."

Sir Anthony was startled to see his grandmother a trifle discomposed. "Nothing has happened, has it?"

"No, of course not." She rose from her chair and wandered to the fireplace and back with a distracted air. Sir Anthony was not sure what to think. He had never seen his grandmother so unsure of herself.

"Come, dearest, it cannot be as bad as all that."

"I hope that it is not. Nevertheless, you are bound to be angry with me."

Sir Anthony felt his heart grow sick with fear. "You haven't done anything to further my engagement to Lucinda?" He could just hear his grandmother promising the precious rose cuttings to the squire in exchange for the peagoose.

"Don't be a fool! You have done very well for yourself in that regard. No, my boy, that coil is entirely of your own making, one which I hope you are as desperate to undo as I."

He enjoyed a momentary surge of relief until a new fear gripped him. "You haven't given your permission for Ginny to marry that lily-livered milk-sop!" he roared. "For if you have, I cannot be held accountable for my actions!"

The duchess treated him to a frosty glare. "What kind of fool do you take me for? I have more in my skull-box than your Lucinda, after all."

Sir Anthony fell into a chair and passed a shaking hand along his forehead. "She is not *my* Lucinda," he ground out.

There was a pause before his grandmama rustled over to a chair across from him and sat. "I do believe you have changed, Anthony."

He dropped his hand and looked her in the eye. "Oh? In what way?"

She pooh-poohed his question with a wave of her hand. "There are too many little details to mention. I can think of only one thing that could have brought about this metamorphosis. I believe you are in love."

Sir Anthony felt his mouth relax into a foolish grin. "Touché, Grandmama. You always were a knowing one."

"And am I right to assume it is not with your intended?"

"Just so!"

"Excellent. Then perhaps you may not be as angry with me as you could be, given the circumstances. You are perfectly aware how I have long wished for you to marry Ginerva."

Sir Anthony winced. Grandmama was sure to gloat, never a pretty sight. He decided to brazen it out with a lie. "No, I can't say that I have. I have been aware that you wished me to marry, though not to anyone in particular."

"Leave it to you not to see what is in front of your very eyes! I have known her to be perfect for you from the very beginning. Nevertheless, my subtle attempts never led to success. Thus, I determined that more, shall we say, desperate measures were in order."

"Of course, the roses. Well, if that is all you are worried about I suspected from the beginning that the whole thing might have been a plot to throw us together," he conceded. "It was a rather unorthodox request."

The duchess sniffed. "There is nothing unorthodox about my love of roses, Anthony. However, there is more. I hoped to throw the two of you together for as long as possible to give the two of you time to find the best in one another."

"You have behaved rather outrageously, Grandmama, especially for something so left to chance. I love Ginny with all my heart but I doubt I would have given the girl a chance if we hadn't had our time together, here."

"I am not a total flat, Anthony. I took steps to ensure a measure of success. What I hadn't counted on was you getting yourself engaged to that Barrington chit, though I knew she would be here. Why else would the squire come pelting back to the country in the middle of the season?"

Sir Anthony shook his head to clear it of his confusion. "You were afraid he was going to take advantage of your absence to pilfer your roses, so you sent Ginny and myself out here, hoping we would fall in love?

Grandmama, forgive me, but it still does not make sense."

"Of course it doesn't," she snapped. "Unless you add the part where I hired those two ruffians to hold you up and take off with your coach within walking distance of Rose Arbor."

Sir Anthony wasn't sure he heard correctly. "You what?"

"I never repeat myself, Anthony. Though I will add that it seems a waste of money to pay highwaymen to hold you up and steal my coach only to see you become engaged to the wrong girl! Not to mention the fact that my roses remained in jeopardy!"

"Grandmama! Forget about the roses! You would do that to Ginny? We could have been stranded out there! Worse, we could have been stranded at the inn! Had you no thought to Ginny's reputation?"

Grandmama winced. "The girl already has a reputation, that of a forthright bluestocking, too lively and intelligent to make anyone a comfortable wife. That is, almost anyone. It has always been my dearest wish the two of you should wed, but you formed such a hearty distate for each other the moment you met. An afternoon together was not going to be long enough for Ginny to see the man of substance you are, or for you to see the generous-hearted woman she has always been. Have I done so wrong?"

Outside her Grandaunt Regina's door, Ginny stood, hesitating to knock. She heard voices deep in conversation and though she had been sent to summon the dowager duchess to the drawing room, Ginny could not bring herself to interrupt.

As Sir Anthony had not yet appeared, she had to assume the masculine voice she heard through the door belonged to him. Perhaps he was discussing his dilemma with Grandaunt, that of being engaged to Lucinda but loving another. She knew it was rude in the extreme, but she must hear what they were saying. She put her ear to the door to listen. As fate would have it, the door was slightly ajar and Ginny was able to widen the crack.

"Does she know?" she heard Sir Anthony say.

"No, she does not, and I would thank you to keep it that way. Before I arrived I hadn't thought she would care. However, after speaking to her this morning it occurred to me how humiliated she would be if she were aware of the situation."

Sir Anthony gave a harsh laugh. "Yes, I can well believe that. As am I!"

What was it she was meant not to care about? What was it that was so humiliating to the both of them? Ginny felt a knot form in the pit of her stomach.

"Grandmama, how could you do such a thing? Those two are idiots and might have done us serious harm."

Harm? Idiots? Who could he be speaking of? What had Grandaunt Regina done?

"Seb and Dobbs?" the duchess cried. Ginny froze. "They wouldn't hurt a fly! They are actors from the traveling troupe. I am sorry if you were frightened, but it seemed the only way to throw the two of you together."

Ginny began to tremble, and her hand on the door felt like ice. What did it mean? Why would Grandaunt ask someone to do such a thing? She wasn't sure what the answer was, but she did know things somehow weren't as they seemed a few moments ago.

"Well, Grandmama," Sir Anthony said. "You should be congratulated! You have surpassed yourself!"

Ginny felt her heart stop. Grandaunt had manipulated the both of them, and he sounded so angry! So lost was she in her thoughts that she didn't hear the heavy footsteps cross to the door until it was too late. He swung open the door to find her hovering in the hall. She could see that he was angry, more angry than she had imagined. He didn't look at her and said nothing, only swept past her and out of sight.

Recovering herself quickly, she stepped into the room. "Grandaunt Regina, it is time to meet in the drawing room for dinner." She prayed her grandaunt didn't realize she had been eavesdropping.

"Ah, darling girl, you look scrumptious! A pink wig! Well I never! It has been years since I have seen one of those. Come, take my arm and let's be off!"

Ginny was grateful for her grandaunt's continuing prattle, as it gave her time to think. She knew how Sir Anthony felt about having been thrown together by his matchmaking grandmama. Didn't she feel the same humiliation? He, however, was so angry. Would his feelings about what had happened transfer themselves to her? Would it be too much on top of his reticence to callously jilt Lucinda? Was it all too much for a newfound love to endure?

Soon she found herself in the drawing room with all the other players in this drama: Sir Anthony, who looked angrier than a polite gentleman should at dinner; Lucinda, who hadn't been shaken from her resolve to marry him, in spite of the psuedo-duel; the Barringtons, who were still adamant that Sir Anthony should do the pretty and make their daughter an honest woman; and Lord Avery, who was looking far too delighted to see her than should a man who was in love with another.

The moment they arrived, the bell was rung and they all proceeded into dinner in order of precedence: Grandaunt at the fore with Lord Avery, Mrs. Barrington as the hostess, on the arm of Sir Anthony, Ginny on the arm of the squire, and Lucinda trailing along behind. Somehow, she was placed across the table from Lord Avery at dinner. Sir Anthony was both across table and one seat down, too far away to make polite conversation.

She felt rather numb through the soup course. Her confidence that Sir Anthony would be able to extricate himself from his engagement before it was announced at the ball began to wane. For what had he been waiting?

She felt positively miserable through the meat and fish course. Would an already humiliated Sir Anthony be willing to bring more humiliation down on his head? As a result, would he find it too distasteful to humiliate Lucinda?

By the fruit and cheese course, she had resigned herself to any possibility. As the female of the species, she could only deny or accept an offer of marriage; she could not make one happen. Before this jaunt into the country, she had been persuaded that there was no one she could care for as much as her life at Dunsmere with her books and roses. However, compared to a life with a man she loved, who challenged her yet loved her just as she was, it now seemed a dreary prospect indeed.

Finally, by the dessert course, she felt angry enough to fight. She knew she could not get Sir Anthony out of his predicament, nor could she force him to offer for her hand. What she could do was disappear. Not forever, of course, just long enough for Sir Anthony to feel that wanting her was his own idea, not his grandmama's. Long enough for him to know that being without her felt far worse than any scandal or humiliation at the hands of scheming females. Long enough for him to decide what he wanted most: to be accepted by the rigid codes of society, or to be loved, wholly for himself, by her.

She only needed to get as far as Dunsmere, but who could she get to help her escape? Such a short distance she could manage on her own, but it was late and soon would be dark. People would be arriving for the ball, and she didn't want to be spotted walking along the road; therefore, she needed a carriage. Stealing one was out of the question, as was asking for permission. No one must know she was leaving. They would only try to stop her.

There was no one she could turn to, unless. . . . Lord Avery! If he were expecting to hear Lucinda's engagement to another man announced to the county, he no doubt planned to leave Rose Arbor soon anyway. He had asked her to fly off with him, had said to only name the time. She hoped a short flight would satisfy him.

With all the courage she could muster, Ginny leaned across the table and said, "My lord. It is time."

Chapter Twenty

Sir Anthony wondered what Ginny could possibly have said to Avery to turn his skin so deathly white. True, he was always rather pasty-faced but never quite so colorless, even when looking down the barrel of Sir Anthony's pistol. Why, the man looked positively ill.

His alarm grew when Lord Avery gasped, choked, and coughed for a full three minutes, forcing Grandmama to halt her discourse on the rare forms of roses to be found in the Dunsmere gardens.

Ginny's behavior was equally puzzling. She at first appeared to be unaware her dinner companion was suffering any distress whatsoever. After a full minute of choking and coughing, she seemed unable to ignore it longer and offered him a napkin, saying, "There, there. You will be fine in a moment."

When the moment had passed and he had not recovered, Ginny actually seemed almost angry. She forced a glass of wine into his hand and bade him drink. He obeyed, too hastily, which only deepened his distress.

By this time Grandmama had stopped speaking and the occupants of the table gave up pretending they were unaware of Lord Avery's difficulties. Sir Anthony supposed it was pure embarrassment that finally gave Avery the strength to force air into his lungs again.

"Are you quite all right, Avery?" Sir Anthony asked.

Avery nodded his head vigorously, his hand clamped tight to his mouth.

Ginny, looking self-conscious, became suddenly very interested in the contents of her plate. Sir Anthony felt sure she hadn't eaten a bite since she sat down, but the food was now disappearing with amazing alacrity.

"You seem to have recovered your appetite, Miss Delacourt," he observed. And he had recovered his equilibrium. He had been angry with Grandmama, but when Ginny entered the drawing room, so lovely in her pink-and-green costume, he had felt his anger melt away.

To his amazement, she dropped her fork with a clatter and folded her hands in her lap. "Actually, I am not very hungry."

"You must eat," he insisted, "if you are to dance with me at the ball." He most desperately needed to speak with her and a waltz would give him the perfect opportunity for a private conversation.

He was startled when five more forks clattered to their china plates. Grandmama glared at him, Lucinda pouted into her lap, and her parents stared at him in open amazement.

"Sir! Your engagement to our daughter is to be announced, I say, announced this very evening at the ball!" the squire protested.

Lord Avery took up choking into his napkin again, the claiming of it having necessitated the dropping of his own fork.

"It would not be appropriate," Mrs. Barrington added, "to be courting another young lady under the circumstances!"

It was difficult to know how to respond to that, but Ginny came to his rescue. "I should be honored to save a country dance for you," she said. "Lord Avery has already requested the waltzes."

Lucinda gasped with dismay, and Avery, whose face had begun to take on some of its usual color, turned purple.

"You seem to be suffering from some kind of distress, Avery. Perhaps another napkin will do the trick. Here, have mine," Sir Anthony said, passing the snow-white cloth down the table.

"Perhaps you should rest for a bit in your room, Lord Avery." Ginny gave him a meaningful glance. A bit too meaningful, Sir Anthony thought. "The guests will be arriving for the ball shortly."

Avery nodded and hastened from the table, a perfect picture of misery while Lucinda watched him go, looking utterly lost. Then she gave herself a little shake and turned to her fiancé.

"Anthony, you haven't complimented my costume."

"It is very lovely. Just the color of your eyes." He smiled the appropriate smile, all the while watching

Avery. He had just reached the door when Avery stiffened and turned to look at Lucinda over his shoulder. He nodded, then left the room.

Something smoky was afoot. Sir Anthony was determined to discover what, even if it meant horning in on one of Avery's waltzes. Especially if it meant horning in on one of Avery's waltzes. He'd be hanged before he sat on his thumbs watching some other man spend the evening with the woman he loved.

Sir Anthony cleared his throat. "Your costume is very lovely also, Miss Delacourt." Well, that certainly didn't come out right. Lucinda was wholly eclipsed by Ginny. He wasn't sure about the wig—he much preferred the chestnut of Ginny's curls—but the gown suited her to perfection. She looked like a princess from another time, like a pink confection of homespun sugar. Then again, there was something about the way the lines of the gown hugged the curves of her excellent figure that was not quite so innocent. The word "goddess" came to mind more than once.

"I . . . thank you," Ginny replied, her eyes fixed to her plate.

"Anthony," Lucinda began in a plaintive voice, but he was saved from hearing her request by Grandmama's announcement that dinner was over.

"Oh, so soon?" Mrs. Barrington asked, clearly bewildered by this takeover by the dowager duchess.

"Yes. It is time we left the gentlemen to themselves. The other guests will be arriving within the hour, and we mustn't deprive these two of the taking of their port."

Sir Anthony suppressed a smile. How many years had the old termagant been after him to give up drink? She wouldn't wish to see him suffer the misery of gout as had countless Crenshaws before him. Apparently the taking of port was permissible if it afforded him the opportunity to speak with the squire about releasing him from his obligation to his daughter.

"Anthony, do take your time," she called. She sailed out of the room with Ginny and Lucinda in her wake, a befuddled Mrs. Barrington trailing along behind.

"Well, my boy," the squire said with a sigh. "It has come to this, to this."

"Yes, sir, I believe it has." What it had come to was perhaps a bit beyond what the squire had anticipated. Sir Anthony rather expected the squire was prepared to speak of dowries and the like, not the possibility of his daughter's second broken engagement in almost as few days. "You spoke of the announcement to be made at the ball tonight."

"Yes, indeed, indeed. A ball is a wondrous time to announce an engagement. Why, my lovely bride and I announced the news of our marriage at just such an event."

Sir Anthony leafed through the pages of his personal code of honor for the proper way to disabuse the squire of the notion that he would ever marry his daughter. Unfortunately, the only help it could proffer was the insistence that he follow through and marry Lucinda as would any proper gentleman in his position.

With the accustomed pang one felt at such a time of loss, Sir Anthony rose to his feet and lifted his drink high. "Squire Barrington. I will never marry your daughter." With that, he quaffed his drink in one gulp and tossed the goblet into the fireplace.

The squire stared at him in unblinking surprise, than said, "You needn't have broken the crystal. It is very dear, you know, very dear indeed."

Crystal? The man was concerned about broken crystal? "Sir, we are speaking of a broken engagement. Are there to be no repercussions, then?"

"Well, Mrs. Barrington is sure to put up a bit of a fuss. That could get a bit nasty, a bit nasty, but I daresay there is something you could do to alleviate my suffering. Life has been so full of woe since my cuttings were left to wither amidst all the ruckus after the duel."

"I see. Would a few fresh cuttings make up for your troubles in that regard?" Getting them out of Grandmama would be almost as bad as wedding Lucinda, but he would face worse for a lifetime of happiness with Ginny.

"Ahhh." The squire leaned back in his chair, much content. "That will take care of my lady wife. As for myself, I have suspected there was some trouble between you and Lucinda. Neither of you behave the least bit loverlike. With the exception of the other night, that is."

"Yes, I feel I should explain about that."

Squire Barrington waved Sir Anthony's protestations aside. "Not at all, at all. It has taken some time, but I have determined that my Lucinda suffers from a major fault."

"Which would be?" Sir Anthony was aware of quite a few but was alive with curiosity to know to which of the many the squire referred.

The squire leaned forward and glanced about to ensure total privacy. "This is a matter of great confidentiality, of course, of course."

"Of course." Sir Anthony nodded.

The squire pursed his lips. "My daughter has a shocking habit of throwing herself at her suitors."

"Oh, really? I hadn't noticed," Sir Anthony politely lied. And for the very last time.

Inside the ballroom, the strains of a waltz were wafting in the air. Where was Ginny? Fortunately, Lucinda and her mama were far across the room. To his chagrin they lost no time in spotting him and rushing to his side, relief written across Mrs. Barrington's face.

Had she suspected that he might turn tail and run? Not that it was such a bad idea. His code of honor may have worn out its usefulness, but at least he had known how to proceed prior to consigning it to perdition. Having commited the ungentlemanly sin of breaking his engagement, he had no idea what to do next. As the Barrington ladies drew ever closer, running was looking better with every passing moment.

"Ah, Mrs. Barrington, Miss Barrington." He greeted them with the hope that he still remembered how to hide his nervousness.

"That is no way to treat your intended, Sir Anthony. I am sure Lucinda has given you leave to use her first name. But really, that is nothing to leaving her to her own devices for so long. Truly, Lucinda." Mrs.

Barrington turned to her daughter. "I do not think you should marry such an insensitive creature!"

"I couldn't agree with you more," Sir Anthony said. It was all so much easier than he had feared, and, even better, he had just spied Ginny deep in conversation with Avery across the room. "Now, if you will excuse me, I believe Ginny owes me this dance."

He suspected Mrs. Barrington was imitating a blow-fish and Lucinda was most likely stamping her well-shod little foot, but he dared not linger long enough to confirm it. The woman he loved had been waiting long enough. Waiting for him. For the real Anthony Crenshaw.

He was across the room in a dozen quick strides, but not soon enough to claim her hand before Avery. Jerking him away by the shoulder, he said, "Pardon me, man, but this is my dance."

Ginny's response was one of pretty confusion. "But I . . . really, I believe . . . I'm sure I mentioned my waltzes were taken." She stared at him through the eye-holes of a black mask. Along with the pink wig and unfamiliar gown, it was as if she were a stranger. A beautiful stranger to whose heart he had no claim. He felt his earlier anger make a reappearance.

"Yes, they are! By me! Take yourself off, Avery. I believe Lucinda is lacking for a partner." Sir Anthony wasn't sure how he should feel about the expression of dismay on Ginny's face when Avery complied. Rather than decide, he drew her into his arms and they began to dance.

He tried to concentrate on the rhythm of the music while willing his fury to recede. It had been a difficult evening, but now that he had Ginny in his arms, things were sure to get better.

"I hear you had a talk with your grandmama today," Ginny said.

Sir Anthony didn't want to think about Grandmama. He found he was still angry with her, but what was a newly made man to do, er, say? Ginny would see through any polite fiction that came out of his mouth. At the same time, Grandmama would never forgive him for telling Ginny about Grandmama's plot to send them off together on her madcap errand and on through to wedded bliss.

"Yes! We, er, we talked." It was the best he could do. He could feel himself frowning, but it seemed he was powerless to stop himself.

"I hope she didn't scold you! I know how Grandaunt Regina can be."

"Why should she scold me?" he snapped. Surely Grandmama was the one who deserved the scolding.

"The roses? I'm afraid we weren't much help in rescuing them from the squire's clutches," she explained.

"Oh, that. No she didn't scold me." He hated to keep secrets from her, but she was right about Grandmama's scolding; it was definitely something one hoped to avoid. Besides, he had promised never to divulge her secret. Afraid Ginny would read his hesitation in his eyes, he looked pointedly away.

Ginny sighed. "You seem rather angry tonight," she said. "Is there anything wrong?"

"What?" The truth was so close to his tongue, but he must never tell her. She would be humiliated. He looked around for inspiration and spotted Avery headed in their direction. "Yes! That popinjay tried to steal a march on me!"

"Anthony, I . . ." But she was stopped short by a shrill voice at his shoulder.

"Sir Anthony, we are waiting for you!"

He turned to see Mrs. Barrington and Lucinda staring at him with great expectation. And just when he thought he had rid himself of that very look for the remainder of his life.

"What is it now!" he barked, causing Ginny to jump under his arm, still draped across her shoulders.

"Why, to announce your engagement to my daughter, you wretch. She is so determined to have you! Every time I suggest otherwise, and believe me, I *have* suggested otherwise, she kicks up *such* a dust."

Before Anthony could reply, Avery appeared at Ginny's side and hooked his arm through hers. Mrs. Barrington and Lucinda were arguing, so he never heard what Avery murmured in Ginny's ear. It must have been most compelling, because she allowed Avery to lead her away without even a backward glance.

Sir Anthony felt the beginnings of a black rage. First Grandmama meddled in his affairs as if he was some kind of child. Then Ginny treated him as if they had barely met! Now the Barringtons were insisting on that wretched announcement while he watched Ginny walk away from him on the arm of another. It was almost as if she were walking out of his life.

Suddenly the Barringtons weren't shouting anymore. That certainly boded ill. Sir Anthony tried to catch up.

"Mama," Lucinda was saying, "I have changed my mind. This does seem like the perfect time, after all. Pray wait until I dash to my room and touch up my hair. I will only be a moment."

Mrs. Barrington puffed with indignation. Did she see how Lucinda's gaze followed Ginny and Avery right out of the ballroom? Sir Anthony certainly did, but what did it mean?

"Yes, do, Lucinda," Sir Anthony insisted, pushing her away. "Your hair looks like a rat's nest." He had no time to lose and certainly none for pleasant banter. If she were insulted by his comment, all the better.

"Oh, thank you, Sir Anthony," Lucinda gushed over her shoulder as if he had just crowned her the most beautiful girl at the fair. Giggling, she clapped her hands and skipped out of the room.

"If you will excuse me, Mrs. Barrington." He didn't wait for her pardon but flew across the room and out the door taken by Ginny and Avery. He searched the hallway, the drawing room, all three salons named after roses, the music room, the dining room, even the breakfast parlor, but they were nowhere. He felt his heart sink like a stone through water. Ginny was gone!

What reason could she have for leaving in the middle of a ball? With Avery? Surely she would never elope with him! Dash it! What did Avery say to her to make her walk out like that? Something was wrong. As he made his way out to the stables, he cudgeled his brain to determine what it could be.

Then he realized. Ginny knew! She had been on the other side of the door when Grandmama told him about the whole sorry mess with Seb and Dobbs. He had even seen her out of the corner of his eye as he stalked off, but he hadn't recognized her in that wig. In his angry state, it barely registered that anyone was there. And now she was leaving.

He couldn't let her leave! He had to tell her it was all right, that it didn't matter that Grandmama had gotten her way. He loved her! And the announcement of his engagement to Lucinda—what must she think? That he hadn't the courage to call it off? That he loved his precious code of honor more than her?

He had to tell her it wasn't so. He had to tell her right now, even though it was clear she wanted to get away from him. The old Sir Anthony would have bowed to his lady's wishes. For once, the new Sir Anthony was no longer in any doubt.

Chapter Twenty-one

The new Sir Anthony found he had a problem. He arrived at the stable just in time to see a coach bowl down the lane. Running inside, he found the stable boy, the one who had been saddling up his horse in the dead of night for the past two weeks.

"Whose coach was that?" Sir Anthony demanded.

"Why, that'd be Lord Avery's, guv."

"Was there a lady with him?"

"Yes, two," he said with a low whistle. "They were in a right hurry to be gone, that's for sure!"

Ginny! And Nan? "Was one of them in a pink gown with a black mask?"

"Ooooh, that one was a beauty, she was!"

Sir Anthony thought fast. "What about this one, here?" He indicated a canary-yellow curricle with a pale blue interior. The color combination was loathsome, but

256

the horses were still in their traces and he didn't have a second to lose. Ginny's heart was breaking.

"Oh, that be Jem Feddleswank's ride. He pulled up just afore Lord Avery's party came in, which is why I haven't had a chance to unhitch . . ."

"It'll do," Sir Anthony said, flipping the boy his last sovereign and hopping inside. As he pulled away he shouted, "Tell Feddleswank . . ." What? He can have mine? Since Sir Anthony didn't have a coach of any kind at Rose Arbor, that would hardly do. "Dash it!" he swore under his breath, pulling away and hoping Feddleswank and his creaking corsets would be otherwise occupied for hours to come.

Which way to go? London was to the south, but Dunsmere was only a short distance away. He turned north. He had a lot of ground to cover, but the curricle was lighter and faster than the coach and it wasn't long before he spotted it lumbering up ahead. With Avery at the reins, Sir Anthony knew he would have little trouble gaining on it and forcing it to a halt. It was the work of a moment, and then Sir Anthony was jumping down from the curricle and approaching Avery up on the box.

"Just what do you think you are about?" Sir Anthony demanded.

"I think what I am about is none of your business." It was a brave speech, but Avery's hands trembled on the reins and the blood had drained from his face.

"I beg to differ." Sir Anthony went to the door.

"She doesn't love you!" Avery shouted in a near panic.

"She won't marry you, if that's what you think, so you may as well just take yourself off!"

"We shall see about that," Sir Anthony snarled, wrenching open the carriage door.

"Ooh, look—it is Sir Anthony come to stop us."

Lucinda! Lucinda? Then where was Ginny?

"It's all right," came her voice from the shadows on the far side of the coach. "He's not here to stop you."

Ginny *and* Lucinda? Avery was a cur!

"Oh, but Ginny, don't you think it is even the teensiest, weensiest bit romantic?" Lucinda replied. "Sir Anthony, I hadn't thought you truly cared about me so!"

Taking Ginny firmly by the wrist, he said, "Miss Barrington, you are free to go wherever you wish—the farther away, the better. Ginny, however, is coming with me."

He had pulled her half across the coach before he realized she was coming of her own free will.

"As you will, my sovereign lord," she said, her eyes twinkling.

Then he grasped her by the elbows, yanking her out of the carriage and into his arms.

The kiss was long and deep. Now that he had her, he didn't want to ever let her go. In point of fact, he held her so tight she began to protest.

"Anthony, we are in the middle of the road!"

"Am I to care for the opinion of the Jem Feddleswanks of the world when I hold in my arms the only woman I shall ever love?"

Smiling, she kissed him on the cheek, turned to

Lucinda, and said, "I wish you happiness on your up-
coming nuptials. Please write and tell me all about it."

"Oh, I will! A runaway marriage is ever so romantic,
don't you think? I can't wait to read about it in all the
papers!" Lucinda said with that infernal clap of her
hands for what he hoped was the very last time.

Sir Anthony could see it was all Ginny could do not
to laugh. Then she turned to Avery still seated up on the
box. "Congratulations! You have won her heart forever.
I look forward to calling on the both of you once you
get settled." Sir Anthony groaned. It would seem that
more of Lucinda's hand-clapping was in his future.

Avery reached for Ginny's hand and kissed it.
"Would it be rude of me to say how glad I am it was you
he was after and not Lucinda?"

This time, Ginny did laugh. "No, not at all! Now go
and be happy," she said waving at the both of them until they drove away.

Sir Anthony had questions. He drew her arm through
his, and they began to walk. "What kind of elopement
is it, anyway, when another woman tags along? I should
have done it quite differently," Sir Anthony quipped.

"It was simply a matter of convenience, that is all.
They were going and I was merely riding along, only as
far as Dunsmere. So," she asked, smiling up at him, a
glint in her eye, "what brings you away from the ball?"

"Minx! If you must know, I was of a mind to collect
myself some illicit rose cuttings."

"Rose cuttings! Whatever for?"

"To buy my way out of an engagement, that's why. I
see now there was no cause as Lucinda is about to run

off to points unknown to escape me. I wish I had been aware of her true feelings! She could have simply said she didn't want to marry me; it would have saved me a deal of trouble." He pulled her closer as they walked. He was right; she did fit perfectly into his side.

"She could hardly say so; that would spoil all the fun! It seems she and Lord Avery have been planning this ever since the duel, which, by the way, was another ruse concocted by Lord Avery in order to give Lucinda more of what she wanted. Meanwhile, she only pretended that she was happy about her engagement to you to keep her parents from suspecting the truth."

"What! She would rather go with that lily-livered gudgeon than with me?" He knew he shouldn't tease her, but she had the most fetching dimple that appeared whenever she smiled. "So, I am not a lord nor have blond curls or write poetry! Ah, but Ginny," he said, turning serious, "one look at you and I could turn out a dozen soppy phrases about the luster of your eyes or the fullness of your lips."

"No! Please no," she begged. "Now that I know just *who* you are, I love you just the *way* you are."

He stopped and drew her once again into his arms. Imagine! He could have walked with her to Dunsmere just this way ten days ago and been the happiest of men that much sooner. Yet Grandmama was right, he had to spend time with her before he could learn to love her. If only Ginny could learn to love him half as much!

The thought of Grandmama reminded him of another of his questions. "My darling girl," he asked, tilting up her chin so she could not look away, "has no one taught you that eavesdropping is odious?"

She bit her lip. "So, you did know it was me kneeling at the keyhole like a schoolgirl!"

"Yes." He gave her nose a flick and once again drawing her arm into his, began to walk. "And no. I saw someone, barely, but with that pink wig—where has it gone, by the way?—I didn't realize it was you. It wasn't until you left that I remembered. Still . . . I don't know why you didn't wait for me to explain."

"I knew you were angry about what Grandmama did. Whether or not you were angry at me, I wasn't sure. It did seem that way, you must admit."

Sir Anthony considered. He had been angry. He didn't try to hide it either. He hadn't realized Ginny would think it directed at her. "All right, I admit it."

"I thought if you were so humiliated that Grandmama had manipulated you into . . . Oh dear! I was about to say 'offering for me' but you haven't. Can I assume it was part of the plan? Your plan, that is?"

"Yes! Assume away!" he said with a flourish of his hand.

"In that case, to continue, I did not want you to feel roped into offering for me. If I left, then you would have a choice, one that was all yours to make. You could either go after me or stay at the ball and become officially betrothed to Lucinda. As it was, I feared you would never put an end to that and I didn't want to hang about to hear it announced."

"My poor darling! Of course I had taken steps to end it! The squire and I came to an excellent understanding right after dinner—hence the rose cuttings—but informing Lucinda and her mother was a trickier matter."

"Well, you can hardly blame me for wondering, just a bit! After all, a gentleman never cries off from an engagement."

"Never?!"

"No, of course not!" She snuggled into his shoulder. "You should know that better than I."

"Me, who has had so little experience in the betrothal area? How can you be so sure I would know how to go about it? In fact, I'm not so sure I know how to go about anything anymore. I have quite given up on my old self and am determined to be made anew."

"No more starched-up, silly old code of honor?"

He shook his head. "No more code of honor. That is, not if it comes in the way of matters that are more important."

"Such as?"

"You are determined to make this difficult, aren't you? Well, then, such as love, affection, and true speaking."

"Truly?" She smiled mistily up at him.

"Truly. In the meantime, you must inform me as to how I am to proceed. Though I have been engaged before, however briefly, I have never proposed, and I find I am at a loss."

"Well," Ginny said, cocking her head, "first you ask for my hand in marriage, and then I accept. I believe that is the usual form one follows."

"Hmmm, and what about kissing? I suppose I will be expected to bestow only polite and chaste kisses for the duration of our betrothal?"

Her eyes twinkled. "Oh, yes. I believe there are times when the rules of convention must be strictly adhered to. That is, unless you want your grandmama to toss you out on your ear."

"Ah, point well taken. Well, then, if you promise not to throw it at me, I shall adhere to the pages of my code of honor and behave the perfect gentleman. When we become officially engaged, that is."

"And in the meantime?" Ginny asked, somewhat taken aback.

"We do our best to get in our fill before we must return and tell Grandmama the news."

Ginny gasped and pulled him to a halt. "We must go back! Grandmama! She will be so worried. We have left the curricle so far behind!"

He took her hand in his and drew her once again along the moonlit road. "Come, Miss Delacourt, it is a beautiful night for walking and Dunsmere is just around the corner. Have you forgotten the task for which Grandmama sent us off?"

"No, I haven't." She smiled and took his arm. "Finally! We are off to smell the roses!"